It appeared as if Noah was about to accept Alyssa's invitation when suddenly a piercing scream shattered the jovial mood, causing heads to turn and hearts to race.

In an instant, the gymnasium fell silent. And then Kat, her face pale with shock, stumbled backward from behind the bleachers, her eyes wide with terror, her hand over her mouth.

Maya and Sandra sprang into action, racing over behind the bleachers, where they were met with a chilling sight. There, lying motionless on the floor, was Tawny, on her back, arms and legs splayed out, her once vibrant personality now replaced with the cold stillness of death. No one at the reunion had ever thought when the evening began that former mean girl Tawny Bryce would be the classmate Most Likely to Die . . .

Books by Lee Hollis

Hayley Powell Mysteries

DEATH OF A KITCHEN DIVA
DEATH OF A COUNTRY FRIED REDNECK
DEATH OF A COUPON CLIPPER
DEATH OF A CHOCOHOLIC
DEATH OF A CHRISTMAS CATERER
DEATH OF A CUPCAKE QUEEN
DEATH OF A BACON HEIRESS
DEATH OF A PUMPKIN CARVER
DEATH OF A LOBSTER LOVER
DEATH OF A COOKBOOK AUTHOR
DEATH OF A WEDDING CAKE BAKER
DEATH OF A BLUEBERRY TART
DEATH OF A WICKED WITCH
DEATH OF AN ITALIAN CHEF
DEATH OF AN ICE CREAM SCOOPER
DEATH OF A CLAM DIGGER
DEATH OF A GINGERBREAD MAN

Collections

EGGNOG MURDER
(with Leslie Meier and Barbara Ross)
YULE LOG MURDER
(with Leslie Meier and Barbara Ross)
HAUNTED HOUSE MURDER
(with Leslie Meier and Barbara Ross)
CHRISTMAS CARD MURDER
(with Leslie Meier and Peggy Ehrhart)
HALLOWEEN PARTY MURDER
(with Leslie Meier and Barbara Ross)
IRISH COFFEE MURDER
(with Leslie Meier and Barbara Ross)

CHRISTMAS MITTENS MURDER
(with Lynn Cahoon and Maddie Day)
EASTER BASKET MURDER
(with Leslie Meier and Barbara Ross)

Poppy Harmon Mysteries
POPPY HARMON INVESTIGATES
POPPY HARMON AND THE HUNG JURY
POPPY HARMON AND THE PILLOW TALK KILLER
POPPY HARMON AND THE BACKSTABBING BACHELOR
POPPY HARMON AND THE SHOOTING STAR

Maya & Sandra Mysteries
MURDER AT THE PTA
MURDER AT THE BAKE SALE
MURDER ON THE CLASS TRIP
MURDER AT THE SPELLING BEE
MURDER AT THE HIGH SCHOOL REUNION

Stand-Alones
MY FATHER ALWAYS FINDS CORPSES

Published by Kensington Publishing Corp.

Murder at the High School Reunion

A Maya and Sandra Mystery

LEE HOLLIS

Kensington Publishing Corp.
kensingtonbooks.com

KENSINGTON BOOKS are published by

Kensington Publishing Corp.
900 Third Avenue
New York, NY 10022

First Printing: June 2025
ISBN: 978-1-4967-5287-1

ISBN: 978-1-4967-5288-8 (ebook)

10 9 8 7 6 5 4 3 2 1

Printed in the United States of America

The authorized representative in the EU for product safety and compliance is eucomply OU, Parnu mnt 139b-14, Apt 123
Tallinn, Berlin 11317, hello@eucompliancepartner.com

Chapter 1

Sarah walks through the park with Rufus, her energetic and beloved German shepherd. The sun filters through the trees, casting dappled shadows on the pathway. Sarah smiles as Rufus happily trots beside her, his leash securely in her hand.

Suddenly, Rufus spots a squirrel, and his instincts take over. With a swift jerk, he breaks free from Sarah's grip, bolting across the park.

"Rufus, no!" Sarah cries.

Sarah takes off after him, her heart pounding with worry. She weaves through the park, dodging trees and benches in pursuit of her runaway pup.

As Sarah rounds a corner, she sees Rufus skidding to a halt in front of a familiar figure. It's Jack, her ex-boyfriend, who is kneeling down, trying to coax Rufus closer.

"Rufus, come here, boy!" Sarah calls out.

Rufus, panting, hesitates for a moment before bounding over to Jack, wagging his tail furiously.

Sarah approaches cautiously, her breath still coming in gasps.

Jack has yet to see her. "Hey there, buddy. Where's your mom?"

Sarah reaches them, her eyes locking with Jack's. There's a mixture of surprise and tension in the air as they stand face-to-face for the first time since their breakup.

"I'm sorry. He broke free from his leash. I hope he didn't cause any trouble," Sarah says cautiously.

"No trouble at all. He just missed me, didn't you, Rufus?"

Jack scratches Rufus behind the ears, and the dog leans into his touch, clearly enjoying the attention.

"Yeah, he . . . he does miss you."

There's a moment of awkward silence as they both remember the bitter custody battle they went through over Rufus.

"Well, I miss him too. And you," Jack mutters under his breath.

Sarah looks up at Jack, her heart fluttering with conflicting emotions.

"Jack, I . . ."

Before she can finish, Rufus suddenly darts off again, this time toward the nearby lake.

Sarah, exasperated, sighs and says, "Oh, for the love of . . ."

Sarah and Jack exchange a knowing look before chasing after Rufus once more, their laughter echoing through the park.

As they reach the edge of the lake, Rufus sits proudly

between them, wagging his tail as if to say, "Mission accomplished."

"Well, I guess it's true what they say . . . dogs really are man's best wingmen."

Jack chuckles, and Sarah joins in, feeling a warmth spreading through her chest as she realizes that maybe, just maybe, there's still hope for them after all.

"Doggone it, Sarah, I still love you."

"Did you really just say that?"

"Sarah, come on, admit it, we're still fetching each other!"

"My God, please, enough with the dog puns!"

"Without each other, we're both still just chasing our tails—"

She stops him with a long, languorous kiss. Jack wraps his arms around her and holds her tight, the tension between them dissipating like the mist in the morning sun, as Rufus, tail wagging, looks on with a triumphant smile.

There was a loud groan.

Sandra elbowed her boyfriend, Lucas, who was sitting next to her in the Nickelodeon Cinemas in downtown Portland, Maine.

"This is so lame!" Lucas chuckled.

Sandra, who was a sucker for any kind of romantic comedy, even a badly written one, was holding back tears. She was not about to let Lucas see her cry over such a schmaltzy movie. Luckily, he was munching on the last few kernels in his bag of popcorn and did not notice her eyes brimming with tears over Sarah and Jack's emotional, heartfelt reunion.

Sandra glanced over at Maya, her BFF and business partner in a private detective agency, who was sitting on her other side. Maya, nonplussed, watched the credits roll, not sure how to react. Next to her was her husband, Max. His head drooped, and his eyes were closed, and she could hear him snoring. He had slept through most of the film.

The lights came up in the theater, and the audience began filing out. Maya shook Max awake, and they stood up, waiting for Sandra and Lucas to lead them out of the row to the aisle. Lucas upended his nearly empty bag of popcorn, pouring what was left into his mouth and tossing the bag into a trash bin as they strolled out.

It was unusually cold for a late-summer night, and Sandra wished she had remembered to bring a sweater. Lucas, almost as if reading her mind, flung an arm around her and rubbed her shoulders to keep her warm.

Sandra turned to Maya and Max. "I hate to ask, but what did you think?"

Lucas jumped in. "I thought it was the worst movie I have ever seen!"

"I wasn't asking you. I know what *you* thought of it. You kept sighing and groaning and making snide comments through the whole thing! I want to know if Maya and Max liked it or not."

Max yawned. "I can't honestly say. I don't remember much. They hadn't even gone to court over who gets to keep the dog before I first dozed off."

"I thought the saucy best friend, the short girl from *Bridgerton*, was pretty funny, but otherwise I was kind of bored," Maya said.

They strolled through the Old Port District on their way to a late dinner reservation at the Little Tap House Restaurant.

"So, what did you think of *her*?" Sandra asked the group.

"She's always the same in every role she plays nowadays. She's never been as good as she was when she was nominated for that movie with what's-his-name where she played the paralegal who became a whistleblower against her own corrupt law firm; I can never remember the name of it."

"I think it was just called *The Whistleblower*," Lucas guessed. "Or something close to it. I saw it when I was a kid."

Sandra cringed.

Of course Lucas had been a kid when he had seen the film.

He was almost fourteen years her junior.

And it still rankled her, even though her close friends were always encouraging her to just forget the large age gap between them.

"She's very likable," Sandra said as they rounded the corner and walked inside the restaurant. Max stepped over to check them in, and a gruff host, who was overwhelmed by a very busy night, escorted them to their table.

Once they were seated and water was poured and their drinks order had been taken by a perky waiter,

Sandra steered the conversation back to the movie, or more pointedly, to the star of the movie, Alyssa Turner, who played Sarah.

"It's going to be very strange seeing her after all these years. Who could have known when we were in high school that she would become this huge Hollywood megastar?"

"She was so shy back then, as I recall, but frankly, I barely remember her," Maya shrugged, perusing the menu.

Alyssa Turner would have been the last classmate that anyone would have assumed would achieve massive wealth and stardom. Sandra remembered Alyssa as a painfully awkward wallflower, sometimes targeted by the mean girl cliques, who hid in the last row in class, just trying to melt into the background. But now, armed with an Oscar nomination from when she was in her early twenties and with a string of box office smashes and prestige television projects under her belt, she was now headlining a mawkish, middling romantic comedy called *Puppy Love.* Sandra, always a sucker for rom-coms, had strong-armed Lucas, Maya, and Max into attending the early-evening showing with the promise of dinner at Little Tap House following the film.

Maya and Sandra had not double-dated often with their respective partners—Max preferred socializing at home—but Sandra thought it might be fun to catch Alyssa's latest Hollywood production before seeing her in person at their upcoming twenty-fifth high school reunion.

"I heard ticket sales to the reunion tripled after

Alyssa announced on social media that she was going to show up," Lucas noted.

"I think her parents still live in the area," Maya said.

Max placed a hand on top of Maya's. "Are you still planning to boycott the reunion, hon?"

"*What*?" Sandra gasped.

"It's not a boycott. I just don't want to go."

"You *have* to go!"

"Says who?" Maya scoffed.

"But you missed the twentieth reunion. We all did."

"Yes, because there was a worldwide pandemic."

"Aren't you just a little bit curious to see everyone?"

Maya scrunched up her nose. "Not especially. A lot of our classmates still live in the area, and I see them all the time."

"Not Alyssa Turner," Max cracked. "I think we should go."

Maya raised an eyebrow at her husband. "Oh, are you a fan?"

"She has certain attributes which I admire, yes."

Maya laughed. "He's not talking about her acting. He's referring to the beach scene in the beginning of the movie where she first meets Jack and Rufus and she's wearing a bikini. The rest of the movie she's fully clothed, which is why he fell asleep and missed the rest of it."

Lucas guffawed, then, with a reassuring smile, said to Sandra, "She's got nothing on you, in my opinion."

"I wasn't asking," Sandra sneered, before fixing her gaze back on Maya. "You have to come. We can all go together. There is safety in numbers." She studied Maya's face, trying to get some kind of readout.

But Maya remained stoic, unmovable, like a statue.

She had always been very upfront about how much she'd hated her high school years. Unlike Sandra, who was head cheerleader, class president, your typical overachiever, Maya was mostly an outcast. She struggled to fit in and spent most of her time loitering in the smoking section, near the school parking lot, when there was one, and dating all the bad boys.

"Okay, if you won't go for me, go for Max," Sandra pleaded.

Max perked up.

"It would be a shame for you to deny him the opportunity to meet one of his favorite actresses."

Max grinned. "She's right, hon. How many chances am I going to get to meet an honest-to-goodness Hollywood celebrity?"

"I even bought a new sports jacket for the occasion," Lucas piped in.

Maya at first refused to be worn down, but by the time they had ordered their entrées and another round of drinks, with Sandra applying even more pressure, Maya finally, reluctantly relented, on the one condition that she be allowed to bolt at any time she started to feel uncomfortable.

It was official.

They were all going to be in attendance at the SoPo High Class of 2000 Reunion.

A decision that would ultimately come back to haunt them.

Chapter 2

"He's a pathetic, lying cheat, and I want you to prove it," Tawny Bryce sniffed, eyes blazing.

She sat on the couch in Maya and Sandra's office, her Gucci clutch bag resting on her lap. Tawny always dressed to impress, wearing an eyelash tweed minidress and sporting some expensive-looking jewelry. Sandra priced the dress at around sixteen hundred bucks, having seen it on the Saks Fifth Avenue website. The jewelry was probably from Tiffany's, she guessed.

Sandra had been surprised to get a call from Tawny. The two hardly ever spoke. They knew each other in high school, but did not stay in touch much after graduation, occasionally running into each other at PTA meetings when Sandra was president.

Sandra tried to keep her distance, remembering Tawny as one of those awful queen bees who liked to cruelly target other girls and make their lives miserable. She was the Regina George of SoPo High during her reign in the late nineties. As head cheerleader and part of the popular clique, Sandra luckily had some protection from Tawny's merciless taunts, unlike Alyssa Turner, who was regularly teased and humiliated by Tawny's band of marauding mean girls.

Tawny had married swoon-worthy football tight end Chad Bryce right out of high school. And, remarkably, they were still married twenty-five years later. None of their friends or classmates, Sandra included, ever thought they would last very long since the rumor was Tawny used a fake pregnancy scare to coerce him into proposing. By the time the rings were exchanged and they were on the plane to their honeymoon in the Bahamas, Tawny broke the news that the first test was a false positive and the second test had come back negative. By then, the deal was sealed, and for his part, Chad decided to stick around to try and make the marriage work. They were married five years before the couple had their first kid, Lianne, who was in Sandra's son Jack's class. Two more followed, all three now living away from home at various colleges across the country.

Sandra was not surprised that Tawny suspected Chad was having an affair behind her back. He was always something of a cad, but what did surprise her was the fact that it took him this long. Or perhaps this was the first one Tawny had become privy to, which was a definite possibility, in Sandra's opinion.

When Sandra called Maya to tell her about the meeting with Tawny, Maya had to consult her high school yearbook to remember who she was, since back then Maya had no use for girls like Tawny, who strutted down the hallway with a perpetual air of superiority and perfectly styled hair and designer outfits, casting disdainful glances at anyone deemed beneath their social standing and belittling others to boost their own egos.

No, Maya was more interested in spending her time with the bad-boy biker types with their smoldering gazes and a penchant for breaking rules and defying authority, which just made them all the more alluring. Maya had always craved danger and excitement, which explained why she later was drawn to her husband Max, a former cop and now ex-convict.

Her taste in men had never changed.

"How do you know Chad's cheating on you?" Sandra asked, crossing her legs and leaning toward Tawny.

"Because whoever this home wrecker is has been sending me text messages flaunting the affair in my face. It's despicable!"

"Can we see these texts?"

"Of course," Tawny replied, opening her Gucci bag and extracting her phone. She handed it to Sandra.

Maya hopped up from her desk and circled around to join Sandra so they could both read the texts in question.

Hope you don't mind me borrowing your husband for a bit. He seems to enjoy my company more than yours. Oops!

Sorry, not sorry. Your husband just can't get enough of me. Looks like you've got some competition, sweetie.

Hate to break it to you, but your marriage isn't as solid as you think. Your man can't resist me.

Sandra handed the phone back to Tawny.

"What kind of person would do something like that? Find pleasure in taunting me, laughing at me?" Tawny sniffed. She turned to Maya. "That's a lovely suede jacket, by the way."

"What? Oh, um, thanks," Maya muttered, flustered by Tawny so quickly shifting gears from devastated spouse to cool fashion critic.

"Tawny, did you confront Chad when you started receiving these texts from this mystery woman?"

"No, of course not!"

Sandra exchanged a curious look with Maya. "Why not?"

"I don't want him to know that I'm aware of his infidelities just yet, because I want to gather more incriminating information on him. I need names and addresses and photos, anything I can get my hands on—incontrovertible proof—in order to build a rock-solid case when I file for divorce. Chad will no doubt try to lowball me in the settlement, so I'm just trying to get the upper hand early. That's where you two come in."

"So you want us to help you take him to the cleaners," Maya remarked, wandering back over to her desk and leaning against it.

"Yes, I'm looking for a fat monthly alimony payment I can use to travel the world with my girlfriends. Do you know I have never been to Europe? Chad was always coming up with excuses why we could never go. Every year, it was the same old vacation. Visiting his parents in Boca Raton and, once every blue moon, a cruise in the Caribbean, where he would overeat at the buffet, drink too many margaritas, and pass out in the state room by nine o'clock. I'm ready to start a new chapter, see more of the world, have some fun without him always dragging me down."

"Sounds like you've really thought this through," Sandra said warily, as it slowly dawned on her that she still did not care for Tawny Bryce all that much.

In Tawny's mind, however, the three of them were now best buds. She smiled conspiratorially. "I came to you two because I think it is imperative that the team responsible for taking down that misogynist weasel are all women. Chad's never truly respected women; he basically sees them as either maids doing his laundry and cooking him dinner to playthings doing his bidding in the bedroom. It will be so richly rewarding to see his face when we ruin him financially and otherwise."

The vindictiveness in Tawny's voice was slightly disconcerting. But if she was painting an accurate portrait of what kind of man Chad Bryce was, then it might be worth accepting the case, in Sandra's mind.

Tawny sensed that she might be coming on too strong, so she softened her stance. "I feel so betrayed. I just want him to be held to account for his actions, see justice served, and then maybe he will understand the pain he has caused me. You have no idea how difficult it's been for me, especially with our twenty-fifth reunion coming up."

"Are you and Chad both planning to go?"

"Chad wouldn't miss it. His ego won't allow him to. And I have no choice. I'm in charge of the planning committee. I tried to get out of it, but I got strong-armed into taking over when Patsy Baumgarten got Covid for the umpteenth time. Honestly, I wish there was someone else. You were class president, Sandra; you should be the one in charge, but you never returned Patsy's emails."

"Maya and I have been so busy with other cases," Sandra fibbed. They had not had a case in a few weeks, but Sandra had no intention of taking on such a thankless task.

"Well, I hope you have time to take on mine," Tawny said, her eyes almost begging.

Sandra was not exactly excited about working for her former cheerleading rival, who had treated her, if not cruelly, then at least dismissively in high school. Why dredge up all those unpleasant memories? But then Sandra glanced over at Maya, who was already jotting down all of Tawny's contact information.

Sandra knew the drill.

Although Sandra was dedicated to their private investigation agency, she was financially independent. She could be choosey when it came to accepting cases.

Maya, on the other hand, was decidedly not.

She and Max had been struggling since his release from prison, especially now that their daughter was enrolled in a very expensive college. She needed every case they could get their hands on.

So Sandra chose to remain mum as Maya readily accepted Tawny's case, rattling off their hourly rate plus expenses and eagerly passing along their own info so Tawny could conveniently Venmo them the retainer fee on the spot.

Chapter 3

Maya and Sandra followed at a safe distance behind Chad Bryce's Midas muscle car, the epitome of a midlife crisis on wheels, an over-the-top manifestation of Chad's desire to recapture the glory days and stand out from the crowd. He had not changed one bit since high school. With each turn, they kept a safe distance to make sure Chad was not aware he was being followed.

It had taken him less than ten minutes to emerge from the house after Tawny left for her monthly book club meeting. He wore an open collar shirt that showcased a forest of chest hair, some casual designer jeans, and a pair of expensive loafers. Maya could almost smell the aftershave he had no doubt slapped on his cheeks, a distinctive blend of invigorating and masculine scents, before taking one last look in the mirror and giving himself a thumbs-up.

They had tailed too many cheating husbands to count in the few years they had been in business together.

Chad was showing all the typical signs of an oblivious, entitled man who thought he would never get caught.

This was going to be a walk in the park.

The Midas swerved to the left.

"Of course he didn't think to use his blinker," Sandra snapped. "Why would he waste time considering other drivers?"

Maya sped up and turned down the street in pursuit. They saw Chad pull his monstrosity of an automobile up in front of the Press Hotel, a meticulously restored newspaper building, now a boutique hotel blending modern luxury with historic charm.

Maya and Sandra pulled over to the curb about a hundred feet from the hotel entrance and exchanged a knowing glance. This was the moment they had been waiting for.

"It's almost too easy," Sandra said with a sly smile.

"We still have to catch him in the act," Maya said, popping an earpiece into her right ear "You wait here in case I lose him and he comes back out. Plus, this is a no-parking zone, and I can't afford another ticket."

"How are you going to do this?"

Maya shrugged. "I've done this so many times. I've learned it's best just to wing it, be prepared for anything." Maya held up her phone. "I'm going to call you. Stay on the line so we can communicate."

Sandra pointed toward the hotel. Chad was handing his keys to a valet and rattling off a stern warning to treat his precious baby with the utmost care before pressing a twenty-dollar bill into the palm of the valet's hand. "You better go now."

Maya jumped out of the car as Sandra unbuckled herself from the passenger seat and circled around to take Maya's place at the wheel of Maya's Chevy Bolt in case a traffic cop came by and ordered her to move the vehicle.

Maya scurried to catch up with Chad, who had already strolled into the lobby and was heading for the elevators. Several hotel guests were waiting for the lift, and she managed to blend in with them as if she was a part of the group. Chad was texting on his phone and took no notice of her.

The elevator bell dinged, and the doors opened. They all crowded in, Maya slipping in and angling around Chad so she was standing directly behind him. She was reasonably sure he would not remember her from high school, but she did not want to take any chances.

An elderly woman who was nearest to the elevator buttons turned to Chad, who was still texting and distracted. "What floor?"

His eyes wandered from his phone to the woman. "Huh?"

"What floor?" she repeated.

"The roof, please," he replied gruffly.

The woman pressed the R button.

Chad did not bother thanking her.

He was obviously going to meet someone at the rooftop bar, with its panoramic views of Portland harbor.

The ride up in the elevator took some time, with stops on four other floors, where people filed off, leaving Chad and three others, including Maya, to ascend to the top floor. There was another ding, and Chad muscled his way off first, nearly bodychecking a woman with a cane. Maya was the last one off, and she casually crossed to the bar, keeping one eye on Chad, who scanned the room before walking over and plopping down in a plush armchair next to the window, eyes glued to his phone, ignoring the stunning view of the city lights and ships in the harbor at night.

Sandra's voice chirped in Maya's ear. "What's he doing?"

Maya lowered her voice as she stood watching from the bar. "It looks like he's waiting for somebody."

"It's got to be her," Sandra said breathlessly.

Twenty minutes passed.

Maya ordered a club soda from the bartender, and when Chad glanced around for any sign of his date, she would turn her back to him and pretend to be engaged in a conversation with a pair of men chatting with each other who were standing next to her at the bar. She could tell Chad was starting to get agitated. He kept checking the time on his Rolex.

Finally, a tall, statuesque blond woman in a shimmering blue cocktail dress and sporting a rocking pair of Jimmy Choos sashayed off the elevator, took a quick look around, and made a beeline for Chad.

Maya held her breath as she watched the woman approach Chad. Sensing her presence, Chad shot to his feet and gave her a warm hug, kissing her briefly on the cheek. He had to play it cool in public. He could ravish her later in the privacy of their hotel room.

After some small talk, and the woman declining to order a drink from the cocktail waitress who stopped by to see if she wanted anything, Chad took the woman by the arm, and they headed for the elevator.

Luckily, there were several people waiting to go down, so Maya was able to blend in again. Chad and the mystery woman got off on the fifth floor. Maya held back for a moment, but then slipped out just before the elevator doors closed.

Chad and his date were already halfway down the hall before the woman plucked a key card from her Gucci bag, the same kind Tawny Bryce had flaunted in their office, and the two disappeared inside. Maya hustled down to get a look at the room number.

503.

"Okay, I know what room they're in."

"What now?" Sandra asked.

"Do you know anyone who works at this hotel?"

There was a pause.

"Plenty. Stephen helped the workers unionize. They idolize him. He has a lifetime of favors he could call in."

Senator Stephen Wallage was Sandra's ex-husband.

But, unlike Chad and Tawny, their divorce had been amicable.

And Stephen still pined to reconcile with his ex-wife.

"I just need to get my hands on a maid's uniform," Maya whispered, heading back down the hall toward the bank of elevators.

"Stephen's on his way back from Geneva with a congressional delegation, but his chief of staff, Suzanne, will be more than willing to help us. She likes me better anyway."

"Great. See what you can do."

By the time Maya located the housekeeping storage room in the basement, away from the guest areas, she was greeted by the beaming night manager, a small, compact man with a receding hairline and kind face.

"Maya?"

"Yes. Calvin?"

He pointed to the brass nameplate pinned to his black jacket. "That would be me."

"Thank you so much for doing this."

"My pleasure. Mrs. Wallage and her husband are heroes around here. We're happy to help. Just keep a low profile because we are technically breaking the rules."

"I promise," Maya assured him.

Within five minutes, Maya was fitted with a gray maid's uniform and loaned a rolling cart with cleaning supplies and fresh towels. She made her way back up to the fifth floor, pushing the cart in front of room 503.

She steeled herself, gripping her phone in one hand with the camera app open and ready to go before she knocked twice with the other.

The blond woman opened the door halfway, peering out.

She was still in her electric blue dress.

"Yes?"

"Would you like turn-down service this evening, ma'am?"

"Um, no, thank you. We're good."

Maya peered past the woman.

She could see wafts of smoke drifting through the room from a smelly cigar.

Even though this was a nonsmoking floor.

Did Chad ever follow any rules?

She heard a man's voice. "Who is it, Bella?"

Bella called back. "It's just the maid."

Just the maid.

Maya liked this woman even less than Chad.

"Hold on!" the man bellowed.

Maya's stomach knotted as she braced herself to come face-to-face with Chad. She had been hoping to catch them by surprise, in flagrante delicto, and take a few quick shots with her phone camera before either could react.

But the man turned out not to be Chad.

He was taller, with slicked-back black hair and a cigar hanging out of the side of his mouth, and he was fully clothed.

"Hey, do you have any more of those chocolate mints you leave on the pillow at night? I've got a real craving."

Flustered, she began fumbling around her cart to find some, her mind reeling. Who was this guy?

As she searched for the mints, she heard the toilet flush, water in the sink run a few moments, and the bathroom door open. Chad sauntered out, wiping his hands with a towel.

"Well, I was wondering when you would show up," Chad sneered, tossing the wet towel on the cart. "We could use some fresh towels."

What the hell was going on here?

"You're Maya, right? I remember you from high school."

How could he?

They had never spoken or had any interaction whatsoever. Had someone tipped him off?

Bella looked at Chad, confused. "What's going on?"

Chad, leering, sized her up and down. "This is

Maya—sorry, I forgot your last name—we were in the same class at SoPo High. She's now a private detective. Isn't that cool?"

The man stiffened. "Private detective?"

"Yes, and apparently, she's undercover as a sexy hotel maid for her latest case. Isn't that right, Maya?"

Maya remained silent.

Bella glared at her. "What's she doing here?"

"My wife Tawny hired her to dig up dirt on me. Tawny thinks I'm having an affair, and so she hired Maya to tail me and get some hard evidence Tawny can use against me. Did I leave anything out, Maya?"

Someone must have tipped him off.

But who?

Chad, a smirk playing at the corner of his lips, ushered her into the room. "Come on in, Maya; let me introduce you to everybody. This is one of my clients, Bill Ashby and his wife, Bella. They're from Buffalo and are staying here at the hotel while they're in town." He waved at Maya to follow him down the hall to the main part of the suite. "Come on; don't be shy."

Maya reluctantly shuffled after him, ready for anything.

They rounded the corner to see two more men, also smoking cigars, sitting around a card table with a deck of cards and piles of coins and dollar bills and glasses of whiskey.

"This is Sid and Danny; they're golfing buddies of mine and also good friends of the Ashbys. We decided to have a little poker night while they're here," Chad said, his voice laced with smug satisfaction.

Maya's heart sank.

She could not have botched this any worse.

"Would you like to search the place, Maya—you know, to make sure I'm not hiding a girl anywhere?"

"That won't be necessary," Maya mumbled.

"Okay then, well, we should get back to our game. Let me show you out."

Chad took her by the arm and escorted her back down the hall to the door. "I must commend you on the whole hotel maid getup—very nicely played."

Chad opened the door and stepped to the side, allowing Maya to pass. Her cheeks burned with embarrassment as she began pushing the supply cart back down the hall.

Chad poked his head out, calling after her. "Oh, Maya, by the way . . ."

She turned to face him.

"You think you can catch me in the act?" he said, his voice taunting. "Think again."

And then he stepped back in the room and slammed the door shut.

Chapter 4

Maya offered to help clear the dishes from the dining room table when they were finished eating, but Sandra insisted that she and Max adjourn to the living room with cups of coffee. She was just grateful to have company tonight. With both her sons away at college, Sandra was officially an empty nester, and this big drafty house could get lonely sometimes. Lucas was always enthusiastic about spending as much time with her as possible and would be more than happy to just move in, but she was still keeping him at arm's length.

It was too soon after her divorce from Stephen.

She was in no rush to dive into a full-fledged relationship, which is why she continued categorizing what she and Lucas were doing as simply dating.

In Lucas's mind, however, they were practically engaged. That was a discussion they were going to need to have sooner rather than later.

The three of them spent most of the evening discussing the next steps in their case involving Chad Bryce. He was a slippery one, and they were going to have to figure out a way to outsmart him now that he was on to them.

Max was eager to help. He was an ex-cop. He had mad investigative skills. But Maya was reticent about bringing him into the firm, even part-time, to help them out. She had long forgiven him for the corruption scandal that engulfed both their careers in law enforcement, sending him to prison and forcing her to resign. He had paid his debt to society and was now trying to start fresh. But she had built this firm on her own, first with her former partner, Frances, and now with Sandra by her side, and she had mixed feelings about Max coming aboard. He had a tendency to take over, be the top alpha dog. After all, he had been captain of their precinct for five years before his arrest.

But this was her thing.

And Sandra could sense he was trying to respect boundaries by not forcing the issue.

As she rinsed off the dinner plates and loaded them into the dishwasher, she could hear Max gingerly offering his advice on how to proceed. Sandra could picture Maya listening patiently with a supportive smile but inside resisting the urge to tell him to butt out of her business.

Sandra's phone chimed with a new email notification. Curious, she dried her hands with a towel and reached for her phone, scanning the subject line with furrowed brows.

How odd, she thought to herself.

She quickly read through the brief email and then

scooted into the living room, where she found Maya and Max sitting side by side on the couch, as Max prattled on about how he would handle a guy like Chad Bryce.

Maya appeared grateful for Sandra's sudden presence, glancing at her expectantly. She instantly noticed the confused look on Sandra's face.

Maya leaned forward. "What is it?"

"I just got an email from Alyssa Turner."

They both sat up straight, their curiosity piqued.

"*The* Alyssa Turner?" Max gasped, eyes lighting up.

Sandra nodded.

"What does she want?" Maya asked.

Sandra handed her phone to Maya so she could see the email for herself. Max scooted closer so he could read over her shoulder.

> *Dear Sandra, I hope this finds you well. As you may have heard, I am in Portland because I plan to attend our twenty-fifth high school reunion on Friday. I know it's been a long time since we last spoke, but I was wondering if you and Maya might have time to chat in person before then. I'm staying at my parents' house in the West End. Please let me know if you two are available at some point tomorrow evening. Looking forward to hearing from you. Love, Alyssa.*

"*Love, Alyssa*? I didn't know you two were that close," Maya remarked, handing the phone back to Sandra.

"We're not. We weren't exactly best pals in high

school. This has to be someone's idea of a joke," Sandra concluded.

"And why does she want to see me too? We never exchanged one word in high school. Like I said before, I don't even remember her."

"Maybe she wants to hire you for a case," Max suggested, downing the rest of his coffee.

"First Tawny, now Alyssa? We'll never have to worry about going out of business if our entire graduating class keeps employing us," Maya joked.

Sandra sat down in a chair opposite them. "But why us? I mean, with her millions, she must have access to every high-end security firm with satellite offices all over the globe. We're just a small potatoes, two-woman operation."

"Maybe this has nothing to do with a case. Maybe it's a personal thing," Maya surmised.

"There is only one way to find out, ladies," Max said. "You should go see her. And I will be happy to tag along."

Maya shot him a warning look, her expression firm. "Forget it, Max."

"Come on, honey. I'll just be there for moral support."

"The last thing we need is you ogling her and making her uncomfortable."

"You don't give me enough credit! I know how to behave myself, Maya," Max protested.

"If that was true, you wouldn't have gone to prison," Maya said with a knowing smirk.

Max fell back on the couch, feigning hurt. "Ouch. She just had to play the jail card."

"Don't worry, Max. You'll get your chance to meet her at the reunion," Sandra assured him.

"If I don't change my mind about you escorting me," Maya warned. "You're on notice. Don't screw it up."

Max threw his hands up in mock surrender.

He was not going to push it.

"Let's see what she wants," Sandra said with a sigh.

Chapter 5

Alyssa Turner was a luminous figure, elegant and timeless, reminiscent of Julia Roberts, but with her own distinct aura. Although well into her forties, she carried herself with the grace and magnetism of a woman untouched by time. Her smile was a beacon lighting up with warmth and sincerity, not just in her roles on screen but in person as well—in fact, more so, Sandra thought to herself. Her eyes, a captivating shade of hazel, held a depth and wisdom gained through years in the limelight. Off-screen, she exuded charisma and charm, effortlessly commanding attention wherever she went.

And yet, when she opened the door to her parents' house to welcome Maya and Sandra, despite her fame, she had been so grounded and approachable, so endearing with her down-to-earth demeanor and genuine kindness.

How could this be the same gangly, painfully shy teenager who had stumbled down the SoPo High hallways, eyes downcast, clutching her textbooks to her flat chest, praying no one would notice her or pick on her.

It had been a miraculous transformation.

Her parents, Doug and Edie, were absolute gems. Sandra had met them once at a fundraiser for her ex-husband Stephen, the senior United States senator from the great state of Maine, during his reelection bid. She remembered them as enthusiastic supporters of Stephen's policies. But, to be fair, she had gone through the motions of a politician's wife that night, glad-handing all of his voters and donors, never falling too deep into a conversation, quickly moving on to the next guest with an open checkbook.

Doug and Edie were still in the same New England house, just outside the city of Portland, where they had lived when Sandra was a kid. It had a quintessential coastal charm, blending traditional architecture with a touch of seaside elegance.

Sandra had not known what to expect when she and Maya showed up, but Alyssa had quickly disarmed them, giving them both warm hugs as if they had just had a girls' night out a week earlier. That's why she was a star. She had the innate ability to make you feel like you were the only person in her thoughts and heart.

Sandra had glanced at Maya when they first arrived and nearly guffawed. She was in such a state of shock at being welcomed by movie star Alyssa, who was such a one eighty from the girl she vaguely remembered in high school, that her mouth hung open, and she barely spoke a word for the first fifteen minutes. But Doug popped open a bottle of his finest Pinot Noir, and they were gathered around the crackling fireplace in the living room, with its large bay windows flooding the room with natural light, offering glimpses of the scenic surroundings, and she had finally let her guard down and relaxed, letting herself appreciate the razor-sharp humor coming from both Alyssa and her father.

Meanwhile, Edie prepared dinner in the kitchen, which was a chef's delight, boasting granite countertops, stainless-steel appliances, and a farmhouse sink overlooking the backyard. Sandra had popped in to see if she could help, but Edie chased her out. Dinner was her show. And she did not disappoint.

As they gorged on New England clam chowder, cornbread, boiled lobster with drawn butter, and finally a homemade apple pie à la mode (Edie even churned her own ice cream), the sun set, and the night sky faded into darkness. Sandra counted three empty wine bottles. Doug and Edie were serious about making certain their daughter's guests went home fat and happy.

As they adjourned to the living room with coffee, Doug had a million questions about their detective agency. He was awed by Maya's sordid tale of how it came to be. How her husband, Max, former chief of police in Portland, had been convicted and sent to prison for corruption. Doug nodded, remembering all the headlines at the time. How Maya was forced to leave the department because of guilt by association. How she had put out a shingle as a private eye simply to try and make ends meet as a single mother raising a young daughter. How she had crossed paths with Sandra five years ago when they were both drawn into a murder investigation and, through happenstance, began working together.

Somehow it had all clicked, and now they were a team and thriving.

Most of the time.

"I had heard through the grapevine that you two were working together as private detectives," Alyssa said, almost breathlessly. "I thought it was so cool. But I didn't believe it at first. I have to ask, Sandra—and please tell me if I'm prying too much—how did your husband Stephen feel about all this? He couldn't have been comfortable with you running around solving crimes, or how it must have looked to his constituents?"

"My extracurricular pursuits were not responsible for the end of my marriage. Stephen and I were already on the path to divorce by that point . . ." Sandra said, then gave Alyssa a wink. "But it certainly didn't help."

Alyssa emitted a small, mischievous chuckle that quickly built into a hearty, unrestrained guffaw. It was infectious, and soon everyone joined in.

Finally, collecting herself, Alyssa shook her head. "I can only imagine how all those uptight DC types must have reacted to Senator Wallage's wife as a private dick. They're just like the power players in my business. You know what they say: Washington DC is just Hollywood, but with ugly people."

More laughs all around as Edie came back to refill everyone's coffee cups and sat down with them. "Alyssa was so excited to talk to you both about your interesting line of work."

There was a pregnant pause.

Maya raised an eyebrow. "Oh?"

Alyssa sighed. "Way to blow my cover, Mom!" She

sat up, hands on her knees. "Okay, time to fess up. I may have had an ulterior motive for inviting you two over for dinner tonight."

Both of them were all ears.

"I'm playing Lindsay Calhoun in my next film."

Maya stared at her blankly. "Who?"

Sandra knew Maya had no clue who Lindsay Calhoun was. She did not have time to read many mystery novels. She was too busy spending her time solving real-life cases. Lindsay Calhoun was a dogged private investigator in a series of best-selling mystery novels by Holly Simason. There must have been nearly twenty books in her series. Sandra had read a handful of them. They were dark and funny and well-written. Readers lapped them up. The character of Lindsay was tough, no nonsense, full of layers and contradictions; she suffered a bit from ADD, had a funny cat, and a dating life that was tragic to the point where it was almost comical.

But she was an ace detective.

There was not a murder she could not solve.

Alyssa's mouth dropped open, almost matching Maya's earlier. "You've never heard of her?"

"Afraid not," Maya shrugged.

As Alyssa explained, Sandra could not help but note how perfect Alyssa was to play that part. She had the depth, the wisdom that came with age, and the sex appeal to breathe life into a role as complicated as Lindsay Calhoun.

"They tried to get a film version of the first book off the ground a few years back with Rachel McAdams, but then it fell apart because she only wanted Bradley

Cooper to play opposite her, and they couldn't get him, so she walked off the project, and it went straight back to development hell. But the studio's got a new script, a hot woman director attached, and now me, and I've already worked with Bradley Cooper, loved him, but been there done that, so they're eyeing a late-spring start date in Toronto." Alyssa took a breath. "So I'm not home just for the reunion. I'm researching the part and was hoping I could pick your brains, maybe get a few tips on how the whole thing works."

Sandra could see that Maya had no clue what Alyssa was talking about. To her, movies were just playacting, pretending to be someone you are not. Why waste time studying anything?

"I've got some time before I have to be back in LA to do chemistry reads with some potential co-stars, so I thought I'd hang around and maybe the three of us could talk."

Maya set her empty wineglass down on the coffee table. "Sure. Why not?" Then she stood up and checked the time on her phone. "We better get going. Doug, Edie, thank you for a lovely dinner. Everything was amazing."

Alyssa shot to her feet. "Do you have to leave so soon? I was hoping you could stay a while."

"It's getting late," Maya replied. Then she noticed Sandra remained seated on the couch next to Doug. "You coming?"

"Come on, we're both empty nesters. We don't have kids to go home to anymore. This has been fun. What's the rush?" Then Sandra eyed Maya's empty wineglass. "Plus we've both had a lot of Doug's favorite Pinot Noir. I'm not sure how wise it would be for either of us to drive right now." She picked up her coffee cup and took a sip.

Maya stared at her incredulously. "Are you serious? You want to stay and have a slumber party?"

Edie chimed in. "We have the attic all made up with three beds and plenty of late-night snacks. And if you liked my dinner, just wait until you experience my breakfast."

Maya was clearly not entirely comfortable with this scenario, but she also knew Sandra was right.

Neither of them should risk driving home.

Alyssa clasped her hands together in prayer and looked at her expectantly.

"I'm going to have to call Max and let him know," Maya sighed.

Alyssa clapped excitedly.

An hour later, the three of them were settled in upstairs in the surprisingly spacious attic, wearing sweats and T-shirts from Alyssa's wardrobe, drinking more wine, and sharing memories from their tortured high school years.

Sandra was struck by just how miserable Alyssa had been in high school. She had no idea how mean her fellow cheerleaders had been to her.

"The worst was Tawny Patterson. Do you two remember her?"

Maya and Sandra exchanged furtive glances.

Alyssa noticed. "What? What am I missing?"

Maya cleared her throat. "She's Tawny Bryce now, and she just hired us. She's a client."

Alyssa sprang upright with keen interest. "No way! What does she want you to do?"

"We can't really divulge any specifics of the case," Maya explained evenly.

"What if I guess? Cheating husband! It has to be a cheating husband! I heard she married her high school boyfriend, Chad. Is it him?"

Sandra fought to maintain her poker face.

But her eyes confessed everything.

And astute Alyssa picked up on it immediately.

"Of course, that's it! You know, I had a huge crush on Chad in high school. I thought he was like this god! So handsome, so self-assured, the big man on campus, in the words of Marcia Brady. I tried desperately to hide it, but I think Tawny somehow sensed I liked him, and so she went out of her way to humiliate me, along with her tribe of mean girls. Writing things like 'whore' on my locker in lipstick, that sort of thing."

Sandra shook her head.

Teenage girls could be so cruel.

Alyssa leaned back, remembering. "But she was right. Every time I saw him, it was like that old Taylor Swift song 'You Belong to Me.' That's exactly how I felt. Tawny wore short skirts. I wore T-shirts. She was a cheerleader, and I was in the bleachers. I would lie in bed at night, fantasizing about Chad waking up one morning and realizing I was the one he belonged with and I was right there the whole time. Isn't that silly?"

"Not to a hormonal teenage girl," Sandra cracked. "We've all been there."

"So you don't have to tell me, but if I get it right, blink twice. Tawny and Chad are going through a contentious divorce, and she's hired you to get dirt on him?"

Maya and Sandra kept their eyes pried open, stubbornly refusing to blink.

"It's okay. I think I nailed it. It really doesn't matter anyway. It's all in the past."

Alyssa's thoughts seemed to wander.

Sandra noticed a slight sadness in her eyes.

As if the pain of her younger years had come rushing back to emotionally traumatize her all over again.

She decided to remind her that the past was just that.

The past.

"And your life obviously turned out *way* beyond your wildest dreams. Or anybody else's, for that matter," Sandra quickly noted.

Alyssa gave her a sly smile. "You're right. I'm not saying it's always been easy. Just not what I expected. And suffice it to say, I'm over Chad. As a matter of fact, I've got a new boyfriend. His name is Aaron Hoffman. He's a hot, up-and-coming film producer, and he's flying in from the set of his movie just to escort me to the reunion, which I find incredibly romantic."

The sparkle in her eyes returned.

And just like that, Alyssa Turner—the movie star, the cultural icon whose influence extended far beyond the silver screen, the epitome of Hollywood glamour—was back as well.

Chapter 6

Maya watched with apprehension as the frumpy woman in the shapeless cardigan, oversized glasses, and a messy bun held in place by a few stray bobby pins entered the Strike City Bowling Alley. Alyssa Turner was totally unrecognizable in her disguise as a nondescript, unassuming, nearly invisible woman who would easily blend into the crowd at the local bowling alley tonight.

Alyssa had attacked her first undercover assignment with gusto and detailed preparation, rivaling Meryl Streep's intense research to play Margaret Thatcher in *The Iron Lady*. She was an actress, after all. This was her job.

How had Maya let this happen?

Her gut had told her right away that this was probably a really bad idea.

Unprofessional.

Reckless.

Possibly even opening them up to a lawsuit, if something went wrong.

But Alyssa had been so insistent.

So persuasive.

And charming.

Like movie stars tend to be.

And Sandra, much to Maya's chagrin, had taken Alyssa's side. And now, Sandra, seated next to her in Maya's Chevy Bolt, appeared far more calm and relaxed about this whole ridiculous charade than Maya.

It had started out innocently enough.

Alyssa had asked to drop by their office and observe them in their daily environment in order to soak up the atmosphere of a real-life private investigation firm. She had been surprised by how small and dingy their office was. She imagined some high-tech enterprise with IT experts and labs with digital footprint analysis, not a tiny office on the second floor of a two-story brick building with a scuffed desk they shared and a worn couch that had seen better days for clients to sit on.

Sandra explained that she had tried to redecorate and even offered to foot the bill, but Maya refused. She could concentrate better in her pared-down surroundings with the same furniture and unreliable coffee maker she had when she first opened her doors for business.

After signing a nondisclosure agreement, assuring them she would not discuss any case they were currently working on, Alyssa quietly took a seat on the couch and listened as Maya and Sandra debated what to do next about the Tawny Bryce case. Chad would be on high alert now that he knew they were trying to catch him in the act. He was so cocky, so brazen, so confident in his own smarts, that he had emailed a picture of Maya's car parked out in front of his office just to let them know he was aware of their every move. There was no way he would make a rookie mistake from this point forward.

Alyssa, who sat in the lotus position on the couch, almost meditating, listened with her eyes closed. Sandra smiled, she found Alyssa's New Agey practices charming.

Maya just thought they were weird.

Hollywood weird.

"Do you think there's the possibility that Tawny's just being paranoid about Chad cheating on her? I mean, Chad was so bold and fearless about challenging us to catch him with another woman, maybe it's because he's not actually cheating and just messing with Tawny, trying to make her think he is," Maya suggested.

Sandra shook her head. "No, definitely not. As you know, I am intimately aware of all the telltale signs of a cheating spouse . . ."

Alyssa popped her eyes open, her face full of sympathy, and mouthed silently, "I'm so sorry, Sandra."

Sandra waved her off. "It's fine. I'm a lot happier now. Our relationship is much, much better now that we're divorced and he lives five hundred and sixty miles away in DC."

Maya nodded in agreement.

"I absolutely believe Tawny is right," Sandra said. "Chad oozes smugness and entitlement. He has all the characteristics of your textbook philanderer. Plus Tawny had those text messages that were supposedly from the other woman."

Alyssa shot her hand up in the air.

Maya and Sandra stared at her blankly.

"May I say something?"

"Of course," Maya laughed. "This isn't high school English class. You don't have to raise your hand to speak. But you will need a hall pass to go to the little girls' room."

Alyssa grinned. "I agree with Sandra. I've dated dozens of men in Hollywood, and I've developed a keen eye for obvious infidelity. And Chad's the poster child. He is exactly like all the actors and directors and executives who live to flaunt their masculinity and virility and general horniness. It's a rare breed that doesn't eventually act upon it. I've seen it all. My trailer on set is like a therapist's office, with distraught women filing in and out, worrying about what their husband or partner or boyfriend is doing behind their back."

Maya gave Alyssa a slight nod. "Thank you, Alyssa."

"Sorry, I know I'm just supposed to be observing. I'll shut up. Pretend I'm not even here."

"It's fine, really. Say anything that comes to mind. We're happy for the help," Sandra chirped.

Speak for yourself, Maya thought. Then she sat up in her chair from behind the desk, folding her hands. "Okay, we need a new battle plan. Chad's going to be on the lookout for us. We can probably tail him, but getting close enough to get any kind of photographic evidence is going to be tough. He'll see us coming a mile away."

Alyssa raised her hand again.

Maya dropped her head. "Yes, Alyssa? You have something you want to say?"

"I can do it."

Maya raised an eyebrow. "Do what?"

"I can get the photographic evidence you need."

Maya sighed. "Alyssa, we appreciate the offer, but if Chad can recognize me and Sandra, you waltzing in is ten times worse. Practically the whole world knows who you are. There's no way Chad would ever put himself in a compromising position if you were around."

"Right. If Alyssa Turner was around. But what if I was someone else? Hello! Girls, in case you forgot, I'm an actress. I can play different parts. Didn't you see *Shadows of Seduction*, where I played Grace, the unhinged serial killer targeting women from her college sorority, including a poor, unsuspecting Anna Kendrick? The critics said I was completely unrecognizable. My manager was so furious when I lost the Golden Globe to Helen Mirren, who's already got, what, like a hundred already?"

Maya felt as if Alyssa was speaking a foreign language.

Sandra perked up. "You want to go undercover?"

"Yes! It's perfect! I can slip in anywhere unnoticed and get you the proof you need to take to Tawny."

Maya clapped a hand down on the desk. "No. Absolutely not. It's way too dangerous."

"Dangerous? We're talking about Chad Bryce. I've handled much worse than him in Hollywood. I nearly snapped the thumb off an Oscar-winning director who got too handsy at the Polo Lounge. Hashtag Me Too!"

Maya shot Sandra a look as if to say, *We need to stand firm on this. Do not waver.*

"I think Maya's right, Alyssa. If we let you put yourself into that kind of situation and something were to go wrong, we'd never forgive ourselves."

Alyssa was not about to give up. "I'll wear a wire. You'll be with me the whole time. And if things go south, we'll just call in Braden."

Maya and Sandra exchanged confused looks.

"Who's Braden?" Sandra asked.

"The guy who drove me here today. You brought him coffee and a danish, which was so sweet and totally you, Sandra. Well, he's not just my driver. He's a trained bodyguard. He comes with me everywhere. Even home to Maine. There are a lot of crazies out there, and I've had my share of stalkers. I call him my head of security, but it's just him. It's not like I'm Tom Cruise or Johnny Depp. I don't need a whole traveling entourage."

Maya remembered meeting Braden briefly when Alyssa first arrived at the office. He was a big, beefy Dave Bautista type, could have been a wrestler, formidable and intimidating. But he did have a kind smile and a twinkle in his eye.

Okay, she had to admit, he was wildly attractive.

But she would not be mentioning that fact to Max.

"Braden can shadow me wherever I go. No one will know who he is, and you can rest assured, I'll be safe," Alyssa pressed.

Maya was still not on board with this cockamamie plan.

Sandra, on the other hand, was wavering.

Just as Maya had predicted.

"I would feel better knowing Braden was close by," Sandra said.

Maya's mouth dropped open. "Are you seriously considering this?"

Sandra shrugged. "What other choice do we have? I'm open to suggestions."

Maya's eyes flicked over to Alyssa, who was bouncing up and down, breathless with anticipation. Maya feared that if she put her foot down, told her it was a hard pass, she might go off and do it anyway.

On her own.

With no supervision from trained professionals.

Against her better judgment, Maya relented. "Okay, but you do exactly what we say, no veering off script."

"Fine. I'm not big on improv anyway," Alyssa cooed with a wink. "Now, as for my character, I'm thinking divorcée, mid-forties, maybe she's named Candy, hardened by life, just trying to make ends meet after getting taken advantage of by a string of bad men and bad choices."

Sandra chuckled.

Maya just prayed nothing would go wrong.

And now, here they were, parked out in front of the Strike City Bowling Alley, watching Alyssa, aka Candy, saunter inside. Just behind her, but at a safe distance, Braden followed in his own local getup. Flannel shirt. Smudged jeans. L.L.Bean hiking boots. A Red Sox baseball cap. Although he looked the part, it would be far more difficult for him to blend into the crowd, given his massive size. Maya suspected the women inside would be eyeing him ravenously, their hearts aflutter.

Tawny had alerted them that Chad had called earlier to let her know he would be working late.

A clichéd excuse but always effective.

They had just hoped that Chad would wind up in a public setting, a place with easy access, although they were not above peeping through the windows of a private residence, if necessary.

Luckily, Chad had driven to Strike City.

After they tested the wire and microphone they had hidden under Alyssa's bulky clothes, the mission was set in motion.

Once Alyssa was inside, Maya and Sandra had trouble hearing anything, given the chatter of the bowlers, all the balls knocking down pins, and the jukebox blasting Luke Bryan country hits.

Alyssa said something unintelligible.

"You have to speak up, Alyssa! We can't hear you!" Maya shouted.

Alyssa must have covered the mic with her hand to drown out the loud ambient sounds because she spoke in a whisper. "I can't. I'm standing right next to him."

"Don't get too close!" Maya barked.

The next thing they knew, Alyssa was engaging with Chad, asking him for pointers on how to bowl, remarking that it was her first time at Strike Alley. Chad's replies were half-hearted and borderline annoyed. He was obviously not impressed with Alyssa's dowdy appearance.

"Is this your girlfriend?" Alyssa asked.

"Yes, this is Lindsay," Chad said.

"Hi!" Lindsay purred.

Maya and Sandra exchanged excited glances.

"I'm Candy. So nice to meet you both. Do you two come here often?"

"Sometimes," Chad said gruffly, pausing before speaking in a low, firm voice. "Listen, Candy, this is our date night, and so, if you don't mind, we'd like to be alone."

"Oh, of course, no problem. I'm meeting some friends anyway. Have a nice evening."

They could hear from the rustling sounds that Alyssa was moving away, far enough so that Chad and Lindsay's voices faded.

Five minutes passed.

Maya and Sandra waited, expectant.

But they only heard balls and pins colliding and more Luke Bryan songs.

Finally, Maya could not take the suspense anymore. "Alyssa, talk to us. What's happening?"

"I'm getting you gold. We'll be out soon . . . if I can tear Braden away from his fan club at the bar."

A few minutes later, Alyssa, aka Candy, came bounding out of the bowling alley. Braden followed closely on her heels. Alyssa slid into the back seat of the car, handing Maya her phone, as Braden stoically stood guard outside.

Alyssa had not been kidding.

It was gold.

All gold.

Photo after photo of Chad canoodling with a much younger woman, Lindsay, who could not have been more than twenty-five. If that.

It was all there.

Hugging.

Kissing.

Pawing each other.

As much as they could get away with in a public setting.

Maya glanced up from the phone and looked at Alyssa through the rearview mirror. "You know, we might be willing to talk about giving you a permanent spot on our team."

Alyssa, ditching the itchy wig and heavy glasses, gave them that megawatt movie star smile. "Sounds intriguing, but you may not be able to meet my quote of seven million a film."

The three of them erupted in laughter.

And Maya could not deny the immense feeling of satisfaction.

Chad Bryce was toast.

Chapter 7

Tawny Bryce's eyes widened in shock, before narrowing with fury, as she watched the clear evidence of her husband, Chad, giving a tongue bath to a buxom local girl at the Strike City Bowling Alley on Maya's phone in their office.

"I knew it," she spat out. "I knew it! I knew it! I knew it!" And then, rather unexpectedly, she burst into tears. Sandra rushed over to comfort her as Maya plucked the phone out of Tawny's grasp, suspecting she had seen enough.

"I'm sorry, Tawny, I know how difficult this must be," Sandra said softly.

Maya shook her head. "I'm confused. You seem surprised by this. When you hired us, you were so certain he was cheating."

Tawny nodded, sniffling. "I guess I held out the slightest bit of hope that maybe, just maybe, I was wrong about all of this, that I was being overly suspicious. That those text messages were just some kind of sick joke. It was foolish of me, I know."

Sandra put a comforting arm around Tawny's shoulder. "No, it's not. No matter how much you prepare yourself, it's still a gut punch when you're actually confronted with it. Trust me, I know. I lived it."

"And he's doing it right out in the open! At Strike City, of all places! We used to take our kids there every Sunday night. They had a discount on the extra-large family-style pizza. How could he be so flagrantly obvious? It's like he's not even trying that hard to hide it! It's as if he *wants* to publicly humiliate me!" She shot out her hand. "Give me your phone. I want to watch it again."

Maya hesitated. "Are you sure that's a good idea?"

Tawny did not bother responding. She just snatched the phone back from Maya and played the video again, shaking her head in dismay, anger building. "How did you get so close to him and his little Lolita? I thought you said Chad was onto you. He would've seen you filming him."

Maya and Sandra exchanged furtive glances.

They knew there was no way either of them was going to cop to the fact that they had enlisted the help of a major Hollywood actress and sent her in undercover.

Maya cleared her throat. "We often hire part-time help if a specific case warrants it."

Sandra gave her a silent thumbs-up.

"So who's the home wrecker? Do we know?" Tawny growled, glaring at the screen.

"Yes. We were able to track her down through Chad's social media contacts. She's, uh, local. Her name is Lindsay Buckman," Sandra said.

Tawny wrinkled her nose and scoffed. "She looks so young. Is she even of legal age?"

"Yes. She's twenty-three," Maya muttered. "Mother is a middle-school teacher, and her father works in construction. She majored in Media Studies at the University of Southern Maine. According to her Instagram posts, her goal is to be the next Jenna Bush Hager hosting the third hour of the *Today Show* and starting her own on-air book club."

"I think I'm going to be sick," Tawny groaned. She tossed Maya's phone down on the coffee table and whipped out her own, googling Lindsay's name, desperate to find out more information.

Sandra gently patted Tawny's arm. "Tawny, it's probably best you focus on Chad and not the other woman . . ."

Tawny shot her a look. "Oh, believe me, I will be focusing on Chad soon enough!" Then her eyes darted back to her phone. "Oh dear Lord, she was second runner-up at the Miss Maine Teen USA pageant. Could she be any more of a cliché? Somebody just shoot me!"

Although Sandra felt completely at home coddling and comforting the client, Maya was done. She was ready to move on to another case. But she knew she had to be tactful, a skill she admitted she was sorely lacking. "So, Tawny, I have already emailed you the evidence and full report, so I suppose the next order of business is the bill. I can invoice you with wire instructions on how to—"

"Oh, I've paid already," Tawny sniffed.

"You have?" Maya asked, taken aback. "I just checked our emails before you arrived and—"

"I Venmo-ed you the fee, plus a sizable bonus for a job well done. Check your business account. It's all there."

"Oh, well, thank you," Maya said as Sandra gave her an eye roll for bringing up money during this obviously difficult time for Tawny. But Tawny did not seem to care. She was now making a phone call.

"Hello, Kendall? Tawny Bryce. It's go time." She paused. "Yes, I'm emailing you everything you need to get the ball rolling. You have my instructions on when and where, correct?" She paused again. "Good. Ciao." She ended the call.

"Who was that?" Sandra asked.

"Kendall James. My divorce attorney. We've been in close contact ever since I hired you to get the goods on my deplorable, faithless husband. Kendall's drawing up the papers now, and we plan on serving Chad at the high school reunion in front of all his former classmates."

Sandra bit her lip, concerned. "Oh, Tawny, do you honestly think that's a good idea? Why create so much unnecessary drama at the reunion?"

"I'm not the one creating unnecessary drama, Sandra," Tawny snapped. "Chad's the one flaunting his disgusting dalliance with Ariana Grande all over town, at family establishments, no less. He deserves everything that's coming to him."

"She has a point," Maya conceded.

Sandra shot Maya an admonishing look.

"Besides, Chad's been making noises about running

for City Council. He actually thinks people like him enough to vote for him. Well, a public spectacle revealing his true character will put the kibosh on *those* plans," Tawny cackled.

She actually cackled, Maya thought to herself.

Like a wicked witch casting a spell.

Maya was pretty confident that Sandra was not going to be able to dissuade Tawny from going through with all this. She was a woman scorned and hell-bent on revenge. And she was determined to inflict as much pain as she possibly could on her lying, cheating husband. Although she would not admit it to Sandra, Maya thought that maybe a messy scene involving infidelity accusations and a process server shoving divorce papers at Chad in front of the SoPo High Class of 2000 might spice up what would most likely be an otherwise dull evening.

"Did you hear the rumor that Alyssa Turner might show up at the reunion?" Tawny gushed, shifting topics so fast Maya thought she might get whiplash.

"It's more than just a rumor," Sandra said. "We spoke to her. She will definitely be there."

"It will be so nice to see her again. I always liked Alyssa. She was such a sweet girl and smart and pretty. I always knew she was going places," Tawny cooed, trying to convince herself that she actually believed this page-one rewrite of history.

Both Maya and Sandra remained tight-lipped about Alyssa's contribution to the evidence presented this morning because Tawny might not appreciate a public figure of Alyssa's stature playing such a crucial role in bringing down Chad.

They had to keep it a secret.

"It will be so rewarding to watch Chad dissolve into a puddle of regret in front of his favorite film actress, whom he has pined for all these years. It will be the worst moment of his life. He'll finally understand that rock bottom has a basement."

Tawny cackled again.

This time louder and more forcefully.

This was starting to feel tragically Shakespearean.

Double, double, toil and trouble.

Let the games begin.

Chapter 8

A hush suddenly fell over the gathered crowd in the decorated gymnasium when word began to spread that Alyssa Turner had arrived at the SoPo High class reunion. The room was bathed in the soft glow of fairy lights and adorned with banners proclaiming WELCOME BACK, CLASS OF 2000! The DJ's music, Britney Spears's pop classic "Oops . . . I Did It Again!" seemed to fade into the background as all eyes turned to the entrance.

Maya and Sandra, standing alongside their dates, Max and Lucas, joined everyone as they all directed their eyes toward the doors that had just swung open, signaling the grand entrance of the girl who was not even close to being chosen for Most Likely to Succeed in the high school yearbook.

Amidst the anticipation, Alyssa emerged, her presence commanding the room instantly. A Hollywood star in every sense, she exuded confidence and grace with every step. Dressed in a stunning designer gown that shimmered under the dimmed lights and hugged her curves in all the right places, she moved with the poise of someone accustomed to the spotlight, her radiant smile lighting up the room, her auburn locks cascading in perfect waves around her shoulders. She was shadowed by her hulking, handsome bodyguard, Braden.

Gasps of astonishment rippled through the crowd of attendees as they caught sight of her. Some whispered excitedly to one another, while others simply stared in awe. A few found themselves clapping in admiration. Memories no doubt came flooding back to most as they recalled the shy teenager who once roamed these halls, transformed now into a vision of success and beauty.

It did not take long for a few starstruck souls to swoop in to say hello, stumbling over their words, gushing about her latest film or television appearance. But most of her former classmates were more reserved in that New England sort of way, pretending she was just like anybody else and did not deserve any kind of special treatment.

Maya noticed that Tawny, the former queen bee, and her two best friends from high school, Kat and Amanda, her ladies in waiting, huddled together in a corner, watching the scene with keen interest. Maya could tell that Tawny was sizing up Alyssa, trying to figure out how long her memory stretched back, perhaps hoping Alyssa, with her glamorous, exciting life, had mostly forgotten how awful Tawny had treated her in high school.

Maya had to suppress a smile.

Bullied girls *never* forget.

Even with all the whispers and stares, Maya could feel a palpable sense of pride in the room, as her classmates welcomed one of their own who had reached such heights of fame and fortune. But for tonight, they were all equals once again, united by the bonds of friendship and the memories of their shared past.

"Honestly, I don't see what all the fuss is about," Lucas remarked before downing the rest of his gin and tonic.

Sandra spun around to face him. "I'm sorry?"

Lucas shrugged. "I mean she's pretty and all, but she doesn't hold a candle to you, Sandra."

Maya could not help but snort.

"You're not seriously doing this right now, are you?" Sandra sighed.

"Doing what?"

"Comparing me to a glamorous movie star? On my best day, I don't even come close to . . ." She gestured toward a perfectly put-together Alyssa, who was floating around the room greeting everyone. "That!"

"Well, I respectfully disagree," Lucas huffed.

"Stop trying to score brownie points, bud," Max said with a sneer. "You're here as her date. You've already won. You don't have to try so hard."

"Don't listen to him, Lucas," Maya said. "I'm lucky if Max even notices me in the room when the Patriots are playing a game on TV. There's nothing wrong with a few well-meaning compliments."

Max pretended to be preoccupied ogling Alyssa. "I'm sorry, dear, did you say something?"

Maya swatted him on the behind. "Thin ice, mister."

"I'm just saying I'm the luckiest guy here tonight. All that Hollywood glamour business is all manufactured and fake, and I've got the real thing right here."

Sandra took a breath and rolled her eyes.

Maya could see Sandra was uncomfortable with Lucas's unbridled devotion. She happened to think it was cute and endearing. But she knew Sandra found it awkward and disconcerting. They had discussed it many times. Sandra was already struggling with the issue of his age. By constantly putting her on a pedestal, Lucas just exacerbated Sandra's doubts about the whole relationship.

Despite his claims of being unimpressed, Lucas could not stop watching Alyssa work the room.

Sandra took the opportunity to pull Maya aside.

"Please don't encourage him," Sandra pleaded.

"Come on, it's adorable."

"No, it's cringy."

"Why are you so hesitant about Lucas? He's a decent guy with a good heart. And he thinks the world of you. Do you how many women would kill for that?"

"We're just so different."

"You mean age-wise."

"Of course that's what I mean. What's going to happen when he's forty and in his prime and I'm an old lady on Medicare?"

"First of all, you're exaggerating the age difference. You're not that far apart. And I read somewhere that it's the woman who hits her prime later in life. Men typically peak in their twenties, so you should enjoy him now while you still can."

Sandra threw her a look. "You're not helping."

"All I'm saying is you two have been dating for almost a year. He's a catch. You're a catch. You can't keep him at arm's length forever. There. I've said my piece. I promise not to mention it again."

Out of the corner of her eye, Maya spotted Alyssa breaking away from a gaggle of admirers and making her way over to their group. Everyone in the room, especially Tawny and her posse, stood frozen, watching, their eyes glued to her. Max suddenly sprang to attention. Lucas continued his campaign, trying to be blasé and bored by Alyssa's presence, but now that she was up close, even he could not deny her star power.

"I was hoping you two would already be here," Alyssa said, hugging Sandra first and then Maya. "There's safety in numbers." She gave them the once-over. "You both look fabulous, by the way."

"She does, doesn't she?" Lucas piped in.

Sandra had to refrain from elbowing him in the rib cage.

Instead, she stepped back next to Lucas. "Alyssa, this is Lucas, my . . ." Her voice drifted off.

"Boyfriend. I'm her boyfriend," Lucas interjected with a bright smile, pumping Alyssa's hand.

Alyssa looked impressed, as if she wanted to say, *You go, girl!*

The young coach was objectively a very handsome man.

And noticeably younger.

Which just made Sandra want to shrink and disappear.

Max stepped forward, saving the day for Sandra. "And I'm Maya's equally handsome and studly husband Max. It's nice to meet you, Alyssa."

"Nice to meet you too, Max," Alyssa giggled.

"I'm not the type to get starstruck or anything, but I gotta tell you, I loved you in *Firestorm: Reign of the*

Dragons! Especially the scene toward the end when you climbed up that monster's back, carrying that sword, and then, bam, you literally went for the jugular! All that blood and guts! It was awesome!" Max gushed.

"Thank you, Max. That was like my second movie. And it was a huge flop, by the way. It nearly killed my career."

"My husband's taste in film is rather limited to mind-numbingly violent action movies. He hasn't seen much of your, shall we say, more critically acclaimed work," Maya said with a wry smile.

Sandra glanced around the room. "I thought you were bringing a date?"

"I am. Aaron had to deal with an unexpected crisis on set. He missed his flight and had to catch a later one to Boston. He's hired a car to bring him straight here after he gets in. Which is soon, I hope. I'm so nervous."

"*You*? What do you have to be nervous about? Everyone here can't take their eyes off you!" Maya scoffed.

"Believe it or not, all this attention just makes me feel ill at ease. I should be used to it by now, but here, with these people, I can feel myself reverting to what I was like in high school, that pitifully shy, insecure wallflower. It's all rushing back."

Her eyes darted over to Tawny, Kat, and Amanda.

"And I can't help but remember those who were responsible for the absolute hell I went through."

Maya was taken aback by the obvious rage in Alyssa's eyes as she glared over at Tawny and her friends.

As if she was silently planning in her mind some sort of sweet revenge.

Amanda noticed Alyssa shooting daggers with her eyes first as Tawny and Kat pretended to be engaged in a conversation, not trying to steal glances in Alyssa's direction. The harshness of her gaze caused Amanda to shiver enough that some of her drink spilled over the sides of her glass.

The coldness in Alyssa's hardened facial expression was so startling, Maya felt the urge to reach over and gently touch Alyssa's arm. "Hey, are you okay?"

And then, like the seasoned actress she was, Alyssa instantly snapped out of it and returned to her usual sunny and sparkling personality.

"I'm fine!" Alyssa chirped. "But in the immortal words of the great Bette Davis, from one of my all-time favorite movies, *All About Eve*, 'Fasten your seat-belts because it's going to be a bumpy night'!"

Chapter 9

Amidst all the buzz of nostalgic chatter and laughter, Sandra noticed two of her former cheerleading teammates, Tawny and Kat, huddled in a corner, engaged in a heated discussion. At one point, Kat had her finger pointing so close to Tawny's face she almost touched her nose. Tawny seemed to brush her off, trying to push past her, but Kat blocked her escape and continued berating her about something.

"Those two are always feuding about something," a woman's voice purred from behind. Sandra spun around to find herself face-to-face with Tawny's other lady-in-waiting, Amanda. She had never liked Amanda much, especially when Amanda fell under the impression junior year that Sandra was secretly dating her boyfriend, Brent, behind her back. There was no truth to the rumor, but Amanda seized the opportunity to systematically ice out Sandra from her circle of friends and try to label her as a slut. Despite Sandra's best efforts to deny any involvement with Brent, there was no convincing Amanda, and so Sandra had finally moved on and found a new circle of friends.

Sandra had to admit that Amanda still looked good, but she was disconcerted by her gaze, as piercing as ever, sweeping across Sandra with a mix of curiosity and something else—something that hinted at old grudges. Sandra could not believe Amanda would still be thinking about that ugly rumor from twenty-five years ago.

"Sandra, I must say, you look positively radiant tonight," Amanda drawled, her smile a bit too sweet to be genuine.

Sandra returned the smile, but hers held a hint of steel. "Thank you, Amanda. You as well." Her eyes drifted back over to Tawny and Kat, who were still arguing. "Is everything alright between those two?"

"Oh, god, yes," Amanda sniffed. "If they weren't constantly at each other's throats, I'd think the world was off its axis. I'm sure it's nothing." Amanda's eyes sparkled with mischief as she leaned in closer. "So where's that charming husband of yours? I expected to see him attached to your arm as usual."

Sandra's expression faltered for a fraction of a second before she recovered with practiced ease. "In DC, I expect. Taking care of Senate business."

"Making the world a better place for all of us, I'm sure," Amanda cooed insincerely. "It's a shame he couldn't come up here to accompany you to your high school reunion."

Sandra's jaw clenched imperceptibly, but she maintained her composure. "I'm sure you're aware that Stephen and I are no longer together. We've been officially divorced for over a year."

Amanda raised an eyebrow, her smirk growing more pronounced. "What? No! I had no idea!"

Of course she did.

It had been all over the local news.

She would have had to be living under a rock not to know.

Amanda was obviously just toying with her.

"I'm so sorry to hear that," Amanda cooed. "Dean and I have been together seven years. But sometimes it feels like fifty. Marriage can be so hard sometimes. But at least this is the second go-around for both of us, so we're a little more prepared. So you came to the reunion on your own?"

Sandra's heart skipped a beat, but she refused to show any sign of weakness. "No, I'm here with . . ." Sandra's eyes darted over toward Lucas, who was standing with Max. They made eye contact, and Lucas blew her a little kiss.

"Is that your son Jack? He's so grown up now! And so adorable. How sweet that he escorted his mother to her high school reunion."

She knew perfectly well that Lucas was not her older son Jack.

They did not even have the same hair color.

And Lucas was about a foot taller.

"No, Amanda, that's Lucas. He's my . . . boyfriend."

"Well, now," Amanda said, with a lascivious grin. "Color me jealous. Way to go, girl."

Maya suddenly appeared by Sandra's side, interrupting the conversation. "Hey, I just ran into Debbie Keebler, remember her? She got suspended for smoking pot on school grounds more times than I did. She is dying to say hello to us."

Sandra pretended to pout. "Sorry, Amanda, would you excuse us? It was lovely chatting with you."

Now it was Sandra's turn to sound insincere.

Amanda straightened up, her smirk widening into an impish grin. "Of course. I wouldn't want to keep you from your fan club."

And with that, Amanda sauntered off.

"It looked like you needed rescuing. I don't think Debbie's even here tonight," Maya chuckled.

"Thank you," Sandra sighed. "Just when you start having fun connecting with old classmates, you get cornered by someone like Amanda Mathers who reminds you just why you hated high school."

"You've got it easy. If I have one more person come up to me and tell me how brave it is for Max and I to show up here tonight, I'm going to go all She-Hulk on somebody!"

Sandra patted Maya's arm.

Even though Max had paid his debt to society for his past sins, his police corruption conviction was still a hot gossip topic in town. And Maya was still paying for her own guilt by association as well. But luckily, she was stubborn and tenacious and had a thick skin, and Sandra could see that she was not about to let it bring her down.

People were always going to talk.

But she did not have to listen.

"Well, Amanda just confused Lucas with my son Jack."

"Okay, I'm out. You win for Most Humiliating Moment."

They shared a laugh.

Maya's eyes moved to the gym entrance. "Wait, *who* is *that*?"

A man had just strolled in fashionably late. He exuded an aura of confidence and success, his tailored suit accentuating his chiseled features and commanding presence, looking as if he had just stepped off a cover of *GQ* or *Men's Health*.

Sandra's mouth fell open. "I have no idea, but he is seriously hot!"

His eyes searched the room and settled upon Alyssa, who was at the bar, surrounded by a group of adoring fans. As he swept across the gymnasium toward her, he seemed to be oblivious to all the heads turning and the whispers erupting from the crowd. People could not help but gawk at the sight of him, their eyes widening in awe at his undeniable allure.

Maya's eyes followed him. "That must be the boyfriend Alyssa talked about. The movie producer. Aaron."

When he reached Alyssa, he embraced her, holding her for a long time before kissing her softly on the lips.

Sandra could tell Alyssa was basking in the attention, her heart swelling with pride as she watched her date command the room with effortless charm. She had once been invisible to most of these people. But now, with her own rocketing, sky-high career and with undeniably the most gorgeous man in the room as her date, she was obviously relishing this personal triumph.

It did not take long for an eager throng of women to work up the nerve to swoop in and engage him in polite conversation. Kat and Amanda were first in line.

But Sandra noticed that amidst the flurry of attention, one figure remained noticeably apart. Tawny lingered on the outskirts, her gaze fixed on the handsome stranger with a mixture of curiosity and apprehension.

Sandra wondered why Tawny, typically a social butterfly and shameless flirt, was abstaining from vying for his attention, unlike all the other women with their seductive smiles and lingering touches.

Perhaps she was more focused on the mission that she had planned on executing this evening: publicly destroying her cheating husband, Chad, who was now buzzed on one too many whiskey sours while reminiscing with his old football buddies, with no clue as to what was about to happen.

CHAPTER 10

Although Tawny continued keeping a safe distance, Kat had no hesitation in rushing up to Alyssa to say hello, as if they had been the best of friends in high school and beyond. Alyssa's whole body stiffened as Kat threw her arms around her, drawing her in for a tight squeeze.

Sandra had to suppress a smirk.

Alyssa looked so uncomfortable.

"I would've come over earlier, but I didn't want to fight my way through the crowd around you! How've you been, girl?" Kat cooed.

Alyssa, shell-shocked, stood numbly, the memories of Kat's abuse from years past rushing back. Of all the girls who had treated Alyssa badly in high school, Sandra recalled that Kat might have been the worst.

"F-fine," Alyssa stammered, regressing back to that painfully shy girl with pigtails and braces.

"I'd say you're doing more than just fine! I still read *People* magazine. I know how much you make per movie!

Did you fly here on your private jet? Where's my invite, girl? Let's take it to St. Tropez in France! Isn't that where all the hot celebrities go to party?"

"I wouldn't know," Alyssa muttered.

"Do you know Jason Momoa? Can you introduce me? I know he's married and all, but I told Scott, my husband, that he's my freebie. If I ever meet Jason Momoa, I get to sleep with him!"

Sandra was quite sure Jason Momoa might have something to say about that.

"Scott's freebie is the girl who played Veronica on *Riverdale*, Camille, Camilla, I can't remember her name, but I'm like, who? Okay, whatever! So do you know him?"

"We've met, but I wouldn't say we were friends," Alyssa answered coolly.

"I remember that we had the same taste in guys in high school. Didn't you have a crush on Chad too? God, I was so in love with him back then, but now? Now I'm like, thank God Tawny won that contest in the long run, because, ew, no thank you!"

Alyssa flicked her eyes over at her bodyguard, Braden, who stood stoically by the door, keeping an eye on things, making sure no one invaded her personal space too much.

Meanwhile, Aaron was trapped in the middle of a gaggle of admirers, mostly women, pummeling him with questions about his exciting Hollywood career and what intoxicating cologne he was wearing.

Alyssa's face seemed to be screaming for someone to rescue her from this awkward conversation with Kat, who had no compunction about rewriting history and casting herself as one of Alyssa's close allies, when, in fact, she had been one of her most brutal tormentors.

"Is that what you were discussing a few minutes ago?" Sandra piped in.

Kat swiveled her head, surprised to see Sandra. "Oh, Sandra, I didn't see you standing there. Hi, how have you been?"

"I've been good, Kat," she said evenly.

"I was so sorry to hear about you and Senator Wallage. That must have been a hard adjustment. I mean, no longer being the toast of Washington."

As bitchy as her comment sounded, Sandra was not the least bit offended, because she could tell Kat was picturing herself in Sandra's position as the ex-wife of the senator and so no longer close to the power center. It said more about her than Sandra.

"I love spending more time here in Maine . . ." Sandra started.

That was all she was going to get.

Kat suddenly remembered something. "Sorry, what did you ask me just now? I forgot."

"I asked what you and Tawny were discussing over there in the corner earlier. Pardon me for being nosy, I was just concerned. You both looked a bit unglued."

Kat cocked her head to the right. "What? No, we were just talking about—" She stopped herself. "It was nothing. A little disagreement, already resolved, ancient history, nothing to worry about. You know how these reunions can be, past drama resurfacing."

She was not convincing in her attempt at a full-throated denial that anything was wrong.

"Yes, I'm acutely aware about past drama resurfacing," Alyssa said pointedly, her stare drilling into Kat. "And how that can make you feel."

Kat finally got the message.

She was not welcome.

"Well, I better go find my husband before he drinks too much and finds a Veronica look-alike to flirt with. It was so nice seeing you again, Alyssa. You too, Sandra."

Sandra gave her a little wave. "Bye."

Kat backed off, then slowly pivoted and skulked away.

"She hasn't changed a bit since high school," Alyssa noted.

"Yes, she still looks terrific."

"I was talking about her awful, grating personality."

"I know. I just wanted to hear you say it."

They giggled.

Unexpectedly a man's thick calloused hand clamped down on Alyssa's bare arm, startling her. She recoiled as she turned to see Chad, Tawny's husband, moving up close, his breath reeking of alcohol. "Hey, remember me?"

Fueled by liquid courage, he covered his name tag with his free hand so she would be forced to guess.

Alyssa tried to wriggle free from his vicelike grip, but he held on tight. "Of course. Chad. How are you?"

He gave her a wink. "I knew you hadn't forgotten mc."

She finally managed to slip out of his grasp, signaling to Bradcn, who had moved closer to intervene, if necessary, that she was alright and he could stand down.

"Hi, Chad," Sandra said, her voice dripping with disdain.

Chad's watery eyes settled on Sandra, and he frowned.

The last thing he wanted was for Sandra to give Alyssa an earful about his cheating ways. He simply gave her a curt nod and then redirected his full attention to Alyssa. He leered at her with a smug grin. His once-boyish charm had faded, replaced by bitterness and regret.

"You look beautiful," he whispered.

"Thank you. And you, it's as if I just saw you yesterday," Alyssa commented.

He completely missed the joke.

Because he had been totally unaware that she had seen him yesterday, covertly snapping pictures of him at the bowling alley while he was cheating on his wife.

Chad stared at her wistfully. "It's times like these you kind of tend to relive the past, you know what I mean?"

"I do," Alyssa answered coldly.

"I remember you had a big crush on me back in high school."

Alyssa nodded slightly. "You're right. I *did*."

Sandra wanted to applaud Alyssa's emphasis on the word *did*.

"Yeah, I totally screwed that up, didn't I?" Chad murmured.

"It's all worked out for the best. You ended up with Tawny, and look, you married her, so it was meant to be."

"Meant to be, yeah, right," Chad spit out.

"Trouble in paradise?" Alyssa asked, feigning ignorance.

Chad's eyes were downcast. "You could say that." He raised them back up and gave Sandra a sharp glance. "She thinks I'm cheating on her, but I'm not."

That was a desperate lie so Alyssa would not think less of him.

But she obviously knew better.

"Anyway, I didn't come over here to talk about my marriage." He paused, trying to work up the nerve, the copious amounts of alcohol in his system helping to urge him on. "I just think you're so . . ." His voice trailed off. "We make choices in life, some good, some bad, and I can't stop thinking about choosing Tawny when I could have chosen . . ."

It was a pathetic moment.

Even Sandra felt sorry for him.

He was proving himself to be what Sandra had already suspected he was: a walking cliché of the high school jock crowned homecoming king whose best days were now long behind him.

He was making a total fool of himself.

And it was sad to watch.

"I guess what I'm trying to say, badly I know, is that maybe one day if I'm available, and if you happen to be available—"

"I'm not."

"What?"

"I'm not available. I have a boyfriend. He's right over there," Alyssa said quickly, pointing.

Chad looked around. "Which one?"

"The incredibly handsome one wearing the Tom Ford suit and Rolex watch surrounded by most of the women here," Sandra interjected, hoping to put an end to his misery.

Chad deflated. "Oh." He gave Aaron the once-over. "Yeah, that makes sense. Of course you'd be with him."

Sandra thought he might cry.

But he just did not want to give up so soon.

"I'm no Hollywood jetsetter. I've worked in construction for most of my life, but I've been trying to find ways to better myself, and I don't know if you know this, but I'm running for City Council. I want to get more involved with the community, do some good, you know?"

There was a deafening silence.

Alyssa finally felt the need to say something, anything. "That's nice."

Kat's husband, Scott, had wandered over, sensing his buddy was embarrassing himself, and swooped in to rescue him before Alyssa's bodyguard did that deed for him. "Hey, Chad, how about we get you another drink?"

Sandra raised an eyebrow. "You think that's wise?"

Scott gave her a rueful look. "Yeah, actually I do. It's probably best he blacks out and totally forgets about everything tonight."

He had a point.

But what Scott did not know was that Chad's night was about to get exponentially worse.

CHAPTER 11

Maya could see Max was having a good time socializing with her former classmates. The problem was Maya did not consider many of those in attendance as close friends.

Or even acquaintances.

The rougher crowd she had run with during her high school years had not even bothered to show up for the reunion. Some had moved to get away from their toxic upbringings, a few were incarcerated, and two were sadly dead. One from a drug overdose. The other in a car crash trying to outrun a speeding ticket. Maya's parents were mostly absent when she was growing up; she was basically raised by her grandmother Lucia, whom she adored, and who passed away when Maya was enrolled in the police academy. At least she lived long enough to see Maya try to make something of herself. She knew on her deathbed that Maya was going to be a positive force in society. And she could not have been prouder. It made losing her slightly less painful.

Although that moment in hospice, when Maya was holding her grandmother's hand and felt her slipping away, had been a gut punch. She had never felt so alone as at that moment.

Remembering her grandmother made Maya smile. She cherished that woman. She had lived a full life. But Maya's only regret was that Lucia did not live to meet Maya's daughter Vanessa, valedictorian of her class, now enrolled in college, determined to make her mark in the world.

A shining star.

In Maya's mind, her greatest achievement.

Max's hand touched the small of her back. "Hey, what are you doing hiding over here in the corner? I'm mingling with more people, and I didn't even go to school here."

"I just don't feel any connection with these people. I mean, I know who they are, mostly the parents of Vanessa's friends from PTA meetings and school events, but I didn't run with this crowd in high school. These are mostly the popular kids. I was more of an outsider. And I still feel like I don't belong."

"You know what they say, it's always the outsiders who go on to greatness."

Aaron suddenly appeared in front of them. "Hey, have you seen Alyssa? I kind of got distracted and lost track of her."

"No wonder you were distracted. We saw all those women buzzing around you," Max cracked. "You were like some rare flower in the garden, and they were bees unable to resist the allure of your beauty."

Maya cocked an eyebrow. "That was good, Max. I

wasn't even aware that you knew what a metaphor was."

Max shrugged. "I heard it on some home gardening show on HGTV."

Aaron's face flushed. "Now you're embarrassing me."

"Seriously, dude, why are you wasting your time behind the camera when you should obviously be in front of it?" Max asked.

"Trust me, an actor's life is not for me. I need to be running things, in total control. That's why I became a producer." His eyes fell upon Alyssa and Sandra, who were now crossing the room to join them, with Lucas shadowing them from behind. When they were all gathered together, Alyssa leaned in conspiratorially. "I think we've stuck around long enough. How about we all ditch the reunion and go have a late dinner at Central Provisions. I love that place."

"But it's a Saturday night. I'm sure they're booked. We'll never get in, and the kitchen probably closes at ten, and it's already nine-thirty," Maya said before catching herself. "Oh, right. You're famous. If we just show up, they'll of course make room for us."

"I can call ahead and give them a heads-up we're coming," Alyssa said. "Do you think we can slip out of here unnoticed?"

Aaron glanced around. "Everyone can't stop staring at you, so, no, I think a quiet exit is off the table."

"Tawny mentioned there was going to be some kind of presentation in a few minutes. Maybe we should stay for that and then leave," Sandra suggested.

"I'm going to need another drink then," Max moaned, waving around his empty glass.

"I'll get it," Lucas said, taking his glass. "Anyone else?"

"I'll just have a bottled water. If I get tipsy, it's suddenly an international news story," Alyssa pouted.

After rounding up everyone's drink order, Lucas hustled off toward the bar.

Alyssa turned to Sandra. "He's so cute."

"Like a rambunctious puppy," Sandra said under her breath.

Maya nudged her side with her elbow and whispered, "Stop it."

"You're right, sorry. I'm being unfair," Sandra admitted.

Tawny stepped up on a riser that had a podium and microphone and was situated in front of a large white screen. She adjusted the mic to her height level and then spoke into it. "Good evening, everyone." There was some feedback that caused a few people to cover their ears. Tawny paused and then continued, speaking at a lower volume. "Thank you all for coming out tonight to celebrate the twenty-fifth reunion of the SoPo High Class of 2000!"

There were applause and catcalls.

Tawny pumped her fist in the air. "Whoo!"

She waited for the applause to die down.

"Now I know typically the class president makes a speech, but we all know Noah Furman is way too busy out in Palo Alto, California, developing the latest AI technology that will soon take over the world and make the human race extinct. So let's have some fun tonight before that happens! Whoo!"

She paused for laughter, but there was none.

Maybe a few titters.

She cleared her throat and continued. "Anyway, I'm not very good at making speeches, so instead of talking about what life was like back when we were seniors, why not just show you? So with the help of my besties, Kat and Amanda, who you all know, right . . . ?"

She paused again for applause.

There was none at first.

But Tawny was not having it.

She waited defiantly until one person clapped, then another and another, until most of the crowd was half-heartedly giving the women a round of applause.

"Let's give it up for Kat and Amanda! Whoo! So the three of us have put together a video highlighting that seminal time in our lives, some long-forgotten memories that we hope will bring us all some laughter, some cheer, and yes, maybe even a few tears. Enjoy, everybody!"

The lights shut off, engulfing the gym in darkness, except for the glitter from the disco ball hanging from one of the basketball nets that was still slowly turning in circles. First on the screen was a title card, Y2K TO FOREVER: A TRIBUTE TO THE CLASS OF 2000. First up was a video of the football team's homecoming victory, the crowd going wild, the players excitedly jumping into a pile of human bodies on the field, the cheerleaders crying and hugging, then the players dumping a jug of water over their stoic coach, causing him to laugh.

Everyone in the gym cheered at the memory.

Then another video followed of the cheerleading team during the half-time show, jiggling and jumping and showing off their sexy dance moves with Tawny and a pony-tailed, fresh-faced, cherubic Sandra front and center, pretending to be Britney Spears and Cristina Aguilera.

Maya chuckled as she turned to see Sandra horrified, covering her face with her hands. Lucas, who had returned with everyone's drinks, with the help of a bartender, glowed as he watched a young Sandra up on the big screen.

The next video was prom night, the gym they were in now decorated with its theme, A Night Under the Stars, including decorations like twinkling lights, starry backdrops, and celestial motifs, creating a romantic and enchanting atmosphere as everyone in their tuxes and dresses danced to "Music" by Madonna. This was followed by a montage of high school yearbook photos. As all the familiar young faces popped up, people in the crowd howled, groaned, and screamed at how much everyone had changed.

When Maya's photo came up, she quickly averted her eyes and shook her head. She hardly recognized that hardened girl, barely smiling and with bangs that seemed to go on forever.

Max turned and whispered in her ear. "Beautiful then, beautiful now."

Maya just prayed they would move on to the next photo quickly.

Following the montage, there were more short videos, and it felt like they were watching a high school version of *America's Funniest Videos* with senior pranks, pratfalls at pep rallies, the French class field trip to Paris.

And then suddenly the mood quickly changed.

After a smiling group shot in front of the Eiffel Tower, the next video was of Chad.

But he was not the eighteen-year-old Chad, the suave handsome big man on campus. This was forty-three-year-old Chad making out with a much younger woman at the Strike City Bowling Alley.

Maya found herself gasping in shock with everyone else in the gym as they watched Chad unable to control himself, mauling this willing woman in front of the Strike City patrons.

Tawny stood off to the side in front of everyone, illuminated by the screen, soaking in all the attention as her classmates turned to her in shock and disbelief, their faces a mixture of horror and sympathy. She held her head high, her façade unwavering as she met their gaze with steely determination.

What they did not realize in the moment was that this surprise had been carefully orchestrated by Tawny herself.

Suddenly a man's booming voice filled the air. "What the hell is going on? Somebody shut it off!"

It was Chad.

He was losing it.

He marched to the front, shooting Tawny a furious look, then began waving his arms in the air. "I said turn it off!"

Somebody finally complied, and the lights came back up.

The room fell to a hush so complete Maya could hear her own heartbeat.

Chad was so mad it looked as if he was going to spit at his wife. "Is this your idea of a sick joke?"

With a trembling voice, Tawny addressed the room, her words cutting through the stunned silence. "It's no joke, dear. I just thought all our classmates would like to see for themselves what you've been up to since high school."

The air crackled with tension as the revelation hung heavy in the room.

Maya could almost feel the surge of empowerment coursing through Tawny's veins as she watched her husband practically melt into a pool of humiliation.

"Why would you do something like this, so publicly, without talking to me first?" Chad whined.

"I'm not doing this just for me. I'm doing it as a concerned citizen. The people in this district deserve to know everything about the man running for their City Council when they go to the polls later this fall. I consider it a public service."

Chad's jaw dropped.

He had obviously underestimated his wife.

Her deceptivness.

Her thirst for revenge.

And it had cost him.

Dearly.

Maya could hear the ice cubes in the drink Chad was holding clinking due to his hand shaking.

A young man in his early twenties, with long wavy red hair and an impish smile that reminded Maya of Olympic gold medalist snowboarder Shawn White, made his way through the crowd to the front of the room, walking right up to Chad.

"Who the hell are you? You didn't go to school with us," Chad snapped.

"No, sir," the kid answered with a laconic smile. "I just graduated in 2022. I'm still in college."

"Then what are you doing here?"

The kid raised his T-shirt up and extracted a white envelope from the waistband of his shorts. He handed it to Chad. "Divorce papers. Consider yourself served."

And then he gave a quick salute to Tawny, as if this had all been prearranged, and sauntered off.

Alyssa turned to Maya. "All this tension and drama. I feel as if I'm watching one of my movies."

Tawny bravely stood her ground, refusing to move.

She was waiting for Chad to leave first.

He glared at her, the fury building up inside him. She had disgraced him, degraded him, and, most importantly, crushed his pride.

He took a step toward her.

She refused to budge.

Smiling at him.

Daring him to further cause a scene.

He took another step closer.

Maya feared he might strike her.

And so did Alyssa's bodyguard, Braden, who left his post near the door and began to slowly approach, ready to intervene at a moment's notice.

But Chad did not touch a hair on his wife's head.

Instead, he hurled his drink in her face.

There were more gasps from the crowd.

Tawny kept the smile plastered on her face, refusing to react.

Maya knew she was praying someone was recording this on their phone.

Another nail in aspiring politician Chad's coffin.

And then he fled the gym.

Wiping her face with her forearm, Tawny made her way back to the podium and spoke into the microphone. “I hope you enjoyed the presentation. The night is young, so come on, everybody, let’s party!”

Mission accomplished.

Chapter 12

Maya had not noticed Marcus Heel lingering nearby, gazing longingly at Alyssa, too shy to approach. He clutched his glass of spiked punch, gulping it down, trying to work up the courage to come over and say hello. Maya remembered Marcus had always been an odd duck in high school. His locker was next to hers, and he had unhealthy obsessions with famous TV actresses of the time, such as Alyssa Milano from *Charmed*, Sarah Michelle Gellar from *Buffy the Vampire Slayer*, and Katie Holmes from *Dawson's Creek*, all of whom adorned the inside of his locker in publicity photos he had collected. Maya could only imagine how mind-blowing it must be for Marcus now to see one of his classmates a bigger star than all of them combined. Any girl in school who even remotely resembled one of his obsessions would inevitably become his object of desire, and he would obsessively write love notes and follow them constantly down the hall like a lovesick puppy and even, it was reported, hang outside their homes trying to catch a glimpse of them through their bedroom window. One girl's parents called the police to complain about his stalking, and he was absent from school for a month. Most people assumed he had been suspended, but there were rumors he had been sent to a psychiatric facility. In any event, when he returned to school, he had not changed at all, and he simply picked up where he had left off, following pretty girls around and acting creepy.

Marcus's eyes darted back and forth nervously, and he had to set his drink down to wipe his sweaty palms down the sides of his dress pants. Maya figured it was only a matter of time before Marcus would make the monumental decision to attempt to start up a conversation with the Hollywood star.

Maya felt the urge to warn Alyssa what she might be in for, and so she breezed over and sidled up beside her. "Fair warning. Marcus Heel is working up the nerve to come over to you."

Alyssa glanced around and made eye contact with him. She smiled and nodded. Marcus was so caught off guard he did an about-face and turned away, as if her star power was too overwhelming, too blinding to handle. "I always had a soft spot for Marcus. I know all the kids made fun of him for being weird, but we were lab partners in Biology class, and I thought he was nice. One time, Mr. Stephens gave us a pop quiz and I hadn't studied the pages he had assigned, and so I got all but one of the answers wrong. We had to switch papers with our partners to score each other's tests, and when

Marcus handed mine back, I had gotten an A. He had erased all my wrong answers and written in the correct ones. I found that so sweet."

"Where's your date?"

"I sent him to get me another drink, but lo and behold, he's been ambushed again by his army of admirers. He's exceedingly polite and would never be rude, so I'm guessing he's going to be stuck there for a while."

Alyssa caught a glimpse of Marcus again standing frozen a few feet away, muttering to himself, as if berating himself for being such a coward, too afraid to come up to Alyssa. "I'm going to make this easier for him. Come on."

Alyssa bounded over to Marcus, whose eyes widened in surprise, his jaw nearly dropping to the floor. Maya followed behind her. "Hi, Marcus! Do you remember me?"

He could not speak.

He just stared at her.

"We were lab partners in Biology. I was just telling Maya how you saved my butt once with that pop quiz that I wasn't prepared for."

He never looked at Maya.

He had no idea she was even there.

He nodded, grinning, baring crooked teeth, the memory of that day seared in his brain. "I-I remember."

"How have you been?"

"F-fine. I work in hospital transportation. I wheel the patients where they need to go. To their rooms. To surgery. Sometimes even to the morgue."

"How nice. That sounds like a good job. I'm happy for you."

"I've seen all your movies. Sometimes twice, even three times. I didn't like that superhero movie you did. I thought it was silly."

"Well, to be honest, Marcus, so did I," she replied with a wink.

"I like your romantic comedies much better. They . . . they showcase your sense of humor. You're very funny. You make me laugh. You always made me laugh in high school."

"Well, I have highly paid writers now who feed me the jokes, so I give all the credit to them."

"You, you look so pretty tonight, Alyssa."

"Why, thank you, Marcus. And you're looking quite dashing yourself in that nice suit."

"I got it on sale at TJ Maxx. It was seventy-nine ninety-nine for the jacket and pants. The tie cost extra. That was twelve dollars. The shirt I already had. I got it last Christmas from my parents. I heard you were coming, so I wanted to look real nice."

"Well, congratulations, Marcus, you definitely scored a win."

She was making his night.

Probably his whole year.

And it spoke volumes about her character that she had been the only one of Marcus's former classmates to engage in a conversation with him.

Suddenly, the DJ spun the Ricky Martin classic from 1999, "Livin' la Vida Loca," and a large swath of the crowd took to the dance floor. Maya could see

Aaron trying to beg off the torrent of invitations from the women around him to join them dancing. Then she noticed Marcus watching everyone bopping up and down, singing along. He desperately wanted to ask Alyssa to dance. Finally, throwing caution to the wind, he opened his mouth to speak, when suddenly Tawny swooped in, blocking him from Alyssa. She was still on a high from her emasculation of Chad.

"Honey, the girls want a TikTok video of us dancing to Ricky Martin. You have to come join us!"

Alyssa hesitated. "I don't know . . ."

This was not something she wanted to do.

Especially with Tawny and her mean girl posse.

But Tawny was not about to take no for an answer. "Please! You must! With you, we'll go viral! Our kids will love it!"

Before Alyssa could answer, Marcus tapped Tawny on the shoulder. She spun around, taken aback by his unexpected presence.

"Oh. Hello."

She did not even bother calling him by his name.

Even though it was in plain sight on the name tag that was pinned to his jacket.

"You have some nerve coming over here and talking to Alyssa like you were best friends in high school, Tawny." He spat out her name like a curse, his voice trembling with pent-up rage.

Tawny took a step back. "I beg your pardon?"

"We all witnessed firsthand how you treated Alyssa in high school, how awful you were, how rude and mean, and now, after all these years, you try to pretend like that never happened? I find you despicable!"

Marcus had clearly found his voice now.

Tawny was so astonished she did not know what to say.

Alyssa reached out and touched his arm. "It's okay, Marcus. Really. Time heals all wounds, as they say. I don't harbor any hard feelings. That was a long time ago."

"She has no right to speak to you like you're old friends. No right," he growled.

Tawny stared at Marcus for the longest time, processing this unexpected attack, and then, she cracked up, her laughing echoing through the gym, cutting through the air like a sharp blade just as the Ricky Martin song finished.

Marcus clenched his fists, his knuckles turning white with fury. "You made her life a living hell, and you think it's *funny*?"

"No, dear, I just forgot what a huge crush you had on Alyssa in high school. I thought they were going to have to cart you away again for more professional help like they did when you stalked Deidre Holloway and followed her family during Christmas vacation junior year when they went skiing at Sugarloaf."

She flipped her hair dismissively.

"Tawny . . ." Maya warned with a stern tone.

There was menace in Marcus's intense gaze.

Tawny instinctively knew she had crossed a line, that Marcus could explode at any moment, and it was time to rein herself back in. "Well, sorry to interrupt your quality time with Alyssa, Marcus." She turned to Alyssa. "We'll record the video another time, so I'll leave you to it."

She floated away.

Alyssa smiled at Marcus. "My knight in shining armor."

Maya wished that Alyssa had not said that.

It was only encouraging him, fueling his emotions.

He took hold of her wrist.

"Dance with me."

She gave a cursory glance at his hand encircled around her wrist. Maya could see she wanted to pull away, but she also did not want to give the impression she was outright rejecting him. "I'm not much of a dancer, Marcus."

"I saw you ballroom dance in *Swing into Love* with Andy Samberg on Netflix. You were amazing."

"I had a trainer for that. It took me months just to get those few moves down. Trust me, I'll crush your toes."

She gently tried to yank her hand free.

He tightened his grip.

Braden, her bodyguard, sensed danger and quickly moved in, appearing behind Marcus, about a foot and a half taller and twice as wide with his muscular chest and intimidating posture. "Time to move on, buddy."

Marcus did not immediately let go.

So Braden clamped a giant paw down on his right shoulder and squeezed enough to make him wince.

Alyssa flushed with embarrassment. "No. It's okay, Braden."

Mercifully Marcus finally released her, and Alyssa rubbed her wrist.

But she remained unfailingly polite. "It was lovely

seeing you again after all these years, Marcus. I had fun catching up."

"Can we have dinner while you're here? I have Thursdays and Fridays off, but I work the night shift on the weekend, so we'd have to do breakfast. I know a place that serves champagne on Sundays."

"Thank you so much, but I'm actually here with my boyfriend, and we're all booked up while we're here, but it was very kind of you to invite me."

Maya feared Marcus was not going to give up and could start causing a scene, so she started to steer Alyssa away. "Speaking of Aaron, he's probably somewhere trying to make his escape, so why don't you go over there and rescue him?"

Alyssa nodded, flashing that megawatt smile, and skittered away, leaving Maya and Braden with a crestfallen Marcus.

"I need some fresh air," Marcus said scowling, stung by defeat. He walked off in a huff.

Braden shook his head. "She can be too nice. These crazy fans. You give them an inch, they take a mile."

"Well, she's got you around to make sure she doesn't get into too much trouble."

"Everyone wants a piece of her. It can be hard to watch. She's such a lovely girl. But way too trusting."

"She is lovely. Beautiful on the inside and out," Maya commented.

Braden nodded. "Yes, Alyssa definitely is beautiful. But I would strongly argue she's not the most beautiful woman here tonight."

Wait, Maya thought. *Back up*.

Was he talking about *her*?

Was he flirting with her?

She looked him straight in the eye.

He winked at her.

A sly smile crept across his lips.

Yes.

He was definitely flirting with her.

And, unfortunately, her husband, Max, had approached them from behind and overheard the whole thing.

He stepped in and put a territorial arm around his wife. "Yeah, I would have to agree with you on that one, buddy."

They stared each other down.

Like two battle-ready lions about to clash for the title of king of the jungle.

Braden finally nodded and smiled and backed away.

And Maya could feel her husband's grip on her relax.

Men.

Chapter 13

"Alright, I think I've experienced enough nostalgia and reminiscing for one evening. Anyone still up for a late dinner? I called Central Provisions, and they're keeping the kitchen open for us," Alyssa said as Maya, Sandra, Max, Lucas, and Aaron all gathered by the bar.

"Good, I'm starving," Aaron said with his impossibly charming smile. "Let's blow this joint."

As they all headed for the exit, Sandra stopped in her tracks. "Wait, look who just showed up."

Alyssa gasped. "I was so certain he wasn't going to make it. I heard on the news he was testifying in front of congress today down in DC."

"Me too," Sandra said. "Which would explain why he's so late."

Maya looked at the man who had just swept into the room. He was tall, lean, with angular features and wavy brown hair; he was casual cool in his pressed jeans and a black dress shirt open at the collar, confident in his stride. He seemed familiar, but she could not quite place him. "Who is that?"

Sandra chuckled. "You don't recognize him?"

"My first boyfriend," Alyssa whispered.

Aaron cocked an eyebrow. "Boyfriend?"

"Yes, sophomore year. We met in the Chess Club. Pretty much the only extracurricular activity I dared to join because I was so shy and I knew you didn't have to talk while playing chess. Noah was the only one who was more socially awkward than me, so we bonded immediately. We were both total nerds."

Maya gasped. "Wait. Is that—?"

Alyssa nodded. "Noah Furman."

Aaron gave them a skeptical look. "I can't imagine that guy ever being a nerd."

"Smartest guy in the whole class and probably the most picked on by the jocks. But he kept his head down and got through high school and wound up at MIT. Now he's like the most revered tech genius in all of Silicon Valley."

"So he's got money," Aaron marveled.

"Maybe not Musk or Gates money, but pretty darn close," Sandra said. "His latest social media app is where all the kids are flocking to these days."

Lucas perked up. "TalkUp? That's his? Oh, man, you're right. He must be so loaded."

Sandra was not surprised Lucas knew what apps all the kids were logging onto these days.

"Sorry, Alyssa, I think you just dropped into second place as the richest person in the room," Lucas said, smirking.

They watched as Noah said hello to a few people, grabbed a drink, and then began scanning the crowd as if he was looking for someone. His eyes finally settled on Alyssa. They made eye contact, and he broke out into a wide smile.

"I don't remember his teeth being so dazzlingly white, do you?" Maya cracked.

"The braces he wore since the sixth grade must have paid off," Sandra laughed.

Aaron visibly stiffened as Noah weaved through the crowd over to them, stopping in front of Alyssa and giving her a warm smile. "Well, look who's here . . . Turanga Leela."

Alyssa beamed. "How's it going, Philip J. Fry?"

Aaron was totally confused. "Is this some kind of secret language you two share?"

Alyssa threw her head back and guffawed. "We were obsessed with watching *Futurama* . . ."

Aaron stared blankly.

"It was a sci-fi cartoon. Philip J. Fry was a pizza delivery boy from the twentieth century who was accidentally cryogenically frozen for a thousand years and woke up in the year 3000, and Turanga Leela was a space ship's captain, a one-eyed mutant who worked as a career assignment officer for Planet Express."

"We must have memorized every episode!" Noah exclaimed. "I think I can still name them all in order."

Aaron turned to Alyssa. "You're right. You two were total nerds back in high school."

Noah gave Alyssa a warm hug. "I'm so glad you're here. You're the only reason I high-tailed it up here from DC. I honestly didn't think I'd make it in time. We had to wait on the tarmac an hour and a half waiting to get my jet refueled."

Of course he came on his own private jet.

Aaron shifted uncomfortably. "We were just leaving."

Alyssa shot Aaron an admonishing look. "I'm sure we can stay a few minutes more. Like I said, the restaurant promised they would wait for us."

Noah put his hands on her arms, causing Aaron to flinch. "You haven't changed a bit."

"Oh, come on, now you're just teasing. Look, I actually have my own hairstylist now. No more greasy split ends."

"Yeah, I noticed. I just didn't want to be rude," he said with a playful wink.

"You certainly have changed quite a bit, Pizza Face," Alyssa giggled, giving him a soft jab in the ribs.

Noah shook his head and turned to Maya, Sandra, Max, and Lucas. "I may have had a slight acne problem in high school."

Maya noticed Aaron growing more and more agitated by the minute. He was not used to being upstaged by a man who, although was by no stretch as traditionally handsome as he was, was arguably a bit more charming. Aaron had enjoyed spending most of the evening playing Pied Piper, casting a spell on all the women in the room with his wit and elegance. But he did not have a private jet. And he did not have the history or, frankly, the connection with Alyssa that Noah had. And it made him very uncomfortable. But in the interest of keeping the peace, he stood by quietly, watching Alyssa and

Noah laugh at old corny jokes and silly memories. He was trying desperately to keep his jealousy in check as Noah got too close for comfort.

When they moved on to the favorite *Mystery Science Theater 3000* episodes they used to watch together, their laughter echoing through the gymnasium, Aaron had heard enough. He stepped forward, his possessive grip tightening around Alyssa's waist. "We should go."

Maya could feel the charged atmosphere.

"I'm not ready yet," Alyssa said through gritted teeth. "Why are you acting like this? You couldn't have cared less when Marcus was all over me earlier."

"This isn't Marcus," Aaron said with a steely gaze.

Noah suppressed a smirk, as if he was enjoying Aaron's inner meltdown. He probably saw Aaron as one of those boys who tortured him in high school, part of the good-looking, popular crowd that treated him like dirt on the bottom of their shoe. And now, with all his power and money and those perfectly white teeth, he was enjoying a completely different dynamic, one where *he* was in control, and it must have been a really good feeling.

"Fine. You let me know when you are ready. I'm going to go get another drink," Aaron seethed, marching off in a huff.

Alyssa's eyes brightened. "We're heading over to Central Provisions for a late dinner. Why don't you join us?"

Noah hesitated.

Even he was not sure he was ready to be subjected to Aaron's simmering temper tantrum.

"Come on, it'll be fun. Besides, is there anyone here you really want to talk to? They were all so mean to us in high school." She slipped her arm through his. "We haven't even got to our *Dungeons and Dragons* epic quests yet! We have so much to talk about!"

It appeared as if Noah was about to accept Alyssa's invitation when suddenly a piercing scream shattered the jovial mood, causing heads to turn and hearts to race.

In an instant, the gymnasium fell silent. And then Kat, her face pale with shock, stumbled backward from behind the bleachers, her eyes wide with terror, her hand over her mouth.

Maya and Sandra sprang into action, racing over behind the bleachers, where they were met with a chilling sight. There, lying motionless on the floor, was Tawny, on her back, arms and legs splayed out, her once vibrant personality now replaced with the cold stillness of death.

From the marks on her neck, they knew someone had strangled her. No one at the reunion had ever thought when the evening began that former mean girl Tawny Bryce would be the classmate Most Likely to Die.

Chapter 14

Detective Beth Hart surveyed the scene behind the bleachers as the CSI team snapped photos of the body and surrounding area, scouring for any clue that might tell the story of what happened. Hart's officers had moved everyone out of the gym and into the auditorium to await questioning, with the exception of Maya and Sandra. Given Maya's history with Hart when she was a cop, Hart had reluctantly given the go-ahead to allow them to stay behind and observe as long as they did not interfere with her initial investigation. Hart had good reason not to eject the pair of private investigators. They had proven useful in past cases. She would even go so far as to categorize their contributions as critical in finding crucial answers that ultimately led to the solving of the cases. But that was not something she was prepared to share with her bosses since she was currently on track to hopefully one day becoming Portland's chief of police, and she did not want to make the impression that she needed anyone's help. It was an unspoken agreement that she accepted their help on the down-low. For Maya and Sandra, it was a win-win. They had an in with the police department and were privy to vital information that could assist with their own cases.

Hart's eyes narrowed as she took in the body of Tawny Bryce, the long-ago popular cheerleader who now lay lifeless. Hart crouched down beside the body. The marks on Tawny's neck spoke volumes, confirming Maya and Sandra's suspicions that this was no accident.

This was a homicide.

Maya and Sandra hovered in the background, trying to stay out of the way, but itching to offer their opinion. Maya found it particularly frustrating that she had to wait to be asked to share her expertise. She was not good at remaining on the outer edges of a real murder investigation.

"What's taking her so long? It's clearly a homicide. Somebody strangled her. End of story. We should be discussing suspects, like Chad," Maya whispered, exasperated.

"She's just being thorough," Sandra said, gently patting her arm, as if calming an agitated horse ready to break free from her stall.

Hart finished processing the scene and popped back up to her feet, signaling to a young officer who was standing as a blockade to separate Maya and Sandra from the crime scene. The officer stepped aside, and Hart gestured for them to come join her.

Maya bolted forward, with Sandra rushing to keep

up. When she reached Hart, she blurted out, "It's the husband. He did it."

Hart cocked an eyebrow. "You seem pretty sure of yourself."

"She's not," Sandra piped in. "The husband just has a very strong motive."

Hart folded her arms. "Well, don't keep me in suspense."

Sandra recounted the earlier events of that evening. The video of memorable moments from the Class of 2000. How Tawny had dropped in the incriminating evidence of Chad's affair, the compromising photos, totally humiliating him in front of all his former classmates at the reunion.

Hart smirked, impressed. "Maybe the misogynists are right about one thing. The whole hell hath no fury like a woman scorned proverb."

"You should've seen his face," Maya remarked. "I've never seen anyone that angry, so full of hate."

"So it's safe to assume their marriage was very much on the rocks," Hart said.

"Oh, you don't know the half of it. After the video presentation, she had some kid serve him with divorce papers. It was all carefully orchestrated to maximize his total humiliation under the judgmental eyes of his peers," Sandra said.

Hart turned to the young officer, who stood at attention, awaiting orders. "Bring me the husband."

A few minutes later, Chad was escorted back into the gymnasium by the young officer and deposited in front of Detective Hart. Chad appeared pale and worn-out, with bags under his eyes. His gaze flicked toward Maya and Sandra, who stood quietly off to the side. He was not happy they were there watching.

Detective Hart held out a hand. "Mr. Bryce, I'm Detective Hart with the South Portland Police Department."

He hesitated, probably because he was uncomfortable talking to a female detective—yes, there were still men out there like him—but then he limply shook her hand, deciding he should not risk ticking her off.

"I need to ask you a few questions regarding the events leading up to your wife's death tonight."

Chad's jaw tightened, but he nodded curtly, a mask of composure slipping into place. "Okay."

"I understand your wife staged quite a show earlier," Hart said brusquely.

Chad shot Maya and Sandra another agitated look, knowing from whom she had gotten that information.

"Yes, she did."

"That must have made you very angry, to be embarrassed and shamed and demeaned like that, in front of your friends?"

"I wouldn't rank it up there as one of the best nights of my life, no. I honestly couldn't believe that Tawny had that kind of venom, that kind of rage festering inside her, and I've been married to her going on twenty-five years."

Hart nodded, taking it all in. She waited until Chad was finished rubbing his eyes with his hands. "Just how angry were you?"

Chad's façade wavered for a moment, a flicker of something akin to guilt crossing his features before he composed himself once more. "I know what you're getting at, *Detective*." His emphasis on the word detective dripped with disdain. "Look, Tawny and I . . . our marriage has been crumbling for years, we've grown apart, found separate interests . . ."

"Like the girl in the video?"

Maya could not believe that had just flown out of her mouth.

Hart shot her a sharp look.

Sandra gave Maya a gentle nudge to control herself.

Maya raised a hand, silently apologizing to Hart.

Chad just glared at her. Then, softening, he continued. "It's no secret we had problems. Everyone knew. And yes, I may have harbored fantasies of escape from the suffocating grip of our marriage, starting over with someone new. I'm sure she did too. We fought all the time. What I didn't expect was her taking it to the next level. Airing our dirty laundry in public, making me the laughingstock of our class, the whole town. That video, those photos she showed everyone tonight, it was like having my soul laid bare for all to see. Every lie, every deceitful moment, all laid out on that giant screen." He paused, trying hard not to lose control. The last thing he wanted was for tears to start streaming down both of his cheeks.

Maya suspected he really wanted to cry over Tawny's devastating betrayal, not the fact that she was dead.

"But *murder*? Just the idea that I would ever stoop so low as to take her life is repugnant to me. That's a line I would *never* cross. Tawny is the mother of my children."

He stopped to check if Detective Hart was buying one word of what he was spilling out of his mouth.

Her face was a mask of indifference, basically unreadable.

Chad flinched slightly and turned his attention back over to Maya and Sandra. There might have been a flash of sympathy from Sandra, but Maya's opinion of him was crystal clear.

Guilty.

And that made him shudder.

He was starting to get more anguished and distressed. He had to convince them. "Look, I need you all to understand. I loved Tawny, flawed as she was. I never would wish her harm, never would want to see her dead."

His words rang hollow.

They came off as desperate.

"Where were you after you were served with the divorce papers? Before Tawny's body was discovered behind the bleachers?" Hart pressed.

Chad's mind raced. "I went outside to cool off. A couple buddies came with me. I was ready to leave at that point, but they talked me into staying. We got another drink. I made the rounds, chatting with people, trying to do a little damage control and explain myself. I can give you names. I'm sure they'll back my story."

"I'll be sure to do that," Hart promised.

"Please, Detective," Chad whined. He turned to Maya and Sandra. "Please, all of you, find who did this. Find the truth, whatever it may be, because I can't bear of the thought of . . ." He swallowed, shaking his head. "I can't bear the thought of being branded a murderer for a crime I did not commit."

Maya calmly took a step toward him. "Funny. I thought you were going to say you couldn't bear the thought of never finding justice for Tawny."

Chad's whole mourning-husband façade suddenly crumbled in the wake of their scrutiny.

He limped away, defeated.

Leaving Maya more determined than ever to prove that Chad Bryce had killed his wife.

Chapter 15

As Sandra searched the hallway of SoPo High for Lucas, she spotted Marcus Heel at the far end of the hall, pacing angrily back and forth. By the look of betrayal and bitterness on his face, Sandra could only assume Alyssa's rejection of him had been festering as the night progressed. He had been so eager for a word, a smile, a memory, only to be cruelly pulled away from her by that towering gorilla paid to protect her from overzealous fans. But Sandra could see Marcus did not consider himself *just* a fan.

He was a friend.

They had a history.

All those Biology classes as lab partners.

Their connection, however fleeting, was real.

Sandra had seen him return to the gymnasium after the incident with Braden, but he had kept his distance, wandering the periphery of the celebration, a forgotten specter amidst the jubilant crowd. But when Tawny's body was discovered, Sandra had lost track of him again during the melee.

Marcus did not notice Sandra, as he seemed to make a decision and then slipped out a side door that led to the parking lot. Detective Hart had been explicit in her instructions. No one was to leave the auditorium until she had a chance to interview everyone.

Sandra instinctively followed him, her Jimmy Choos clicking on the floor as she hurried to the exit and pushed on the door handle, flinging it open to complete pandemonium. Reporters swarmed outside SoPo High, initially there to cover Alyssa's high-profile return. But the discovery of Tawny's body had transformed the event into a media circus. Since no one up to this point had been allowed to leave the building, the excited reporters descended upon Marcus like he was POTUS giving an impromptu press conference.

Sandra, who, as the former wife of a US senator, was famous in her own right and did not want to be recognized, quickly closed the door, but left it open a crack so she could still see everything going on outside.

The usually shy Marcus was suddenly basking in the attention of all the reporters and influencers, armed with their cameras and phones, who descended upon him. He stated his name, how he had been a classmate of both Alyssa Turner and the murder victim, Tawny Bryce.

The name of the victim was new information.

Up until now, most news outlets were reporting a death at the SoPo High Reunion, but the police had not yet released a name.

Thanks to Marcus, it was now public knowledge.

Detective Hart was not going to be happy about this.

Then Marcus took a dramatic pause before blurting out at the top of his lungs, "I saw Alyssa and Tawny arguing earlier, right before she was killed!"

Gasps echoed throughout the throng of press.

Chaos erupted.

Everyone started snapping photos of Marcus and shouting more questions all at once, sensing a sensational scoop.

One reporter's eyes lit up. "Really? What did you see?"

"They were by the bleachers. It looked heated. I couldn't hear what they were saying, but it seemed very serious."

The reporters needed no more. Within minutes, the story was live, flashing across screens and social media feeds: ACADEMY AWARD NOMINATED ACTRESS ALYSSA TURNER LINKED TO FORMER RIVAL'S DEATH AT HIGH SCHOOL REUNION!

Sandra's own phone started blowing up with breaking-news alerts.

All the same story.

Alyssa Turner was a suspect in a homicide.

Sandra shut the door and dashed back toward the auditorium, where she found Maya, Alyssa, Aaron, Lucas, and Max all gathered out in the hall, eyes glued to their phones. Braden hovered nearby, stone-faced.

Alyssa's face drained of color, and her whole body sagged as the firestorm of media coverage exploded in real time.

Aaron tried to make light of it. "So I guess dinner's off the table?"

No one laughed.

Alyssa's hand was visibly shaking as she held her phone. "This is not good. Who is out there talking to the press?"

Sandra took a breath. "Marcus Heel."

Alyssa's eyes widened. "But why would he—?" She did not have to finish her thought.

She knew why.

Sandra could see a hint of guilt on Braden's otherwise stoic face, fearing he might have somehow caused this by the way he had treated Marcus earlier.

"We need to get you out of here," Maya whispered urgently, already scanning an exit strategy.

Max spoke up. "But Detective Hart said—"

"Beth will understand. It's not like she won't be able to track down Alyssa whenever she wants. She's got almost as many eyes on her as Taylor Swift," Maya said.

"I'm sure they've got the school surrounded. Surely, they'll spot us trying to leave," Aaron barked, his agitation growing.

"Right, so we just take her out the front," Sandra said.

Aaron's mouth dropped open. "Are you crazy? They'll eat her alive!"

"Not if we create a diversion," Sandra suggested, mind racing. "We switch places. Alyssa and I are about the same size, same hair color. So we trade outfits, jewelry, everything. It's dark outside. Alyssa keeps her head down and goes out the front with Lucas, Maya, and Max; they'll just assume it's me, and I sneak out the back with Aaron and Braden, where I'm sure some intrepid reporter will spot us. Who do you think the press will chase?"

Maya cracked a smile.

Her partner had come up with the perfect plan.

Lucas gazed admiringly at her. "Isn't my girl smart? God, how did I get so lucky?"

Alyssa nodded tentatively. "I think it's a wild enough plan that it might just work."

They scooted off to the ladies' room, where Sandra and Alyssa swapped ensembles, while Maya went to find Detective Hart to explain what was happening. Hart was already aware of the media frenzy speculating about Alyssa's involvement in the case and immediately gave her stamp of approval to the escape plan. She considered Alyssa a low flight risk. No one with her high profile could easily flee the country. As long as Alyssa promised not to fly back to California before they had a chance to speak. Maya promised to deliver Alyssa to Hart for questioning at a place and time of her choosing.

When the two women emerged, Aaron and Lucas both did a double take. Sandra, all glammed up in Alyssa's designer dress, was a dead ringer. And Alyssa in Sandra's more subdued attire was acting the part to the hilt. The transformation was startling and disconcerting for both their boyfriends.

Once everyone was in place, Braden went ahead to get Aaron's rented sedan and position it near the back exit for a speedy escape.

It was go time.

The group moved swiftly. Sandra watched as Alyssa

took a deep breath and prepared to face the media circus outside. With Lucas at her side, she joined Maya and Max, who flanked her protectively.

Sandra spied through the narrow slits of the window blinds.

The front entrance was a chaotic scene. The crowd had ballooned in size, journalists and photographers jostling for position, eager to capture a shot of the star at the center of the controversy. As Alyssa, posing as Sandra, stepped into the fray, the flash of cameras and the barrage of questions were almost overwhelming.

"Do you know where Alyssa Turner is now? Has she been arrested?" one reporter shouted.

One savvy reporter thought he recognized Sandra. "Mrs. Wallage, do you have any comment on the allegations Alyssa Turner murdered someone here tonight?"

Sandra watched as Alyssa kept her head down, letting Lucas and Maya and Max guide her through the sea of press. The plan seemed to be working—no one suspected that the woman in the middle of the media storm was actually the woman they were so feverishly hunting.

Sandra felt a hand on her shoulder.

It was Aaron.

"I just got a text from Braden. We should go."

They made their way to the back entrance, where it was quieter, almost deserted. Aaron led Sandra out a side door, slipping into the cool night air. They navigated the darkened grounds of the high school, avoiding the main entrance, where the press was gathered en masse. The sedan was parked nearby, next to the football field. They could make out Braden behind the wheel. They moved swiftly, hoping to avoid detection.

But one reporter, a keen-eyed young woman who had been covering the event from all angles, spotted them as they passed by her.

"Hey, isn't that Alyssa Turner?" she muttered, grabbing her camera and sprinting after them.

Sandra heard the footsteps behind her and quickened her pace. Aaron, realizing they were being followed, positioned himself to shield her.

The reporter closed in, her camera flashing.

"Alyssa! Alyssa!" she called, breathless.

Sandra turned just as they reached the sedan. The reporter skidded to a halt, camera raised, ready to capture the moment. But as she focused, she realized something was off.

"Wait a minute," the reporter said, lowering her camera. "You're not Alyssa Turner."

Sandra flashed a quick, knowing smile. "No, I'm not. Looks like you were chasing the wrong person. Bummer."

The reporter stood stunned, the realization dawning on her. She had been outmaneuvered. Sandra and her group quickly slipped into the waiting car, and Braden drove off, leaving the reporter standing in the parking lot, fuming at her missed opportunity.

As they sped off into the night, Sandra received a text from Maya, confirming they had been able to break free from the media crush and escape virtually unnoticed.

Mission accomplished.

Chapter 16

The glare of the spotlight did not dim as the days passed, but only grew in intensity. The press camped outside Alyssa's parents' house, and the constant barrage of phone calls and knocks at the door became unbearable. Alyssa knew she could not stay there and subject her parents to this onslaught of attention for much longer. Her father was already dealing with a heart condition, and she did not want this circus to exacerbate his stress level. Desperate for some semblance of peace, she moved to a secure hotel downtown, a temporary refuge from the madness.

Maya and Sandra had received a desperate early-morning phone call from Alyssa, begging them to come see her in the top-floor suite of the Press Hotel in downtown Portland. By the time they arrived in the lobby, word was out that the local prosecutor, Robert Haskell, was calling a press conference at ten o'clock. It was already five to ten. Maya and Sandra rode the elevator up to the suite where Alyssa had sought refuge and found her and Aaron, wearing matching white terry-cloth robes, having just finished breakfast from room service.

"Thank you for coming," Alyssa said as she greeted them at the door, holding a mimosa in her hand.

Sandra took Alyssa's free hand in her own as she entered the suite. "How are you holding up?"

Alyssa took a sip of her mimosa. "I've had two already to calm my nerves. Let's hope the third one's the charm."

Maya held up her phone. "Alyssa, we got a report on our way over here that—"

"We know," Alyssa nodded. "The press conference."

Aaron stood up angrily. "Why is the prosecutor already talking to the press? Shouldn't the police be the ones giving updates about the investigation?"

"Yes, that's usually the protocol," Sandra noted. "But Haskell's a bit of a grandstander. I'm sure he sees this case as an opportunity to make a name for himself, raise his profile, maybe give him the boost he needs to throw his hat in the ring to be the next state attorney general."

"Sandra's being diplomatic," Maya scoffed. "He's a world class a-hole with an inflated opinion of himself."

Alyssa's heart sank. "Then I'm toast."

Aaron crossed over and put a comforting arm around her. "Let's not panic yet. We should hear what he has to say."

Maya did not want to dash their hopes of fair treatment by the prosecutor, so she kept her lips sealed. But she knew Haskell. She had dealt with him many times before when she was a cop and he was a bottom-feeding defense lawyer. He saw this as his ticket to the big time, going after a famous Hollywood actress despite an obvious lack of evidence, throwing all scruples out the window.

Maya checked the time on her phone. It was ten. She picked up the remote and turned on the television. Gayle King was just breaking away from her usual "Talk of the Table" segment on *CBS Mornings* in New York to go to live coverage of the press conference in Portland, Maine.

The morning sun glared down on the steps of the county courthouse, casting long shadows across the throng of reporters and cameramen jostling for position. The air was thick with anticipation, the hum of murmured conversations underscoring the tension. All eyes were fixed on the podium set up at the top of the stairs, where a row of microphones stood ready to capture every word.

At exactly ten o'clock, the courthouse doors swung open, and Haskell, a tall, confident man in a sharp suit, strode out. He approached the podium with a practiced air, adjusting the microphone and scanning the crowd with a determined gaze.

"Good morning, ladies and gentlemen," Haskell began, his voice resonating with authority. "Thank you for being here today. As you all know, the tragic murder of Tawny Bryce has shocked and saddened our community. I am here to provide an update on the investigation and to address the concerns and questions that have arisen."

Maya glanced over at Alyssa, who sat on the edge of the bed, nervously chewing on her fingernail, a habit she had probably had since childhood. Aaron was beside her, his protective arm still around her tense shoulders.

Watching Haskell, who had always had a flair for drama ever since the day she had first met him, made even Maya's stomach twist with dread.

Haskell continued, his tone growing more somber. "Tawny Bryce was found dead at South Portland High School during a twenty-fifth class reunion celebration, a time that should have been filled with joy and nostalgia. Instead, it has become a scene of tragedy. We have been working tirelessly to uncover the truth, and our investigation has led us to certain troubling facts."

He paused for effect, letting the tension build before delivering the punch. "One of the key figures in this investigation is Alyssa Turner, a well-known actress and former classmate of the deceased. We have received credible reports that Ms. Turner was seen arguing with Ms. Bryce shortly before her body was discovered."

The reporters erupted in a flurry of questions, but Haskell raised a hand to silence them. "I understand the public's curiosity and concern, but I want to be clear: we are not jumping to conclusions. Ms. Turner is a person of interest at this stage." He paused, feeling the need to add, "As are several others who knew the victim. We are exploring all leads and following the evidence wherever it takes us."

A reporter from the front row shouted, "Do you think she did it? In your opinion?"

Haskell's eyes gleamed as he seized the opportunity. "At this time, we are not labeling anyone a suspect until we have sufficient evidence. However, I must emphasize that no one is above the law, regardless of their fame or social status. We are committed to finding justice for Tawny Bryce and will pursue this case with the utmost diligence."

The questions continued to fly, each one more probing than the last, but Haskell maintained his composure, answering selectively to keep the press hanging on his every word.

"I assure you," he said finally, "that we will provide further updates as the investigation progresses. Thank you."

With that, he stepped away from the podium, leaving a storm of speculation and conjecture in his wake. The cameras flashed, and the reporters clamored for more, but Haskell had already made his impact.

"I'll say it again. World class a-hole," Maya spit out. "I'd say the whole word but Sandra doesn't like me swearing."

The little joke lightened the mood slightly, but Maya could see Alyssa spiraling.

Haskell's performance had been masterful, casting just enough doubt to keep the public intrigued while leaving her in a perilous limbo.

She turned to Maya and Sandra, who had been watching with her. "He's not going to stop until he sees me behind bars."

"No one's arresting you. He's got nothing," Maya said confidently. "Listen to me, Alyssa; that was a performance. It had nothing to do with facts. He's just enjoying his fifteen minutes of fame."

The television continued to broadcast the frenzied reactions of the reporters, but Alyssa picked up the remote and muted the volume, unable to bear hearing any more speculation about her involvement.

"Don't worry, Detective Hart is in charge of the investigation, and she is decent and fair," Sandra assured her.

Alyssa shook her head despondently. "I know how these things usually go. How the police can get swept up in all the press coverage, the hysteria, until they lose sight of the evidence and become desperate to pin the blame on someone, anyone, to wrap up the case. And what a story. Former high school outcast, now Hollywood A-lister, is triggered at her class reunion and offs her mean girl, queen bee tormentor. It writes itself. Soderberg can direct the film, and I'm sure they'll find someone big to play me, like Emily Blunt. Maybe she'll take home an Oscar for her riveting performance. She certainly deserves one."

"That is *never* going to happen," Sandra insisted.

"Even so, if all this rampant speculation continues, I may never recover. I'm sure to get canceled, and my once-illustrious career will be nothing but a dumpster fire." She paused, then turned to Maya and Sandra. "I need people on my side who know me, who trust and believe in me. I need you two."

"We are here for you," Sandra promised.

"I want more than that. I want to hire you to find whoever killed Tawny and prove to the world I'm innocent."

"Alyssa, I can't stress enough how good Beth, I mean Detective Hart, is at her job. I've worked with her. She'll solve this case, and you *will* be cleared, I promise," Maya said.

"With all due respect, I don't know her. I know you. I need you. Please, I'll pay double your going rate, triple."

"We're not going to charge you," Sandra said.

Maya wanted to give Sandra a sharp elbow to the ribs.

Sandra was rich.

Maya was not.

Triple their going rate would pay her bills for the next several months.

But she kept mum.

They would discuss it later.

Maya and Sandra looked at each other, a silent conversation passing between them.

Finally, Maya nodded. "Okay."

Alyssa released a huge sigh of relief. She still looked scared and overwhelmed, but Maya could see she now felt she had a fighting chance.

Alyssa checked the time on the clock by the bed and glanced over at Aaron. "Shouldn't you be getting to the airport?"

Aaron reacted with surprise. "What are you talking about? I'm not going anywhere. I need to be here to support you."

"No, Aaron, you should get back to the set," Alyssa urged.

Aaron looked at Alyssa, his eyes filled with determination. "I want to stay and help. I can't just leave you to deal with all of this alone."

Alyssa gave him a sad smile, grateful for his support, but knowing it was not practical. "Aaron, you have your own responsibilities. The movie needs you, and if you stay, the press will just use it against us. They'll say you're interfering with the investigation."

He sighed, running a hand through his hair. "I hate leaving you like this."

"I know," she whispered, squeezing his hand. "But I need you to trust me. We'll get through this. Maya and Sandra are here, and they know what they're doing."

Maya nodded in agreement. "We'll do everything we can to find the real killer, Aaron. Right now, the best thing you can do is keep the press off Alyssa's back by being visible on the set of your film."

Reluctantly, Aaron stood up, pulling Alyssa into a tight hug. "If you're sure this is what you want."

Alyssa kissed him softly on the lips. "I'm sure."

He hugged her again and then tightened the tie around his robe. "I better take a shower then."

He went into the bathroom and shut the door.

Alyssa's eyes locked on Maya and Sandra, and she raised her hands in prayer. "Thank you."

Maya and Sandra exchanged concerned glances. They had been through many investigations together, but this felt different—more personal, more urgent.

Alyssa Turner's life and career were on the line.

They had to get this one right.

Chapter 17

Stan Robbins, balding and wiry, fiddled with his tie in Maya and Sandra's office, a bundle of nervous energy. He had arrived on an overnight flight from LA to Boston and had rented a car to drive up to Portland for an early-morning meeting. He was on Alyssa's PR team, whose mission was to do damage control after Robert Haskell's devastating press conference. Alyssa's career and the millions of dollars her agents, manager, and publicists reaped from her success were all on the line if they could not clean up this mess and fast.

Alyssa had disguised herself in a maid's uniform Braden had borrowed from a willing housekeeping staffer, who was a huge Alyssa Turner fan, and was able to slip out the employee exit from the hotel, where Braden was waiting with a nondescript Kia he had rented from a car rental agency a few blocks away. He spirited her incognito to Maya and Sandra's office.

Now they all sat around with coffee, discussing next

steps. Stan, who loved hearing himself talk, took the lead. "Obviously, this Marcus guy is lying, so we need to deny, deny, deny. Am I right?" His eyes flicked over to Alyssa, who nodded slightly. "I mean his whole story is a complete fabrication. Alyssa had no contact with this Tammy person—"

"Tawny," Sandra corrected him.

"Whatever. It's nonsense, and we can scare the bejesus out of him by threatening a libel lawsuit against him in order to get him to retract his story. I've already called our lawyers in LA to draft the papers, and we can file them here in state court by midday. Okay? Everyone on board with this plan?"

He looked at Alyssa again.

Sandra could see she was hesitating.

So did Stan. "In my professional opinion, Alyssa, this is the best course of action. Nip this guy in the bud. Call him out as a liar."

Sandra leaned back in her chair, arms crossed, her intense gaze fixed on Alyssa, who sat across from them, looking every bit the Hollywood starlet, despite her distressed state. "What is it, Alyssa?"

Her lip quivered.

"You can tell us anything," Maya urged from across the office where she was leaning up against the wall, coffee cup in hand.

"He's not lying," Alyssa mumbled.

"*What?*" Stan screeched.

"He's not lying. He's telling the truth. I did have an altercation right before Tawny was found dead behind the bleachers."

Stan sucked in air. "Okay, we can still publicly deny it. Besides, Aaron has already tweeted that you were with him the whole night and you couldn't possibly have slipped away to commit a murder."

"Aaron just posted that to protect me," Alyssa sighed. "He was too busy getting hit on by half the women at the reunion."

Sandra leaned forward, the office chair creaking. "What happened with Tawny?"

Alyssa paused, gathering her thoughts, and then raised her eyes to meet Sandra's. "She approached me, maybe ten or fifteen minutes before her body was discovered. She said she needed to talk to me, that it was urgent, and wanted to go somewhere private."

Maya raised an eyebrow. "Did you go with her?"

Alyssa shook her head. "No. When she came up to me, I felt like a seventeen-year-old all over again. Something similar happened in high school. She came up to me in the hall and said she had something important to talk to me about, and I followed her into the girls' bathroom, and then she pushed me and threatened me, said to stay away from Chad, and then she ripped off my favorite charm bracelet and tried flushing it down the toilet. I ran home crying that day. I was so afraid of her after that, I avoided her at all costs. So when she cornered me at the reunion, it was so triggering, and I just wanted to get away from her."

"Did you find out what she wanted to you talk about?" Sandra asked gently.

"No, I didn't give her a chance. I tried to walk away,

but she was so insistent, and she grabbed me by the arm so hard I still have a mark. I just lost it. I screamed at her to leave me alone. Braden was by my side in an instant, and so she finally gave up and stalked off. I didn't think anyone had heard or seen it happen because the music was so loud and we were kind of off in a corner, but I guess I was wrong. Marcus must have slipped back inside the gymnasium in time to witness the whole thing."

Stan exhaled fretfully. "We need to get ahead of this. Discredit Marcus. Paint him as a bitter, lovesick nerd who is trying to get his fifteen minutes of fame."

Alyssa shot him a look. "We're not doing that, Stan."

"We have to do *something*!" he huffed. "Staying silent will only fan the flames and turn this little brush-fire into a raging inferno."

Maya crossed the room and sat down next to Alyssa. "Did anyone see you after the argument? Anyone who can confirm your whereabouts?"

Alyssa bit her lip, thinking. "I went to the bathroom to cool down. No one else was in there. I'm sure Braden was keeping an eye on the door from outside."

Stan jumped in again, his voice more urgent. "Yes, but a little reminder, Braden is your paid protector. Good luck getting twelve people on a jury to agree he's telling the truth. Alyssa, listen to me. We seriously have to spin this somehow."

Sandra stood up from the desk. "If Marcus saw Alyssa arguing with Tawny, others might have too. We need to get to the truth, not just spin a story."

Alyssa gave Stan a look of warning to stand down. He threw his arms up in the air, frustrated, but did not press the issue.

"You hired us to clear your name, find out who really did this, so give us a little time," Sandra advised. "It won't do anyone any good to go off half-cocked, calling witnesses liars and making denials that could come back to haunt you. Just keep your head down, stay out of the public eye for a bit, and let us do our job."

Alyssa turned to a discombobulated Stan. "She's right."

"So I flew all the way across the country for what? To just sit on my hands and do *nothing*?" Stan roared.

"Yes," Alyssa said cooly. "I'm paying you to work for me, and if that's what I want you to do, then you will do it."

That shut him up.

If puffing his chest out and yelling was going to cost him one of his firm's top clients, then Stan Robbins was not going to risk it. He plopped down in a chair and wiped the sweat off his face with a handkerchief he yanked out of his breast pocket and then glanced around. "Is there any more coffee?"

Alyssa tilted her head toward him. "Are you sure you can handle more caffeine?"

Sandra circled around the desk to fetch him another cup. She felt confident in her recommendation but was also a little wary. This was the highest-profile case she and Maya had ever worked on, and she was concerned they might not be up to the task. She had grown so fond of Alyssa in the short time she and Maya had gotten reacquainted with her; the last thing she wanted was to disappoint her or give her bad advice that would just make her situation worse.

But they had to follow their instincts.

And deep down, Sandra knew Alyssa Turner was innocent.

And there was someone else at that reunion who was fully capable of murder.

Chapter 18

The first thing Maya saw was the sweat glistening on his muscled arms as she entered the hotel gym. Alyssa's handsome bodyguard, in all his washboard-abs glory, was lifting weights in front of a wall mirror, wearing a tight red tank top and form-fitting navy blue shorts. His physical beauty nearly took Maya's breath away, but she managed to rein it in as she marched over to him. He did not hear her because he had Bluetooth plugs in his ears as he listened to music on his nearby phone. She patiently waited until he was nearing the end of his reps when he suddenly noticed her reflection in the mirror, standing a few feet behind him with her arms folded.

Braden placed the weights on the rack, wiped his face and arms with a white towel before tossing it over his shoulder and plucking out the earplugs. He caught Maya's eyes sweeping across his butt.

"Enjoying the view?" Braden cracked with a sly smile.

Maya's eyes instantly shot back up to his face, ignoring his question. "I didn't want to interrupt your workout. I was just waiting for you to finish."

He turned around and slowly approached her, coming up so close he was almost invading her personal space. "I'm all yours."

Maya instinctively took a step back.

"I know I get pretty ripe when I'm at the gym, so I probably reek. Should I take a quick shower first before we chat?" he asked in a deep, gravelly voice.

Maya was certain he had intentionally created the image of himself naked in the locker room in her mind. "No, you're fine. I just have a few questions."

"Shoot," he said with a flirtatious wink as he took a small step forward, muscles flexing.

"I, uh, I wanted to ask you about the night of the reunion. You were shadowing Alyssa, like always, so you must have been observing everyone around her."

He nodded. "That's my job. To be a buffer between her and all her adoring fans, who might get a little too excited being around her."

"So, you saw Tawny Bryce approaching Alyssa to try and talk to her?"

"Yes, I mean no. I didn't see her actually walk up to her. I was busy getting rid of the nerdy, stalker-y guy."

"Marcus."

"Yeah, the creep who's been mouthing off to the press and making Alyssa's life miserable. What's his deal, man? For someone who supposedly worships her, he sure does seem to be wanting to hurt her." He paused, trying to keep his fury in check; then he took a deep breath and continued. "I thought I had gotten rid of him, but he must have slipped past me when I wasn't looking. By the time I got back to the gym and located Alyssa, Tawny what's-her-name was already accosting her."

"What do you mean by accosting? Was she a physical threat?"

"No, nothing like that. She was just all up in Alyssa's face, trying to talk to her, and I could see it was making Alyssa very uncomfortable."

"Did Tawny seem angry to you?"

Braden shook his head. "Not angry, more like upset. As if something was on her mind and she desperately wanted to talk to her about it."

"Do you have any idea what she was upset about?"

Braden shrugged. "Not a clue. You'd have to ask Alyssa."

"She says she never let Tawny get the words out. She was just trying to get away from her."

"Yeah, she was relentless. She wouldn't leave poor Alyssa alone, even after she politely asked the woman to back off, so that's when I had to intervene."

"You mean you had to forcefully remove her?"

"No, I just had to walk over and insert myself between her and Alyssa. I'm six five and two hundred and fifty pounds. What's she going to do? Challenge me to a wrestling match? She was barely five feet tall, maybe a hundred and ten pounds. She pretty much got the message and immediately backed off. And that's the last I saw of her until, well, you know, her body turned up."

Maya went over the sequence of events in her mind.

"Okay, after you got rid of Tawny, you had eyes on Alyssa for the rest of the evening? You never lost sight of her at any time?"

Braden thought about it, and Maya could see his face flinch slightly, as if he had remembered something, perhaps a brief time he had lost track of Alyssa, but as her loyal bodyguard, there was no way he was going to expose his boss to more wild speculation. "That's right."

He was lying.

"And you would be willing to testify to that in court, if it ever came to that?"

He locked eyes with her and replied firmly, "Yes."

"Why do I get the feeling you're covering for her?"

"Because you probably have an overly suspicious nature."

She stared at him.

Wanting to press further.

But she knew she was never going to get anywhere with him. He was never going to betray Alyssa. Braden was literally trained to take a bullet for her, so why would he ever consider blowing up her alibi?

"If it comes out that Alyssa did have more contact with Tawny after that point, and you lied about it, it will just make things worse for her."

"Let's say, and I'm not admitting anything here, let's say I got distracted by all the drama unfolding with Tawny's husband in the aftermath of that video for a few minutes, and wasn't totally focused on Alyssa for maybe a minute or two, that doesn't mean she snuck off and strangled her old high school rival. That's ridiculous."

He was admitting it without admitting it.

He did lose track of Alyssa for a brief time.

A detail that would most likely come back to haunt her if it ever got out.

"Would you want to go out sometime?"

Maya snapped out of her thoughts.

What did he just say?

She had to think for a moment.

"I'm sorry, what?"

"Go out. Together. You know, on a date?"

Maya stiffened and raised her ring finger. "In case you hadn't noticed, I'm married."

"Oh, I noticed."

"Then you know my answer."

"Everyone's story is different. People have all kinds of arrangements these days. An Army buddy of mine lives with two girlfriends, like a thruple, or triad, who knows what they call it now?"

"Well, my husband and I have a very traditional marriage, just the two of us."

"Look, I did two tours of Afghanistan. My unit was ambushed by the Taliban. Twice. I barely made it home alive. I've learned not to leave anything to chance. If you see something you like, you don't wait around. You go for it. If it doesn't work out, so be it. But no matter what, you gotta try. Otherwise, what's the point? You'll end up just sitting around and wondering if you let something great pass you by."

Maya softened.

She could not deny she was flattered.

He was disarmingly handsome.

Even charming to an extent.

Definitely aggressively forthright.

But he was not Max.

"Well, I appreciate your interest, but again, the answer is no," Maya said firmly.

"Roger, that."

Maya turned to leave.

"Hey, before you go, would you do me a favor?"

Maya spun back around expectantly.

"Would you not mention to Alyssa that I tried asking you out? I don't want to get fired."

Maya smirked. "I'll think about it."

She pivoted and headed to the door.

"Think about it? You're going to think about it? Come on, man, don't leave me hanging. I love this job!"

Maya made it to the door before cranking her head around. "I was just messing with you. Your secret's safe with me."

He breathed a sigh of relief. "Thank you." He paused, unable to resist. "Hey, this flirtatious back and forth? It's kind of hot, right? You can't deny we have chemistry."

"Don't push it!" Maya barked before fleeing the hotel gym.

She was never going to admit that she had enjoyed their playful sparring. But she had enough on her plate as it was.

Chapter 19

As Sandra pulled her black Mercedes into her driveway, she suddenly noticed a familiar figure standing on her front lawn, arms crossed and a stern look on her face.

Detective Beth Hart.

Sandra stepped out of her car, closing the door, and adopted a warm smile. "Detective Hart. This is a surprise."

Hart's expression did not soften. "We need to talk."

"Sure, why don't you come inside and I'll make us some coffee?"

"We can do this right here."

Sandra braced herself. "Alright."

"I hear you and Maya are on the Alyssa Turner case."

Sandra hesitated before answering. "I can't really speak to that since we have a strict client confidentiality policy—"

"Which means you're working for Alyssa Turner,"

Hart spat out. "It doesn't matter whether you want to admit it or not; it's all over social media."

Sandra's eyes widened. "*What*?"

"Somebody found out and leaked it online. One of my younger officers who spends way too much time on TikTok brought it to my attention."

Sandra knew there was no point in denying it any longer. "She's a friend. She came to us for help." She paused, trying to read Hart's stone expression. "What can I do for you?"

"You can start by staying out of my way," Hart said, her voice cold. "This is my investigation, and I don't need you two meddling and complicating things."

"I think you know the two of us well enough to know—"

Hart cut her off. "This isn't the usual cheating spouse or threatening note in a kid's locker at school kind of case, Sandra; this is very high profile, involving a major public figure. All eyes are on my department. I can't afford any missteps, so the last thing I need is to bump up against *Romy and Michelle's High School Reunion* murder investigation."

Sandra took a breath and spoke evenly. "We are not trying to make your job harder. You should know that by now, given our past interactions. But we're also not going to abandon a friend in need just because you're worried we might beat you to the punch and find the killer first."

"Trust me, I'm not worried about you two showing me up."

Her words rang hollow.

And Hart knew it.

She decided to take a different tack.

More subdued and reasonable.

"Look, Sandra, you can't imagine the pressure I'm under right now from the commissioner, the press, everybody. I feel like I'm living under a microscope. I need to do everything by the book."

"I know exactly how you feel. I was married to a United States senator, remember? None of this is new to me."

"All I'm asking is for you and Maya to keep a respectful distance and not get in my way. But if you do come across any helpful information, I would appreciate you passing it along to me."

"So you expect us to share everything we discover with you, but it's a one-way street, and we get nothing from you?"

Hart did not have a ready answer.

Because Sandra was absolutely right.

"We can discuss that arrangement at another time. Just be careful. And professional," Hart advised.

"Always."

Hart whipped around to leave.

"Oh, Detective Hart?"

Hart stopped, slowing turning. "Yes?"

"I'm just curious. Why did you come to me?"

"What do you mean?"

"You and Maya have a long history together at the department. You came up in the ranks together. You two are so much closer. Why not just go to her with your concerns?"

Hart shrugged. "Your house was nearby. Maya's is across town."

"We have an office a few blocks from the precinct. Why didn't you just pop by and speak to both of us?"

"I honestly didn't think about it."

"So it had nothing to do with you thinking I'm more of a pushover, more susceptible to your request that we steer clear of your investigation, and that Maya would probably just tell you to go to hell?"

Hart's face was inscrutable. "Of course not. Like I said, coming here was more convenient."

"Uh-huh," Sandra grunted, knowing she was lying. "Have a nice day, Detective."

Hart bounded away to her car, which was parked across the street, and Sandra watched her go, shaking her head slightly.

She was always being underestimated.

Ever since her ex-husband Stephen's first swearing-in ceremony as a Maine state congressman, she had been stung by all the fervent whispers about her. Trophy wife. Lack of substance. Empty-headed. An accessory that luckily polls well. She had heard it all. And over the years, she had managed to build up a resistance to the point where she was now immune to it all.

She did not care what anyone said about her anymore.

Especially a self-doubting, insecure homicide detective who fully expected to intimidate her into backing off a case she had every right to accept.

Hart's impromptu visit only emboldened her to prove herself once again to those who habitually underestimated her.

Sandra walked up the lawn to her front porch, eager to get inside and squirrel away for some peace and quiet.

But first she needed to call Maya and update her on Hart's warning. She barely made it through the front door, phone in hand, when her son Ryan barreled toward her from the kitchen.

"Mom, you're home!"

Sandra stopped in her tracks. "Ryan, what are you doing here? What happened?"

"Nothing happened. I decided to come home for the weekend. Rehearsals don't start until Tuesday, so I took the train up to see you."

Ryan was a theater major at NYU's Tisch School of the Arts in Manhattan. He had been recently cast as Corny Collins in a student production of the musical *Hairspray*.

"Is that Mom?" a voice cried out from upstairs.

The next thing she knew, her son Jack, a sophomore at Boston College, came bounding down the staircase.

"Jack, what?"

"I know I said I wouldn't be home again until Thanksgiving break, but one of my fraternity brothers, the one who lives in Auburn, was driving up to Maine this weekend, and I thought, why not tag along, spend some quality time with Mom?"

"Why didn't you two text to let me know you were coming? I would've gone shopping. I have no food in the house."

"Don't worry, Dad's taking us to dinner tonight," Ryan said.

Sandra reared back. "Your *father's* in town?"

"Not only is he in town; he's in the other room," Jack said, grinning.

Sandra glanced around. "*What*?"

Stephen, looking like the consummate professional politician with his perfect hair, pressed shirt with the rolled-up sleeves, and slightly askew necktie that seemed to say he's always working for the American people, strolled out of Sandra's home office. Of course, it had once belonged to him, but that was before the divorce papers were final.

"Sorry, hon, I needed to make a few calls, so I confiscated your office. Hope you don't mind."

She cringed.

She hated it when he called her "hon" like they were still married. She had no ill will toward him; it had not been a contentious divorce, but he still refused to respect her boundaries as they began life without each other.

"Why aren't you in Washington?"

"Senate went on recess today, and good news for you, I'm in escrow on a condo in Freeport, so I won't be imposing on you anymore by crashing here whenever I'm in town."

Sandra's mouth dropped open. "You bought a condo?"

"Yeah, the inspection is tomorrow," Stephen explained.

"You came all the way up here for an inspection? Couldn't your realtor handle that without you being there?"

Stephen's smile never faltered.

But it appeared as if his mind was racing to come up with a plausible explanation.

"It was a good excuse to come home and take my sons out for a meal," Stephen blurted out quickly.

"So you already knew they were coming home this weekend? Did you all coordinate this surprise attack?"

None of this made any sense to Sandra.

She folded her arms, trying to assess the situation.

"Man, ever since you got your PI's license, you never stop with the questions!" Jack complained.

Finally, a lightbulb went off in Sandra's head. "Alyssa Turner."

Jack's face reddened.

Ryan averted his eyes.

Stephen, who was used to keeping his cool on the Senate floor, remained calm and unflappable.

But, she knew she had hit pay dirt.

"You all came home hoping to meet a movie star!"

"Sandra, do you know how many world leaders, tech billionaires, how many Hollywood celebrities, I have met in the course of my senate career?" Stephen scoffed.

"Yes, and none of them are Alyssa Turner," Sandra said, folding her arms.

Ryan snorted, giving himself away.

"I'm right, aren't I?"

Jack shrugged.

Stephen pressed on like a true politician. "I am here to supervise the inspection of my new condo. That's my story, and I'm sticking to it."

Sandra shook her head, a reluctant smile tugging on her lips. "Did you three come here thinking we might be having a coffee klatch in the kitchen, me and Alyssa Turner? You're all ridiculous. She's not here, and even if she was, she's a client. We're trying to help her, not turn this into a fan club meeting."

"Okay, Mom, but if she does drop by, you'll introduce us, right? I mean it's not every day we get to meet a superhot famous actress like Alyssa Turner!" Ryan opined.

"Out," Sandra ordered.

They all stood their ground.

Jack spoke first. "What?"

"Your dad said he's taking you out to dinner, so go."

Ryan and Jack exchanged a look.

"Oh my god, she's coming over," Ryan gasped.

"That's the only reason she'd want us out of the house," Jack concurred.

Sandra opened the door, gesturing for them to leave.

The boys sighed, but did as they were told.

Stephen followed but stopped at the door. "Is she really coming over—?"

"Out!" Sandra cried, shoving him through the door and slamming it behind him.

Chapter 20

Maya and Sandra stood on the creaky wooden porch of Marcus's run-down house, its paint peeling and windows grimy. A faint odor of stale smoke and mildew permeated the air. They exchanged glances, then knocked on the door, the sound echoing in the otherwise silent street.

After a long pause, the door creaked open just a crack, revealing Marcus's wild eyes peering out suspiciously. "What do you want?" he demanded, his voice tense.

"We need to ask you a few questions, Marcus," Maya said calmly. "It's about Tawny Bryce."

"I already told the police everything I know," Marcus snapped. "Leave me alone."

He went to slam the door on them, but Maya shot her right foot out, blocking him from closing it all the way.

"What do you think you're doing? This is private property!" Marcus wailed.

Sandra glanced over her shoulder, spotting a familiar figure stepping out of a sleek black car parked at the curb. "If you refuse to speak to us, maybe you'll talk to our friend," she suggested, her tone casual but firm.

Marcus's eyes widened in panic as he saw Braden, Alyssa's imposing bodyguard, get out of the driver's seat of the Tesla parked behind Maya's Chevy Bolt.

Marcus visibly flinched, backing away from the door. "Get him away from me!" he shouted. "I'll call the police!"

"Wait, Marcus," Sandra said, raising her hands in a calming gesture. "Look who's with him."

Marcus opened the back door of the Tesla, and Alyssa Turner stepped out of the car, her presence radiating a tranquil, reassuring aura. She walked up the path with a warm smile, her eyes filled with understanding.

"Alyssa!" Marcus gasped, his hostility melting away. He swung the door open, all traces of his earlier defiance gone. "I'm so sorry! I never meant to cause you any trouble. I just—"

"It's okay, Marcus," Alyssa said gently. "We just need to talk."

This had all been carefully orchestrated. Despite Marcus's calculated and angry interview with the press, in which he claimed to have seen Alyssa arguing with Tawny shortly before she was found strangled to death, Maya and Sandra knew he was still hopelessly infatuated with her; no doubt, he was vying for her attention when he mouthed off to the gaggle of reporters swarming outside the school on the night of the reunion. It was Alyssa's idea to accompany them when they showed up at Marcus's house, confident he would relent and open up more if she was in his presence. His puppy-dog eyes as he watched her approaching confirmed that she was right.

"Please, come in, come in," Marcus cooed, his adoring eyes fixed on Alyssa's beguiling face. And then, as his gaze flicked over to Braden, who stood on the front lawn, watching, his mood darkened. "Not him. He stays outside."

"Of course," Alyssa agreed. "He's just here to protect me."

Marcus looked crestfallen. "From who? Me? You know I would never hurt you in any way, Alyssa. I think the world of you."

"I know, Marcus. You've always been very sweet and kind to me. But the press is dogging me; they're relentless, Braden's just here to make sure they keep their distance. Do you know, I had to take the hotel service elevator and slip out a back-alley door and lie on the floor of the car just to come over and see you today?"

"Savages! Why can't they just leave you alone? It's like they learned nothing from the Princess Di tragedy. They've only gotten worse!"

Marcus gave Braden a bit more side-eye before grimacing and shutting the front door after ushering Alyssa, Maya, and Sandra into his home.

Inside, Marcus's house was a cluttered mess. Stacks of old newspapers and magazines covered the worn furniture, and the faint smell of birdseed mixed with the lingering scent of smoke. A brightly colored parakeet sat in a cage by the window, chirping intermittently.

"Take a seat," Marcus mumbled, clearing a space on the couch. "Sorry about the mess."

Maya and Sandra sat down, and Alyssa chose to stand, her presence seeming to brighten the dingy room. Marcus fidgeted nervously, his eyes darting between the detectives and Alyssa.

"You said you saw Alyssa arguing with Tawny minutes before she was found dead," Sandra began. "Can you tell us more about that?"

Marcus's face flushed with guilt. "I shouldn't have said anything. I just—I don't know what I was thinking . . ."

"You were angry and embarrassed. Braden never should have manhandled you like that," Alyssa said softly, letting him off the hook.

Marcus nodded in agreement. "It brought up a lot of traumatic memories from when I was a kid. All the rotten thugs who took such joy in stuffing me in my locker, or pushing my face in the toilet, or stealing my lunch money. It was a living hell."

"I understand. We both suffered from bullying back in the day," Alyssa said with a sympathetic gaze.

"And just because I was really good at dissecting the frogs in Biology class, they all called me Marcus the Serial Killer! They all laughed and said I was going to graduate to humans next! That's just *sick*!"

"Horrible," Alyssa whispered.

"Marcus, we don't blame you for sharing what you saw with the press. Alyssa has already admitted she and Tawny had an altercation at the reunion, and pretty much everyone within shouting distance saw you go after Tawny," Maya said. "But we need you to tell us what happened after that?"

"You mean when He-Man Master of the Universe kicked me out?" Marcus growled.

Sandra nodded. "Yes. Where did you go?"

"After Muscles dragged me out, away from Alyssa," Marcus said, glancing nervously out the window at the bodyguard, who stood silently on the lawn, "I snuck back inside when he wasn't looking and went straight to the gym. That's when I saw Alyssa arguing with Tawny."

"So you were alone, with no one to verify your alibi," Maya said, more a statement than a question.

"Yes, no one paid attention to me; no one ever does," Marcus admitted, his voice shaking. "But I didn't do anything to Tawny. I swear."

Alyssa stepped closer, her eyes meeting Marcus's. "We believe you, Marcus. But we need to be thorough. Did you say anything to anyone else about Tawny that night?"

Marcus shook his head. "No. After I told her off, I didn't speak to anybody except you."

"Are you sure about that?" Sandra pressed.

Marcus threw her an annoyed look. "I'm telling the truth."

At that moment, the parakeet began to chirp loudly, repeating a phrase over and over. "Tawny deserved to die! Tawny deserved to die!"

Marcus's face went pale. "Shut up, Skittles," he muttered, rushing to cover the cage with a cloth.

Maya and Sandra exchanged a look, their suspicions reignited. "Where did Skittles learn that?" Maya asked, her voice firm.

Marcus swallowed hard, his eyes wide with fear. "I—maybe I said it once. I was mad, okay? But I didn't mean it. I would never—"

Alyssa placed a reassuring hand on Marcus's shoulder. "We just need to know the truth, Marcus. Please, help us clear this up."

Tears welled up in Marcus's eyes. "I swear, I didn't kill her. I just wanted to scare her off, make her leave you alone. That's all. I never touched her! Never got near her!"

Maya and Sandra nodded, their expressions serious. "We believe you, Marcus," Sandra said. "But we need to check out every angle. Can you think of anyone else who might have wanted to hurt Tawny?"

Marcus wiped his eyes, taking a deep breath. "Just open up the yearbook and point at any graduation photo and you'll have somebody who hated Tawny Bryce, and maybe a few teachers too. Remember Coach Garten? They fired him after Tawny claimed she caught him watching her undress in the girls' locker room. Everyone knew she was lying. She was just ticked off he was failing her in Phys Ed for never showing up."

"Coach Garten died years ago," Maya reminded him.

"Okay, I'm just saying Tawny had a lot of enemies. Most of whom are still alive. Try her henpecked husband, or her high school posse she still bosses around like servants, especially Kat. I overheard something at the reunion about there being bad blood between them. Or what about that poor girl Jennifer she humiliated in front of everyone at the homecoming school dance senior year for having hair on her legs?" Marcus huffed. "I saw her glaring at Tawny when she made her big speech that night. There are dozens, maybe hundreds of suspects you can focus on. But I'm not one of them. You've got to believe me. I didn't do it."

"We'll follow up on those leads," Maya said, standing up. "Thank you, Marcus. You've been a big help."

As Alyssa turned to go, Marcus sprang forward. "If there's anything you need, Alyssa, please don't hesitate to call me. You have my number, right?"

"Yes, Marcus, thank you," Alyssa replied, hesitating a moment before deciding to give him a brief friendly hug.

Sandra could see his whole body melting in her warm embrace.

As they left the house, where Braden was patiently waiting for them outside, Alyssa turned to Maya and Sandra. "Do you think he's telling the truth?"

"He seems genuine," Maya said. "But we'll have to verify everything he said. And we can't ignore Skittles. Parakeets don't lie."

Thanks to his talkative pet parakeet, Marcus was still very much a possible suspect in Maya's mind.

Chapter 21

The cheerful chaos of the Old Orchard Beach Pier in southern Maine was a stark contrast to the dark events that had unfolded at Maya and Sandra's twenty-fifth high school reunion. The air had a crispness to it, signaling the early days of fall. Children, bundled in light jackets, raced along the boardwalk, clutching dripping ice cream cones, while couples strolled hand in hand, enjoying the festive atmosphere. The scent of fried dough and saltwater mingled in the air, creating a heady mix that seemed to lift everyone's spirits.

Everyone except Maya and Sandra.

Maya, dressed in a cozy yet stylish fall outfit, scanned the crowd. "Kat's supposed to be around here somewhere," she murmured to Sandra, who was adjusting her scarf to keep the chilly breeze off her neck.

"Over there," Sandra said, nodding toward the end of the pier, where a woman leaned against the railing, watching the waves crash against the shore. Kat, still as striking as she had been in high school, seemed lost in thought as she sipped a hot apple cider.

"Let's do this," Maya whispered, and they made their way over.

"Kat! Hello!" Sandra called out, injecting a false cheeriness into her voice.

Kat turned, her expression shifting from surprise to guarded curiosity. "Maya, Sandra. Didn't expect to see you two here."

Maya and Sandra exchanged a glance.

"We, uh, came here looking for you," Maya confessed.

Kat cocked an eyebrow. "How did you know I'd be here?"

"I follow you on Instagram. You've been coming here a lot lately," Sandra said.

"I've always found solace in the ocean. I practically grew up on this pier. Listening to the waves. It makes me nostalgic and calm. Lately, it's been a refuge, a place to clear my mind from all the madness."

She was no doubt referring to Tawny's death and the ensuing media frenzy.

"My husband says I post way too much, as if I'm a Kardashian. I know I overshare on social media. The world doesn't really need to see a photo of every loaf of sourdough bread I've ever tried to bake. But I enjoy connecting with people, reading everyone's supportive comments." She paused, then added ruefully, "It's a lot more than I get at home."

Maya smiled. "Mind if we join you?"

Kat shrugged, gesturing to the empty space beside

her on the railing. "Go ahead. I'm guessing you two following me has something to do with your investigation into Tawny's murder. I know Alyssa hired you to clear her name."

"The whole world seems to know we're working the case at this point," Maya sighed.

"So what do you want with me? Am I a suspect now, too?"

Their silence spoke volumes.

Kat's smile faded, and she set her drink down.

"No, seriously? You think *I* did it? Come on, Tawny was my best friend!" Kat protested.

"We're talking to everybody who was at the reunion," Sandra reassured her.

Maya cleared her throat. "But . . ."

Kat bristled. "But what?"

"We heard about your business venture with Tawny," Maya said evenly, carefully gauging Kat's reaction.

Kat's shoulder sank at the memory. "Yes. We were going to start a company for party planning and made-to-order decorations. We were going to name it Happily Ever After Events, which is ironic, because that's the last thing I experienced going into business with Tawny, happily ever after."

Maya leaned forward, her tone gentle but insistent. "Can you tell us what happened?"

Kat sighed, her defenses lowering slightly. "We were so sure it was going to be a huge hit and we'd make millions, like Kate Middleton's mother did with her party supplies business. But it didn't work out. We were both going to put in something like fifty grand each, enough seed money to get us started. I invested my money first, which we used to set up the LLC and buy supplies and advertising, but when it came time for Tawny to deposit her money, she sent me an email to say she was backing out of the whole enterprise. I couldn't move forward without her, so I was left holding the bag. All my money had already been spent. I trusted her to come through, and she screwed me. So you can imagine why I would be angry with her."

She glanced at Maya and Sandra. Both of their faces were inscrutable.

"But again, not angry enough to do her any physical harm," Kat insisted.

"Did she explain why she was pulling out?" Sandra asked.

"Not really. Believe me, I demanded to know, but she never really gave me a satisfactory answer. She mentioned something about investing in a stock she was sure would pay off big, but it tanked and she lost a huge amount of money, even more than she promised to invest with me."

"And Chad?" Sandra asked.

"Oh, he was furious," Kat said, her voice dropping. "Tawny didn't tell him before buying the stock, and when he found out, well, it just added to the troubles of their already failing marriage. Apparently, it was a huge chunk of their savings. It nearly wiped them out. And Chad was already in debt from spending big on vacations to St. Barts with Dua Lipa."

Maya appeared confused. "Who?"

"That's what we call her. The girlfriend."

Sandra leaned forward. "You know about Lindsay?"

"We all did. The whole clique. It was no big secret.

We just didn't talk about it with Tawny because things were so tense and messy at home, and she was in such a bad place, we didn't want to push her over the edge. We weren't aware that she had already hired you to find proof she could use in the divorce."

"What do you know about Lindsay?" Maya prompted.

"Not much," Kat shrugged. "But I did hear she was more upset than Chad when she found out how much money Tawny had lost in the stock market. She was worried about her future and how Chad would take care of her if he was broke?"

"True love," Maya cracked.

"You get what you deserve," Kat spat out. "And believe me, those two deserve each other."

Maya exchanged a look with Sandra. "Did you mention any of this to the police?"

Kat hesitated. "I didn't want to get involved and draw attention to myself. If they found out what Tawny did to me, do you not think I would shoot to the top of the suspect list? But if you think it can help Alyssa, I'll tell you what I know."

Sandra leaned back, considering. "Do you know anything about Tawny's mental state before she died?"

Kat's eyes darkened. "She was unraveling. The money, the affair, the pressure of the reunion—it was too much. She was spiraling, and none of us knew how to help her."

Maya nodded, understanding the complexity of the situation. "Thanks, Kat. You've been a big help."

Kat looked relieved, but there was still a hint of worry in her eyes. "Just find out who really did this. Tawny wasn't perfect, but she didn't deserve to die like that."

As they walked away, Sandra glanced back at Kat, then turned to Maya. "Do you believe her?"

Maya shrugged. "I'm not sure, but it's a start. We need to talk to Chad and Lindsay next. I have a feeling they're the missing pieces in this puzzle."

The sun began to set, casting a golden glow over the pier and the Atlantic beyond. Maya and Sandra knew they had to move quickly because, with so many unanswered questions, the possibility loomed that the killer might strike again.

Chapter 22

Oscar Dunford's face lit up at the sight of Maya entering the diner near his apartment where they had agreed to meet. She plopped down in the booth opposite him and grabbed a menu, quickly perusing it before setting it down and ordering a coffee and blueberry muffin from the passing waitress. Then she focused on Oscar, who stared at her besotted.

"I've missed you. You never call; you never come around the precinct to say hello," Oscar whined. "I'm getting the feeling you don't love me anymore."

"I will always love you, Oscar, like a pair of comfortable ratty old slippers I can't bring myself to toss out."

"Not the most romantic response I had been hoping for," he huffed.

"That's the best you're going to get. I'm a married woman."

"A guy can dream, can't he?"

"What have you got for me today, Oscar?"

He leaned back with a self-satisfied grin.

Oscar Dunford had always harbored a not-so-secret crush on his former colleague Maya when she was still working at the precinct before she was forced to resign after Max's conviction on corruption charges. In the eyes of her new superiors, Maya was guilty by association and could not be trusted, even with a sterling record and concrete evidence that she had nothing whatsoever to do with Max's crimes and had been completely in the dark. Oscar was the department's go-to IT whiz; he was called in whenever there was anything computer-related during an investigation. Maya had relied on him heavily during her years with the department, and they had remained friends, although his borderline sexual harassment could be an irritant at times. Still, she knew he was a decent guy at heart and was dependable. When Oscar called and left a voicemail on her phone, asking her to meet him at a tucked-away place, safe from the prying eyes of any fellow officers and detectives, Maya knew she was about to get something juicy.

And Oscar did not disappoint.

"We got some interesting voicemail messages off Tawny Bryce's phone I thought you might like to hear," Oscar said, hunched over his laptop on the table in front of him, his fingers flying across the keys. He then tapped a key to play a recording.

A woman's charged and angry voice could be heard through the laptop speaker. "You're pathetic, Tawny. A sad, pathetic, useless woman who doesn't deserve to live. When are you going to wake up and finally realize no one wants you around? You might as well do the world a favor and kill yourself."

Maya sat back in the booth, her mouth open in shock.

"That was just the opening salvo. Wait until you hear this one," Oscar said excitedly.

The same woman spoke again on the recording, this time even more vicious and threatening. "I saw you today, but you didn't see me. In the parking lot at the supermarket. Slumped over your grocery cart, with bags full of junk food so you could go home and eat your feelings. It took every ounce of self-restraint not to hit the gas pedal and mow you down and end your misery once and for all. Why are you still on this earth, Tawny? Why do you insist on still taking up space when no one, especially your poor husband, even wants you around?"

Maya shook her head. "She's horrible."

"Oh, they get progressively worse. And the later ones include a lot of four-letter words I would never dare repeat in your presence. I love and respect you way too much."

"You don't have to protect me, Oscar. I've been a cop most of my adult life. I've heard it all. So do you have any idea whose voice that is?"

"Maya, you hurt me deeply when you question my innate talent. It took me less than ten minutes to trace it, even though she tried to block the number. It's the girlfriend."

"Lindsay?"

"Yes, the answer to Chad Bryce's raging midlife crisis."

Maya was not surprised.

Lindsay had sent those taunting texts to Tawny.

But these voicemails were so next level.

A major escalation in the hateful threatening rhetoric.

"Apparently she didn't think too much of the wife," Oscar noted.

"Who is now dead. Has Beth heard these?"

"Not yet. We just got the data from the phone this morning. But I'm meeting with her this afternoon."

"You could get into a lot of trouble for letting me listen to these voicemail messages before the detective in charge of the investigation."

"What can I say, love makes you do stupid things."

"I'm serious, Oscar. You could be fired."

He waved his hand dismissively. "Please. They need me more than I need them. Haven't you heard? I'm a genius."

The waitress returned with Maya's coffee and muffin. She took a quick sip and pushed the muffin back toward the waitress. "Can I get this to go? I've got to go find Sandra. Could you email me files of those voice messages?"

"Already done, my love."

"Thanks, Oscar. You're a prince among men."

She jumped up and hurriedly bussed Oscar on the left side of his face.

He lovingly stroked his cheek where she had just kissed him. "Even the smallest innocent gesture of affection makes it all worthwhile."

"You really need to get out more," she said with a wink as she headed to the register, where the waitress was just putting her muffin inside a paper bag. She grabbed it and thanked her before dashing out the door.

She picked up Sandra at the office, and they drove

straight over to Lindsay's address, which Sandra was able to research in the time it took Maya to drive to her. Lindsay lived in a pleasant residential area with several apartment houses near the waterfront. Her top-floor apartment was modern and chic, with floor-to-ceiling windows and a view of the harbor.

Lindsay was surprised to find Maya and Sandra standing there when she opened the door. "Yes?"

"Lindsay, I'm Maya Kendrick, and this is—"

"I know who you are. You're the two who secretly recorded me and Chad at the bowling alley. You were working for his wife. I think it was disgusting what you did. Spying on us like that."

"We were hired to do a job, and we did it," Maya said flatly.

Lindsay stood at the door, keeping it halfway closed, defiantly refusing to allow them inside her apartment. "What do you want now?"

"We want to talk to you about Tawny Bryce," Sandra said.

Lindsay crossed her arms defensively. "I barely knew her. I think I met her once, maybe twice. Obviously, given the circumstances, we were never going to be friends, but I never wished her any harm."

Maya raised an eyebrow. "Is that a fact?"

"Yes, it is," Lindsay huffed. "I know Tawny became unhinged when she found out about us; she painted me as some home-wrecking monster, but their marriage was already on life support when Chad and I met."

"So you claim you didn't harbor any resentment toward Tawny?" Sandra asked.

"No, none at all," Lindsay insisted. "I'm a good person. Holding onto anger isn't healthy for the soul."

"Uh-huh," Maya grunted, wanting to laugh. "Then how do you explain these?"

Maya raised her phone in front of Lindsay's face and played the most cruel and harsh message from the playlist.

Lindsay spitting out a litany of insults and threats.

Lindsay took a step back, gutted. It appeared as if she might faint. Not from guilt or remorse, rather over the fact she had just been caught.

"T-That's not me," she stammered.

"Oh, Lindsay," Maya moaned, shaking her head. "Not only does it sound just like you, even though you attempted to disguise your voice; these messages were traced directly back to your phone."

"That's impossible because I—" Lindsay stopped herself.

"Blocked your number? That's never a foolproof way of hiding your identity. There are experts who know exactly how to get around that. You were always going to get caught, Lindsay," Maya said. "It was only a matter of time. And time's up."

Maya played another message.

The sound of her own cold-blooded, callous voice caused her façade of composure to finally crack. Tears welled up in her eyes. She backed away from the door, allowing them to step inside. She sank onto the couch, burying her face in her hands. "I-I don't know what came over me. I don't even recognize the person who left that message."

"It wasn't just one message," Sandra reminded her. "You left half a dozen messages, each one meaner and more ferocious than the last."

"I know," Lindsay sobbed. "I just snapped. I was so jealous of Tawny, how she still had this hold over Chad. She was making him so miserable. I just wanted her to go away and leave us in peace, so we could start our life together. But she was always on his mind; he was constantly obsessing over her. I thought . . . I thought if maybe I scared her, she'd back off."

Sandra's voice softened, but her tone remained firm. "Jealousy is one thing, Lindsay. But those messages were beyond the pale. You encouraged Tawny to commit suicide."

"I know, it's awful! I was awful!" Lindsay looked up, her eyes red and puffy. "I didn't mean for it to go this far. I swear, I never wanted her dead. I just wanted her out of my life." Her eyes widened as she read the skepticism on their faces. "I didn't kill her! I was nowhere near the reunion that night. I told Chad I couldn't deal with seeing Tawny. Me being there on his arm would have just made things worse. I was trying to bring down the temperature on the whole situation!"

Maya gestured toward the voicemail she had played previously on her phone. "These are not the best way to bring down the temperature, Lindsay."

She nodded, sniffing. "I know. I'm so ashamed. I was in a terrible place."

"Does Chad know you sent those messages to Tawny?"

"He didn't know at first. I was afraid he would be appalled and think I was as crazy as the wife he was trying to escape from. But after Tawny was murdered, I confessed everything. I felt he had to know so we'd be ready if they ever came back to haunt us."

"You mean get your stories straight?" Maya asked sharply.

"We didn't kill Tawny," Lindsay wailed.

"Because you're a good person and holding onto anger isn't healthy for the soul," Maya repeated.

Lindsay dropped her head and sobbed some more.

She knew she was now a major suspect.

And there was very little she could do about it.

But still, there was a gnawing feeling in the pit of Maya's stomach telling her that, although Lindsay's despicable actions countered her claim of being decent at heart, it was not enough evidence to prove that she was a killer. And if it was true she was nowhere near the high school on the night of the murder, she could not have physically carried out the crime.

However, that did not mean she could not have at least been involved. Her boyfriend, Chad, was certainly in the vicinity, and he had yet to offer up any solid alibi for the time his wife had been brutally strangled.

And he'd despised his wife almost as much as Lindsay.

Maybe more so.

Chapter 23

The morning sun cast long shadows across the quiet suburban street as Maya and Sandra canvassed the neighborhood, hoping for a breakthrough in their investigation. They had spent the past hour knocking on doors and asking questions, but so far, no one had seen or heard anything unusual in the days leading up to Tawny's murder, other than one man walking his dog who had overheard a loud fight between Tawny and Chad, which was not unusual since the couple fought most of the time they were together.

Their spirits were starting to flag when they reached a house a few doors down from the Bryces'. Maya rang the bell, and a spry woman in her late seventies answered the door with a warm smile. "Hello, how can I help you?"

Sandra took the lead. "Hello, I'm Sandra Wallage—"

"Oh, I know who you are, dear. I didn't vote for your husband, but I always thought you were so lovely and had such a flair for fashion. Every time I saw you on the news, I thought to myself, look at how beautiful she is. She has such grace and poise and style."

Sandra was taken aback. "Why, thank you."

Then the woman leaned forward conspiratorially and whispered, "You were right to leave him. He was never good enough for you. You deserve better."

Maya smirked, as Sandra was at a loss as to how she should respond.

"I-I appreciate that . . ." she stammered.

"Florence. Florence Gatsby. Please, do come in."

She opened the door, waving them inside.

She led them into a cozy living room filled with family photos and the comforting scent of fresh coffee.

"Can I get you anything? I've just made a pot of coffee, and I have some homemade banana bread I can offer you."

Sandra had to speak loudly because the volume on the TV was up high and blasting an episode of *The Price Is Right*, which was right in the middle of the climactic Showcase Showdown. "No, thank you, Mrs. Gatsby, we're fine."

"Are you sure?" Mrs. Gatsby shouted as she snatched the remote off the coffee table and mercifully lowered the volume. "I wish they made more shows like *The Price Is Right*. Of course, the new host isn't anywhere near as handsome as Bob Barker. He was so charming. I'd plan my whole day around him. Nowadays, it's always rich, spoiled housewives yelling at each other and throwing champagne glasses, making complete fools of themselves. I miss *Match Game* and *Pyramid* and *Hollywood Squares*, and don't get me started on the soaps, how they've all become unwatchable, except maybe for *The Young and the Restless*. That one can still hold my attention occasionally."

Maya and Sandra patiently waited for the end of her diatribe on the state of daytime television.

Mrs. Gatsby suddenly seemed to remember they were in the room. "Are you sure I can't get you anything?"

"We're sure, but thank you," Maya said softly. "Mrs. Gatsby, the reason we stopped by is because—"

"You're investigating Tawny's murder."

Maya nodded. "Yes."

"I read something in the paper about Alyssa Turner hiring you to clear her name. Yes, I still read an actual newspaper. I refuse to keep up with current events on my phone! A phone is for making and receiving calls! Although I rarely answer an unknown number these days, with all those scammers out there targeting the elderly, trying to talk them into just handing over their credit card or Social Security number. Doris Foster down the street got one of those calls, and she ended up losing twenty thousand dollars! Can you believe that?"

Sandra got the feeling Florence Gatsby did not get many visitors and loved having company.

Maya attempted to get her back on track. "So, did you know Tawny Bryce well?"

"Oh, Tawny was like a daughter to me," she said, her voice heavy with sadness. "It's just so terrible what happened."

Sandra leaned forward, her expression serious. "What about her husband, Chad?"

"The lying cad? Oh, he would pour on the charm, always offering to shovel my walk after a snowstorm or help me carry in the groceries, but I saw him for the lout that he truly was. I didn't buy his stand-up guy act for one second."

"Did Tawny ever talk to you about her marriage troubles?" Sandra asked.

"Never outright. But she would make little comments. I could tell she was miserable. Once I tore out an ad from the paper for a divorce lawyer and left it on her windshield, but I never told her it was me. I didn't want to embarrass her."

"In the days leading up to Tawny's death, did you happen to see anything unusual, anything suspicious, maybe a physical altercation between Tawny and Chad?"

"No, he really wasn't around much during those final days. I suspect he was shacking up with his whore," she sniffed.

It was obvious who Mrs. Gatsby was siding with in the War of the Bryces.

"But I remember one morning I saw her crying when she went outside to get her mail, so I took over a coffee cake I had made to cheer her up. I asked her what was wrong, and she explained she'd had a fight with Chad earlier, which was par for the course, but then she mentioned something else."

Sandra grabbed a notebook and pen from her bag and began jotting down notes as Mrs. Gatsby continued.

"She told me she had been on edge lately because she felt like she was being watched and followed."

"By whom?" Sandra asked.

Mrs. Gatsby shrugged. "She didn't know who he was. But she was certain he was stalking her."

"*He*? So she saw him?" Maya gasped.

Mrs. Gatsby nodded, her eyes clouding with concern. "Yes. She was really scared. I could see why. He was a huge man. Very tall. Broad-shouldered. Quite intimidating."

Maya's eyes widened. "Wait. You saw him too?"

"Just once. He showed up one morning, about a week before the reunion," Mrs. Gatsby recalled. "I saw Tawny confront him on her front lawn from my kitchen window. Tawny was taking out the garbage bins to the curb when she saw him passing by. He was so big, wearing a hoodie. They argued, and I could hear her yelling at him. He eventually walked away, but Tawny was very shaken."

Sandra's pen paused over her notebook. "Did you get a good look at this man?"

"Not really," Mrs. Gatsby admitted. "He kept his hood up, and his back was to me most of the time. But he seemed . . . threatening."

"This is the first we've heard of this," Maya said, exchanging a look with Sandra. "The police didn't mention any altercation."

"They don't know about it," Mrs. Gatsby said, shaking her head. "I didn't think it was important at the time. Now I wish I had said something."

Maya and Sandra thanked Mrs. Gatsby for her time and promised to keep her updated. As they walked back to their car, Sandra spotted a security camera mounted on the corner of Chad and Tawny's house. "Look," she said, pointing.

Maya's eyes followed Sandra's finger. "Chad's car is in the driveway; he's probably home. Let's go have a little chat."

Chad Bryce answered the door with a scowl and a hardened look in his eyes. He was clearly agitated. "What do you want now?" he snapped, his voice cold.

"We need to see the security footage from the camera you have set up outside the house," Sandra said firmly. "It's crucial for the investigation."

Chad's eyes narrowed. "Why should I help you? All you want to do is pin this murder on me."

Maya remained calm. "We've come across some information that just might help clear you. So the sooner we find the real killer, the sooner you can move on with your life."

Chad glared at them, but finally relented. "Fine. Follow me."

He led them to his office, where the security system was set up on his desktop computer. "Make it quick."

Maya sat down behind the desk and expertly navigated the security footage, fast-forwarding through the days leading up to the reunion.

"There," she said, pausing the video. "That's him."

On the screen, a large man in a dark hoodie walked up and down the street in front of Tawny's house. He lingered by the driveway, watching the house intently. Chad's expression shifted subtly, his eyes widening for a split second before he regained his composure.

"Rewind to the morning of the confrontation," Maya said, watching Chad carefully.

The footage showed Tawny dragging the garbage bins to the curb. As Mrs. Gatsby had described, the hooded man was passing by, somewhat surprised by Tawny's sudden appearance. She charged up to him. They exchanged some heated words, Tawny's gestures becoming more animated as she pointed toward the street, clearly telling him to leave. The man never touched her, but his presence was intimidating enough. After a few tense moments, he turned and walked away, disappearing down the street.

Chad's face paled slightly. "I . . . I don't know who that is," he stammered, trying to mask his discomfort. "Never seen him before."

Maya's eyes narrowed as she scrutinized the footage. "Sandra, doesn't that build look familiar to you?"

Sandra leaned closer, her brow furrowing. "Yes, it does. He looks a lot like Braden."

Chad's eyes darted between them. "Who's Braden?"

"Alyssa's personal security," Maya explained, her voice growing more intense.

"Wait, you mean Godzilla from the reunion? That guy? You think *he* killed Tawny?"

"We don't even know if that's him on the footage. It just looks like him," Sandra sighed.

Chad shrugged attempting to play it cool. "Well, you need to go find out. What was Tawny even doing with that guy? There could be a whole other side to her that we don't know about."

"Relax, Chad. We plan to do just that," Sandra sighed.

"Who knows how many enemies she had? She was a very unlikable person," Chad insisted, unable to resist one more dig at his dead wife.

Maya leaned in closer, her eyes boring into Chad's. "Why didn't you show this footage to the police?"

Chad's jaw tightened. "They never asked," he replied defensively. "And I didn't think it was relevant. I never knew footage of Tawny with that guy was even on there until just now."

"We need a copy of this," Maya said, her voice firm.

Chad hesitated, but then nodded, handing over a USB drive. "Here. Take it. Just get out of my house and focus on finding the real killer so everybody will leave me and Lindsay alone."

As they walked back to their car, Sandra glanced at Maya. "He's hiding something."

"Definitely," Maya agreed. "And we need to find out what. He was way too spooked by that footage."

There was an unspoken tension between the two women.

If Braden was the hulking man on the security footage, what was he doing there?

And did Alyssa know about it?

Chapter 24

The afternoon sun filtered through the blinds of the small office on the second floor of the two-story brick office building, casting slanted shadows across the cluttered desks and the rows of file cabinets. Maya paced nervously, her sharp eyes occasionally darting to the door as she waited for their guests to arrive. Sandra, always the calm and composed one, sat at her desk, her fingers flying across the keyboard as she pulled up the security footage once more.

There was a quick rap on the door to the office, and Maya spun around to see Alyssa Turner, Hollywood starlet turned prime murder suspect, enter the room. Her eyes were wide with stress, her usually impeccable makeup doing little to hide the strain of the past weeks. She had picked up on the seriousness of the situation when Sandra had called her requesting that she and Braden come to their office immediately. Braden followed close behind her, his massive frame filling the doorway. He moved with the cautious grace of someone used to being on high alert.

"Thanks for coming," Maya said, her voice steady. "We felt it would be easier to do this at our office rather than try to coordinate it at your hotel with the press crawling everywhere."

Alyssa looked at them pensively. "We're here. What's this all about?"

Sandra stood up from the desk. "We need to go over something with you both."

Alyssa nodded, her lips pressed into a tight line, and took a seat on the couch. Braden stood next to her, his presence imposing and protective.

Sandra clicked a few buttons, casting the video from the computer to a television screen on the wall. The footage from Tawny's lawn appeared on the screen. The grainy black-and-white video showed Tawny, animated and angry, shouting at a large man in a hoodie.

"We found this footage at Tawny's house; it's from a few days before the murder," Sandra explained. "Chad handed it over, hoping it would clear him as a suspect. We noticed something . . . familiar."

As the video played, Sandra hit pause at a crucial moment, zooming in on the man's face. "Braden, this guy looks a lot like you."

A nervous laugh escaped Alyssa's lips. "What?"

Braden walked over and stared at the television, his brow furrowing as he scrutinized the screen. "It's not me," he said flatly, his tone carrying the weight of certainty.

Sandra adjusted the zoom, trying to enhance the image further. The blurred pixels gradually formed a more distinct face. "Let's see if we can get a clearer look."

"Where's Oscar when we need him?" Maya sighed.

Minutes ticked by as the technology did its work. The face that emerged was similar, but there were differences in the jawline and the nose.

Braden exhaled, relieved. "See? Not me."

Before anyone could react further, the door swung open again. Max, Maya's husband, strode in, his rugged face set in a grim expression as his eyes narrowed at the sight of Braden.

Maya cocked an eyebrow. "Max, what are you doing here?"

"I have the day off from the garage, remember? I thought I'd swing by and take you to lunch."

Max worked as a mechanic at a car repair shop.

It was a long way from his days as captain of the South Portland Police Department. But given his status as a paroled felon, a job was a job, and he was grateful to have it.

"Sorry, I can't. We're in the middle of something."

He glanced at Alyssa curiously. "What's going on?"

"Max, you know we can't discuss our investigations," Maya said evenly. She had the feeling Max had somehow known Braden would be at the office and purposely dropped in to make sure he did not try to make a move on his wife.

Or perhaps she was just being paranoid.

"Right, sorry," Max said with a wave of his hand.

Alyssa did not seem to care one bit about confidentiality. "They found some security footage of a man they thought was Braden interacting with Tawny right before she was murdered."

"But we were wrong," Maya quickly added.

Max glared at Braden, who remained stone-faced;

then he glanced over at the television screen at the frozen image of the man with a hoodie, his ex-cop instincts kicking in immediately.

Sandra instantly noticed his expression registering with recognition. "Max, what is it?"

He walked over to get a closer look. "Wait a second," he muttered, staring at the image. "I know that guy. That's Shrek."

"Shrek?" Sandra echoed, her fingers pausing over the keyboard. "Who's Shrek?"

"Local thug," Max explained, his eyes still fixed on the screen. "I had a few run-ins with him back in the day. Real piece of work. Arrests for multiple assaults, bar fights mostly, illegal gun possession, a couple DUIs. I'm sure I'm forgetting a few."

Alyssa's eyes widened. "What would he have to do with Tawny?"

Max shrugged, but his jaw tightened. "I don't know; they don't exactly run in the same circles, but it's worth finding out."

"Why do they call him Shrek?" Sandra asked.

Max chuckled. "Look at the guy. Big, robust, intimidating, wide flat nose, large round ears, bald, fond of wearing green hoodies. What else would you call him?"

The tension in the room was palpable, thick enough to cut with a knife. It did not help when Braden shifted closer to Maya, offering her a reassuring smile, as if to say, *See? Not me.*

Max's eyes darkened, his hands clenching into fists. "What was that?"

Maya turned to Max, surprised by his confrontational tone. "What was what?"

"That little exchange between the two of you. Is there something you'd like to share with the rest of us?" Max spit out.

Maya's mouth dropped open. "Please tell me you are not doing this right now, Max."

"Doing what?"

"Playing the jealous husband."

"I'm not playing anything," he seethed.

Alyssa sat on the couch, eyes wide, up to now totally in the dark about Braden's attraction to Maya.

"You got a problem with me?" Braden asked, his voice low and challenging.

Max took a step forward, and for a moment, it seemed like violence was inevitable. "Yeah, I do. I want you to stay away from my wife."

Maya, embarrassed, wanted to disappear. "I can't believe this is happening." She took a beat, then moved to defuse the escalating situation by quickly sliding between them, her hands on Max's chest. "Stand down, Max. This isn't helping."

"He's obviously flirting with you," Max hissed, his eyes locked on Braden. "This time right in front of my face."

"It means nothing," Maya whispered urgently, her eyes pleading with him to see reason. "Don't risk violating your parole over this."

Max's muscles were taut with barely restrained anger, but he took a deep breath and stepped back, raising his hands in the air. "Fine." There seemed to be a release of some of the tension in the room, but then Max could not resist adding, "But I'm watching you."

Braden merely smirked in response.

Which almost set Max off again.

Sandra cleared her throat, intervening with a change of topic. "We need to focus on Shrek. Max, do you think you could find him?"

Max finally tore his fiery eyes away from Braden and softened as he glanced over at Sandra. "I can try. He's not exactly low profile."

Alyssa stood up, her resolve firming. "Okay, we have a lead. What can I do?"

"Go back to your hotel, avoid talking to the press, wait to hear from us," Maya instructed.

She could tell Alyssa wanted to do more to help clear her name, but she understood Maya's reasoning.

She nodded, resigned. "Okay, let's go, Braden."

Alyssa headed toward the door as Braden lingered, tossing a little more unspoken attitude in Max's direction before following her out. Maya dug her fingernails into Max's arm to stop another outburst.

When the door closed behind them, there was a long, awkward pause.

"Anyone care for some more coffee?" Sandra asked in as perky a voice as she could muster.

Maya ignored her as she looked at Max, eyes flaring. "What the hell was that?"

Max at this point knew he had overstepped. He averted his eyes from her, ashamed. "I'm sorry; that was out of line."

"Out of line? Don't undersell yourself. That was completely inappropriate, childish, and downright dangerous. If that had escalated into a shoving match or fistfight, you would have bought yourself a one-way ticket back to prison. You don't think news of a brawl with Alyssa Turner's security guard wouldn't make it back to your parole officer? You can't take stupid chances like that, Max. You've worked so hard to build your life back since your release, and now you're willing to risk it all because some random guy looked at me in a way you didn't approve of? God, Max, how could you be so dumb?"

"You're right, you're right," he muttered, shuffling his feet and staring at the floor like a child caught shoplifting a comic book.

"Well, I for one, could use some coffee, so I'm going to make a fresh pot, over there in the kitchen area, where I can still hear you arguing, but where I can pretend that I don't," Sandra whispered, scuttling over to the coffee maker and filling the pot with water.

"Promise me you'll take a breath and think about that the next time you want to pop off like that, okay?" Maya took him by both arms. "It's not just you anymore in a six-by-eight-foot cell. It's me. It's Vanessa. We're counting on you to be there for us. Don't screw it up."

She had finally gotten through to him.

He nodded, red-faced and chagrined, still shuffling his feet. "So I guess lunch is off the table?"

Maya could not help but crack a smile. She swatted his shoulder playfully. "We have work to do. Now get out of here."

"I'm going to go put some feelers out, try to locate Shrek," Max said, dashing for the exit before he put his foot in it again, leaving Maya and Sandra alone.

"That man loves you so much," Sandra said wistfully.

"Which won't do either of us any good if he winds up back in the slammer," Maya exhaled.

A very real thought she just could not escape.

Chapter 25

Max's heavy footsteps echoed down the deserted alleyway, the dim evening light casting long shadows against the brick walls. Maya and Sandra followed closely behind, their faces set with determination. Max had tracked down "Shrek," a hulking figure known for his resemblance to the famous animated character, and they were about to confront him in the most unexpected of places.

Max had gotten a tip from a local informant, a petty thief who owed Max a favor from his days on the local police beat. The informant had seen Shrek pulling his typical mail-theft scam in this alley multiple times over the past week, and Max knew it was the perfect opportunity to catch him red-handed.

Kurt Maloney, aka Shrek, was hunched over a series of mailboxes at the end of the alley, prying them open with a crowbar. The gleam in his eye suggested he was hoping to score some easy cash or credit cards. Max raised a hand to signal Maya and Sandra to hang back as he slowly approached the man.

"Evening, Shrek," Max called out, his voice carrying an authoritative edge that spoke of his years on the force.

Shrek froze, then slowly turned around, the crowbar dropping to his side. His face twisted in a mix of surprise and annoyance. "They let you out?"

"Yup. Served my time. Paid my debt to society. Trying to stay on the straight and narrow."

"How's that going for you?"

"So far, so good. Haven't been tossed back in yet. Wish I could say the same for you."

Shrek's eyes flicked to the crowbar in his hand. "I was just trying to get a letter back I never meant to mail. Had a fight with my girlfriend, Rochelle, and afterward, I wrote her a nasty letter about how I really felt about her. But then we made up, you know how things change, I missed her, and well, I didn't want her to see what had been going through my head."

"Wow, I'm impressed with how fast you came up with that very detailed story," Max mused.

"It's the truth," Shrek pushed back.

"The thing is, Shrek, I heard you've been vandalizing mailboxes in this area the past few weeks. That's a lot of girlfriends and a lot of Dear Jane letters, and also, there's this crazy new thing called texting, which all the kids are doing nowadays."

Shrek's face darkened. "Who told you about that?"

"Let me put this as gently as I can. Your friends, they're not really your friends. They'll sell you out without blinking twice," Max said with a sneer.

Shrek shifted uncomfortably, still gripping the crowbar that Max kept one eye on just in case the guy decided to try and use it on him.

"What do you want, Max?"

"Just a friendly chat," Max replied smoothly. "Got some questions about Tawny Bryce."

Shrek's eyes narrowed, but he did not move. The muscles in his neck tightened as he looked past Max to see Maya and Sandra hovering a few feet behind him. He knew he was cornered. He sighed, set the crowbar down, and leaned against the mailbox, crossing his arms over his chest. "Make it quick. I've got places to be."

Maya stepped forward, her keen eyes not missing a detail. "We saw you on the security footage, Shrek. You were scoping out Tawny on her front lawn. Care to tell us what that was about?"

Shrek let out a bitter laugh. "That? I was just walking the neighborhood. I have a friend who lives nearby. She jumped to conclusions. Thought I was casing her house, planning to break in when she wasn't home and rob the place. You know how these suburban Karens are. One unfamiliar face in the neighborhood, and suddenly it's stranger danger!"

"Try again," Sandra pressed, her voice steady but insistent. "We heard she had spotted you several times in the days before she was murdered. At various locations. This story, like your girlfriend, doesn't add up."

Shrek's eyes lingered on Sandra a moment too long. "Well, hello there," he said, a sly grin spreading across his face. "I don't think we've been properly introduced. I'm Kurt."

"And I'm profoundly not interested," Sandra snapped back.

Max took a step closer to Shrek, his expression hardening. "Eyes over here, Shrek. Why were you stalking Tawny Bryce, who mysteriously wound up dead shortly thereafter?"

Shrek shrugged, averting Max's intense gaze.

"I still got a lot of buddies at the police department. One text and they'll be here in two minutes to scoop you up and whisk you away to the station for questioning. And we both know I'm a hell of a lot nicer than they are."

"Oh, you playing good cop now?" Shrek spat out.

"Whatever you're hiding is gonna come out eventually, Shrek, so why not save us all the time and trouble and just be straight with me?"

"I don't want to go back to jail, man," Shrek whined.

"I promise, whatever you tell me, whatever reason you had for tailing Tawny, I won't go to the police with it," Max said.

Shrek's eyes darted back and forth, contemplating; then, with a heavy sigh, he whispered. "I had a meeting with her husband a couple weeks back."

"Chad?" Maya gasped.

Shrek nodded. "Yeah, one of his drinking buddies is a pal of mine and put us in touch. Chad was looking for somebody to help him with a project."

"What kind of project?" Maya pressed.

"His wife was causing him a lot of problems, and so he was interested in, how should I put this, finding someone who could help him remove her from his life?"

"A murder-for-hire plot?" Maya asked.

"I wouldn't put it quite like that!" Shrek protested.

"Then how would you put it?" Max barked.

Shrek thought about it. "No, you're right. That pretty much sums it up. But I didn't go through with it! I didn't touch a hair on her head! I had nothing to do with killing her!"

"But you considered it," Sandra said with a scowl.

Shrek could not help but stare at Sandra lustily. "Man, you are one of the most beautiful women I've ever laid eyes on, like Beyoncé beautiful . . ."

"Don't make me throw up," Sandra retorted.

"So what happened?" Max demanded to know. "Why didn't you go through with it?"

Shrek gestured toward Sandra. "Barbie Doll over there is right, man, I did consider it. He offered me twenty grand. And I had some outstanding debt that needed to be paid off, or I might have an accident and end up in the hospital or worse. I wasn't thinking straight. I was desperate for cash. Chad Venmo-ed me ten grand, promising to send the other ten when the deed was done. I was checking her place out, her habits, schedule, deciding if I was going to do it or not."

Max raised an eyebrow. "And she noticed you following her?"

Kurt looked around, his eyes darting to the shadows, as if expecting someone to jump out at any moment and surprise him. "Yeah. I thought I was being all stealth and shadowy, like James Bond, but damn if she didn't spot me a couple of times. That morning, I was walking by when she came out to take her garbage bins to the curb for the trash collector. She threatened to call the cops and report me as a stalker. Said she'd seen my face and wouldn't hesitate."

Maya's heart raced. "So you backed out?"

Shrek nodded. "Yeah. I played it off, told her she didn't know what she was talking about, that I was just passing through on the way to a friend's house. But it scared me enough to wash my hands of the whole deal. Kept the advance, though. Figured Chad wouldn't dare ask for it back, knowing the kind of people I hang with."

Sandra stepped closer, her voice a whisper. "And when you heard she was dead, you thought Chad did it himself?"

"Yeah," Shrek admitted. "Of course. Who else? I just figured he got desperate and took matters into his own hands."

Maya exchanged a glance with Sandra. This was the break they had been looking for. If they could concretely prove Chad's involvement, they might be able to finally clear Alyssa's name.

"How did you stay in contact with each other?" Maya asked, her mind racing with possibilities. "Are there texts on your phone between the two of you?"

Shrek shook his head. "Nope. My buddy arranged the initial meeting in a crowded bar. We sat in a back booth where nobody could overhear our conversation. After that, we kept our distance. We couldn't be seen with each other in case something went wrong. We didn't want to risk the cops ever connecting us."

"So there is no communication between you, but what about the ten grand?" Maya asked. "You said he Venmo-ed you. There would have to be some kind of receipt or payment trail. Did he use a third party to pay you the advance?"

Shrek took out his phone and scrolled down through a list of emails. "Here it is." He scanned the receipt. "Looks like he transferred the funds from his own account."

Maya laughed. "Of course he did. Chad's hardly what I would call a criminal mastermind."

"So we got him," Max concluded.

Shrek studied Max closely. "So you're not going to say anything about my role in all this, right, Max? I mean, you promised."

"Of course, Shrek. My lips are sealed," Max assured him.

He glanced over at Maya and Sandra. "And what about them?"

Max shrugged. "I can't speak for them."

The blood drained from Shrek's face. "What do you mean? You promised!"

"Max promised. We didn't promise," Maya said evenly.

Panicked, Shrek's eyes fell toward the crowbar propped up against the mailbox.

"Don't even think about it," Max warned.

"If the DA builds a case against Chad, they're going to need an eyewitness, so I'm sure there is some sort of deal they can offer for your testimony. It may even keep you out of jail."

"But there's no guarantee!" Shrek wailed.

"There are never any guarantees in life, Shrek" Maya said sharply. "But there is some good news."

"What?" Shrek sneered.

"We promise not to report you for the mail theft,"

Maya said, marching forward and reaching around to snatch a stack of letters and bills out of the back pocket of his jeans. "As long as you promise to stop stealing other people's mail, which is a federal offense by the way, lots and lots of jail time. I'm sure you can find a more reputable way to pay off your outstanding debts." She opened the mailbox and dropped the letters back inside.

Shrek's mind raced.

His whole world was about to blow apart.

Maya ignored Shrek's pleas for them not to give his name to the cops and was already mentally working through the next steps.

With Shrek's testimony and the evidence of the money transfer, they had a real shot at proving Alyssa's innocence. But they had to move fast. The press was like a pack of wolves, and every second counted.

This was far from over, but for the first time, Maya felt a glimmer of hope. They were getting closer to the truth, and soon, everyone would know what really happened to Tawny Bryce.

Chapter 26

Maya and Max sat on the worn-out couch in their cozy living room, illuminated by the flickering light of the Zoom call with their daughter Vanessa, who was chatting away from her dorm room.

"Ryan's coming up to see me this weekend," Vanessa said. "Which is perfect because I'll need to celebrate after this chem exam I have on Friday," Vanessa sighed.

"Did you study?" Maya asked pointedly.

Vanessa sighed again. "Mom! I was at the library until close to eleven last night. They had to kick me out."

"How's Ryan doing at NYU?" Max asked.

"Good, I think. We talk as much as we can. But this whole long-distance thing is proving to be harder than either of us thought it would be."

Sandra's younger son, Ryan, and Vanessa had been dating since their junior year. Maya had suspected the relationship would be challenging when both of them set off to attend separate colleges the previous fall. Most adult relationships could not survive prolonged absences, and these kids were just out of high school.

"Well, you should be focusing more on your studies anyway, honey," Max said emphatically. "Forget about boys for now. There will be plenty of time for that later when you're a doctor."

"Ryan isn't just any boy, Dad," Vanessa huffed. "We've been together almost three years."

Maya rolled her eyes. "When you say stuff like that, Max, you know you're having the exact opposite effect, right? She'll just want to prove you wrong."

"Mom's right," Vanessa snickered.

"Fine, I'll keep my opinions to myself just as long as you make sure you ace that chem exam on Friday," Max said.

"I know, Dad. I got it under control," Vanessa replied with a smile. "Hey, Dad, do you think you can send me that cookie recipe from Grandma? My roommate Kimmy's nineteenth birthday is next week."

"Of course, honey. I'll email it to you tonight," Max replied, smiling.

"You sure you don't want mine?" Maya joked.

"Thanks, Mom, but I'd like Kimmy to live to see her next birthday when she turns twenty!" Vanessa laughed.

The doorbell rang.

Maya raised an eyebrow. "Who's here this late?"

Max shrugged.

Maya stood up, out of frame on the laptop screen that was angled toward Max on the coffee table.

"Where's Mom?" Vanessa asked as she took a bite out of a candy bar.

Maya was already making her way to the door. "I'll be right back, Vanessa," she said, hearing the doorbell ring again.

As Max continued the conversation with their daughter, Maya opened the door to find Detective Hart standing there, her expression serious.

"Beth," Maya greeted, stepping aside to let her in. "What brings you here?"

Hart's eyes scanned the room briefly before focusing on Maya. "Shrek denied everything. He claims he never admitted to anyone, especially you, that Chad was trying to hire him to kill Tawny. He completely stonewalled us when we brought him in for questioning. Bottom line, he's not willing to testify against Chad, so the prosecutor has no case, at least right now."

"What about the Venmo payment, the ten grand?"

"Chad says that was for a used motorcycle Shrek was selling online. I sent an officer over to check, and he saw the bike in Chad's garage, and Chad showed him the receipt."

Maya had no doubt the motorcycle transaction happened once Shrek alerted Chad that they were onto him.

Maya's heart sank. "He's contradicting everything he told us last night. What changed?"

Hart's jaw tightened. "He insisted you're trying to frame him and Chad so you can clear Alyssa Turner and get a big payday and lots of free press."

Maya's mind raced. "I think he's working another angle. I bet Shrek went to Chad and extorted him for more money to keep quiet. He's covering his tracks now."

Maya glanced back at Max, still engrossed in the Zoom call with Vanessa. "I need to talk to him again. Max can't get involved; you know his situation."

Hart nodded. "I get it. Look, Shrek hangs out at that bar on Congress and Pine, The Rusty Nail. Be careful if you decide to go. I'd go with you, but we just had him in an interrogation room for six hours today. He'll cry police harassment."

Maya was relieved Hart was not giving her the usual "don't go poking your nose in my cases" speech. She knew if Hart had any hope of tying Shrek and Chad to Tawny Bryce's murder, she was going to need Maya's help.

"You know where to find me," Hart said, walking out.

"Thanks, Beth," Maya said, closing the door behind her. She returned to the living room, grabbing her purse and jacket.

"Where are you going?" Max asked, suspicion creeping into his voice.

"Just running an errand," Maya replied smoothly, forcing a smile. "I'll be back soon."

Max sat back and folded his arms across his chest. "At this time of night? Who was at the door?"

"Do I need a permission slip to go outside the perimeters of this house?" Maya asked sharply.

Her tone caught Max off guard.

She could hear Vanessa chuckling on the computer screen.

"I need to pick up a few things at the Circle K. Would you like me to provide you with a complete list?"

"Fine. Sorry. Go," Max mumbled, sufficiently chastised.

She glanced at the screen. "Good night, Vanessa."

"Bye, Mom!"

Maya left the house, her mind racing with possibilities and strategies. The evening air was cool, and she pulled her jacket tighter around her as she walked briskly to her car. She needed answers, and she needed them now.

The Rusty Nail bar on Congress and Pine was a dingy dive with a reputation for attracting the city's less-savory characters. Maya parked her car a block away and approached cautiously, the hairs on the back of her neck standing up. She readied herself for anything.

Inside, the bar was dimly lit and filled with the smell of stale beer and cigarette smoke. Maya's footsteps were muffled by the worn carpet as she moved deeper into the shadows. She spotted Shrek at the bar, nursing a drink. There were only two other customers in the whole establishment since it was going on eleven o'clock on a Tuesday night.

She saddled up to the bar and ordered a vodka tonic from the bartender. Shrek did not seem to recognize the voice, at least not at first. When the bartender set Maya's drink in front of her, and she picked it up to take a sip, she slowly turned toward her mark.

"Shrek," she called out, her voice steady but firm. "We need to talk."

Shrek looked up, a sneer forming on his lips. "Well, well, if it isn't Detective Rizzoli. Where's your partner, Isles?"

Rizzoli and Isles.

A TV reference.

Cute.

But lame.

"She was so hot. Totally my type. So why isn't she here? Where is she?"

"I'll tell you where she is. She's way, way, way out of your league," Maya cracked, setting her drink down. "You know why I'm here. You lied to us. Why, Shrek? Did Chad pay you off?"

Shrek's eyes narrowed, and he turned to fully face her. "You think you can come here and accuse me? You coerced a confession out of me. I made the whole thing up. That dirty cop husband of yours was trying to scare me. Intimidate me. I thought he was going to get violent. Mess me up bad. Coming up with that lame murder-for-hire story was just a way to get you all off my back, keep myself from getting hurt."

"That's a lie," Maya shot back. "No one physically threatened you. You're protecting Chad. Why?"

Suddenly, Shrek's demeanor shifted, becoming aggressive.

"Lady, you don't know what the hell you're talking about."

Before she could react, Shrek lunged at her, grabbing her by the arm. Maya struggled, trying to break free, but his grip was ironclad.

Maya glanced around. The bartender had gone out back, and there were only two customers; one's face was buried in his phone, oblivious, and the other's head rested on the bar, passed out. No one was close by to help her.

"Let go of me!" she seethed, her heart pounding in her chest.

"Mess with the bull, you get the horns!" Shrek growled, his face inches from hers, his breath rancid, squeezing her arm tighter.

Just then, a shadow moved behind Shrek. Max appeared, his face set in a determined scowl. "Let her go, Shrek."

Shrek turned, surprised, but did not release Maya. "Look who decided to show up. The dirty cop trying to redeem himself by playing the hero."

Max did not wait. He swung a punch at Shrek, connecting with his jaw. Shrek stumbled back, releasing Maya, who quickly moved out of the way. The two men grappled, exchanging blows in a fierce struggle.

Maya watched in horror as Max, despite his strength, began to falter. She knew if this escalated, things could go spectacularly wrong in so many ways.

She had to do something.

"Max, stop!" she screamed. "It's not worth it!"

Suddenly, without warning, the bar patron who had been so focused on texting just moments earlier rushed over and broke up the fight, pulling Max away from Shrek. "That's enough!"

The man pulled a wallet out of his back pocket and flashed a badge. "Officer Ramos, I work with Detective Hart."

"You're off duty and just happened to be here?" Maya asked skeptically.

Ramos shook his head. "Detective Hart asked me to tail this guy, in case he tried to get in contact with Chad Bryce."

"Detective Hart was just at my house. She never mentioned you," Maya said.

"It's not her job to keep you apprised of every assignment she hands out," Ramos replied. "Maybe she thought I'd be helpful if you found yourself in trouble."

Shrek, panting and nursing a bruise on his face, pointed a finger at Max. "He assaulted me! Attacked me without provocation!"

Maya stepped forward, her voice trembling with anger. "That's a lie! Shrek grabbed me first. Max was just coming to my defense! If you hadn't been on your phone, you would've seen what really happened."

Ramos looked between them, his expression hard. "I'll need statements from both of you. But if Shrek presses charges, Captain, I mean Mr. Kendrick, you're in serious trouble."

Shrek smirked. "She'll say anything to protect her husband. You can't trust her."

Max looked at Maya, his eyes filled with guilt and frustration. "I followed you because I thought you might need me. I couldn't just sit there."

"I told you I was going to the Circle K!"

"Yeah, and I knew you weren't telling me the truth," Max said sheepishly.

"See! She's a serial liar! You can't believe a word that comes out of her mouth! She's obsessed with pinning me with a conspiracy to commit murder charge!"

Maya's anger flared. "Shut up!" She whipped around to her husband. "You risked your parole for this! Do you have any idea what could happen now?"

Max hung his head. "I couldn't just sit home and hope you came back unharmed. That's not who I am."

"What you're about to be is a convict back behind bars! Is that what you want?" Maya snapped.

Ramos sighed, pulling out his notebook. "Let's get this sorted. But, Max, you should know better. This is going to be a mess."

As they gave their statements, Maya could not shake the feeling that the shadows around them were closing in, tighter and darker than ever before. The stakes had never been higher, and now, not only was Alyssa's future at risk, but so was Max's freedom.

Chapter 27

Max shifted uneasily in the hard plastic chair, his fingers tapping a restless beat on his knee. The parole office's waiting room was a stark contrast to the life he had built since his release—a life he feared might be slipping away because of one rash decision.

Maya sat beside him, her presence a comforting anchor in a sea of uncertainty. She squeezed his hand, but the worry in her eyes mirrored his own.

The door to the inner office creaked open, and a stern voice called out, "Max Kendrick."

Max took a deep breath, exchanged a glance with Maya, and stood up. They walked into the office, where a woman in her late fifties with sharp features and a disapproving expression awaited them. Her nameplate read DEE KAPLAN. She motioned for them to sit without a hint of warmth.

"Mr. Kendrick, Mrs. Kendrick," Kaplan began, flipping through the file in front of her. "I've reviewed the report from last night. It doesn't look good for you, Max."

"Ma'am, I was just trying to protect my wife," Max started, but Kaplan cut him off with a raised hand.

"I've heard it all before. You were on parole, Max. You know the rules—no violence, no exceptions. The fact that you were involved in an altercation, regardless of the reason, is a serious breach."

Maya leaned forward, her voice steady despite the tension in the room. "Ms. Kaplan, with all due respect, Max wouldn't have acted if he didn't think I was in real danger. Shrek, the man he confronted, was threatening me."

Kaplan's eyes flicked to Maya, with an unreadable expression. "I'm aware of Kurt Maloney, aka Shrek, and his reputation. But this isn't about him. This is about Max violating his parole conditions."

"Ms. Kaplan," Maya persisted, "I'm a private detective. My partner and I are working on a case, trying to clear an innocent woman's name. Tawny Bryce's murder has the whole town on edge, and we believe Shrek is involved. Max acted out of instinct to protect me while I was gathering evidence."

Kaplan sighed, a deep, weary sound that spoke volumes about the number of similar stories she had heard. "I get it, Mrs. Kendrick. I really do. But my job is to ensure parolees follow the rules. Max, you were given a second chance—a chance many people don't get. And now you've jeopardized it."

Max tried to protest. "But—"

"Do you have a private investigator license issued by the state of Maine, Max?"

Max bowed his head. "No, ma'am."

"I know you just wanted to protect your wife, but

she was doing the job she's paid to do, and you never should have been there."

Max's jaw tightened, the weight of his past mistakes bearing down on him. "I know, Ms. Kaplan. But I've worked hard to stay on the right path. I made a mistake, but it was one moment of bad judgment. Please, don't let it undo everything I've done to turn my life around."

Kaplan leaned back in her chair, her gaze hardening. "I believe you, Max. But that doesn't change the fact that you broke the rules. I'm setting a court date to address this violation. Your fate is in the judge's hands now."

Max leaned forward to try to press his case one more time, but Maya knew it would fall on deaf ears. She gripped him by the hand and stood up, signaling him that it was time to leave.

Max's heart sank, but he nodded. "Thank you, Ms. Kaplan."

As they left the parole office, the weight of the situation pressed heavily on their shoulders. They stepped into the bright sunlight, feeling anything but free.

Maya squeezed Max's hand again, her determination rekindled. "We'll figure this out," she said, her voice resolute. "We have to."

Max nodded, though doubt gnawed at him. "What's our next move?"

"First, we need to get more dirt on Shrek. If we can prove he's been extorting Chad and lying to cover it up, it might help your case too. Let's talk to Sandra and see what she's come up with while we've been dealing with this latest crisis."

They climbed into Maya's car, the silence between

them thick with unspoken fears. As they drove, Max stared out the window, his mind obviously racing with worst-case scenarios.

"Maya," he said finally, his voice barely above a whisper, "What if I get sent back? What will happen to us? To Vanessa?"

Maya gripped the steering wheel tighter, her knuckles turning white. "We can't think like that, Max. We have to believe we'll find a way to keep you from having to go back to prison."

"But you heard Kaplan. It doesn't look good."

"We need to stay positive," Maya insisted.

"But if we don't," Max insisted, turning to look at her, "the next time we do a video chat with Vanessa, please don't say anything. I don't want to upset her. She doesn't need this hanging over her head while she's at college."

Maya's eyes softened with sorrow and resolve. "I promise, Max. We won't say a word to her until we have to. But we will find a way. I won't let you go back to prison."

Maya could see her husband's shoulders relax.

She had always been a calming influence on him.

But she could not stop feeling the gnawing in the pit of her stomach. She was grappling with the fear that she just made a promise to her husband that she might not be able to keep.

And it worried her deeply.

They arrived at their office. Sandra was already there, surrounded by stacks of papers and a laptop open to a spreadsheet.

"Hey, how'd it go with the parole officer?" Sandra asked, looking up.

"Not great," Max admitted. "A court date's been set. But we're still in the game."

Sandra glanced at Maya, who was working hard to project optimism, but Sandra could see right through it. Maya was scared. And it was rare to see Maya scared.

Maya quickly changed the subject. "What have you got?"

Sandra's eyes lit up with the thrill of new information. "I've been working with your buddy Oscar—who is amazing and adorable, by the way—digging into Shrek's background and his recent activities. Oscar managed to hack into his bank account. In less than two minutes. It wasn't hard. His password was 'Shrek.' Kind of on the nose, huh?"

She managed to get Maya to crack a smile.

"Not the brightest bulb in the chandelier," Sandra continued. "Other than the initial ten-thousand-dollar Venmo payment, there are no other reportable transactions from Chad Bryce. So if Shrek is extorting him now, he's receiving the money in cash. We also found a few shady transactions that suggest Shrek's been involved in more than just small-time extortion and mail fraud."

"That's no big surprise," Max said. "He's always running some kind of scam."

Maya's eyes narrowed. "Can we tie any of this directly to Tawny's murder?"

"Not yet," Sandra admitted. "But it's a start. We need to pressure Shrek, get him to spill the truth to the police. If we can prove Chad was trying to hire him as a hitman, it'll shift the focus away from Alyssa."

Max frowned. "But Shrek's not going to budge. As long as Chad's paying him to keep his mouth shut, he'll never talk. Especially not after last night."

"Then we'll need to get creative," Maya said. "If we can catch him in a lie, or find someone else who knows about the murder-for-hire plot, then we'll have some leverage on him."

Sandra nodded, her mind already working through the possibilities. "Who are Shrek's friends? Who does he hang out with?"

"Most of them are probably either in jail or awaiting trial," Max guessed.

"Maybe the DA would be willing to cut a deal with one of them in order to get them to turn on Max," Sandra suggested.

Maya shook her head. "That will take too long."

"And we're not even sure any of them are aware that Chad was trying to hire Shrek as a hitman," Max moaned.

Sandra thought some more. "Does he have a girlfriend?"

Max shrugged. "Not that I'm aware of, and even if he did, she would know that it would be in her best interest not to talk to the cops about Shrek. The guy can get pretty rough if he has to. Let's face it, Chad and Shrek may be the only two people in the world who ever knew about the hitman scheme before he spilled the beans to us the other night."

"So we have to get one of them to talk," Sandra concluded. "Once we do, it will only bolster the case against Chad."

"Shrek's already backtracked his story; he's never going to say a word to us ever again," Maya said.

"And what about Chad?" Sandra asked with a sly smile.

Maya folded her arms. "What about him?"

"What if we focus on getting *him* to talk?"

"To us? How?" Maya scoffed. "Sandra, have you forgotten we're the two who confirmed his affair with Lindsay at the bowling alley? He detests us! He would never talk to either of us willingly ever again."

"What if he didn't know it was one of us?"

Maya shook her head, confused. "I'm not following."

Sandra hesitated for a moment, then spoke up. "I've got an idea. It's risky, but it might be our best shot. I could go undercover to get a confession out of Chad."

Maya's eyes widened. "Undercover? As what?"

"Shrek's girlfriend, who heard some interesting pillow talk about Chad and his desire to rid himself of his nasty wife."

Max's eyes widened with concern. "That's dangerous, Sandra. We don't know what Chad is capable of."

"I know," Sandra replied, determination in her eyes. "But it's the only way to get close enough to him. We need a confession, and this might be our best chance."

Maya remembered the last time Sandra had played dress-up and gone undercover. It was before she had taken her under her wing, long before they became partners. And it was still very fresh in Maya's mind that Sandra's overzealousness and inexperience had almost gotten her killed.

Maya looked at Sandra, worry etched across her face. "Sandra, I'm not comfortable with any of this. Max is right. Chad was planning to hire someone to kill Tawny, and when that failed, he may have just gone and done the deed himself out of frustration. If he feels backed into a corner, there is no telling what he might do."

"Which is why I'll be wired and you'll be close by to swoop in and rescue me if things get too hot," Sandra said. "By the way, is it illegal to record someone without them knowing in New England?"

"Only New Hampshire and Massachusetts," Max answered.

"Well, we're in Maine, so we're good to go!" Sandra exclaimed.

Maya wanted to keep arguing.

This was a silly plan.

Sandra, a former US senator's wife, playing a dimwit, greedy, low-class girlfriend?

The whole idea was utterly ridiculous.

And yet, what other choice did they have?

It was the best shot at moving the case forward.

Maybe the only shot.

Make Chad believe the proverbial cat was out of the bag.

His murder-for-hire plot was no longer the world's best-kept secret. Make him think Shrek was a Chatty Kathy confessing all to his girlfriend even as Chad was paying him his hard-earned money in order to keep his mouth shut.

Whip him up into a panicked frenzy because panicky people nearly always make mistakes.

Chapter 28

The air inside the bowling alley was thick with the mingled scents of stale popcorn and cheap beer. Flashing neon lights reflected off the polished lanes, casting an eerie glow on the faces of the patrons. Laughter and the steady rumble of bowling balls striking pins filled the room, but Sandra's focus was solely on Chad Bryce, who sat a few lanes down with his girlfriend, Lindsay.

Sandra adjusted her wig—a platinum-blond bob that made her almost unrecognizable. Her outfit, a tight, leopard-print dress paired with sky-high heels, completed the transformation into Shrek's fictitious girlfriend. She took a deep breath, steadying herself for what was about to unfold.

"Can you hear me?" Sandra whispered.

"Loud and clear," Maya's voice crackled through the tiny earpiece she had placed inside her right ear.

Sandra took a deep breath. "Here we go."

* * *

At the bar, Chad laughed too loudly at something Lindsay said, his arm draped possessively around her shoulders. Sandra took her chance, sauntering over with a confident stride, hips swaying just enough to catch Chad's eye. She perched herself on the stool next to him, casually ordering a drink.

She could tell Chad was hyperaware of her presence but was pretending not to notice with Lindsay around. He waited until Lindsay scampered off to the ladies' room before swiveling around on his stool to see Sandra nursing her drink.

"Hey there," Chad greeted, his eyes lingering a bit too long. "Haven't seen you around here before."

Sandra turned toward him, flashing a sultry smile. "Maybe you haven't been looking hard enough," she replied, her voice dripping with faux flirtation. "I'm Cinda."

"Are you here on your own tonight, Cinda?"

Sandra gave him a pout with her ruby-red lips. "My boyfriend stood me up, so yes, I'm here all by my lonesome. Why? Are you the welcoming committee?"

He winked at her. "I could be." He glanced around to make sure Lindsay was not making her way back from the restroom.

"Your boyfriend's an idiot to let you out of his sight for one second, let alone a whole evening," Chad said in as deep a voice as he could muster.

"I wish Shrek appreciated me like you seem to," Sandra whined.

The mention of Shrek's name had the intended effect. Chad's easy demeanor vanished, replaced by a nervous twitch. He glanced quickly over at Lindsay, who had emerged from the ladies' room but was engrossed in her phone, oblivious. Chad then flicked his eyes back toward Sandra. "Shrek, huh? That's too much of a coincidence, if you ask me."

Sandra feigned innocence. "Oh, you know my Shrek?"

Chad wavered, not sure how much he should say.

"He can be a pill sometimes, and he snores all night long, which can be really annoying when I need my beauty sleep, but he takes good care of me when he wants to." Sandra gestured toward Lindsay, who was still texting on her phone. "Is that your wife?"

Chad shook his head.

"Oh, your girlfriend? She's very pretty. No wonder you wanted to get rid of your wife."

The blood suddenly drained from Chad's face.

Sandra leaned in closer, lowering her voice. "Not only does Shrek snore, he also talks in his sleep, you know. Says some pretty interesting things. Like a certain job he was supposed to do but didn't. Now, I'm thinking there might be some profit in keeping quiet."

Chad's face paled. He cleared his throat, trying to regain composure. "I don't know what you're talking about," he said, but the tremor in his voice betrayed him.

"Oh, come on," Sandra said, her tone sharp. "You don't think I know about the little arrangement you two had? The one involving your wife? How could I not? We sleep in the same bed."

Chad swallowed hard, his gaze darting around the

room, as if looking for an escape. "Alright, alright," he hissed, keeping his voice low. "How much more does he want?"

"Shrek? Oh, he's good. I'm not talking about him. I'm talking about me. I think I deserve a little reward for keeping these gorgeous lips sealed."

Chad sighed. "Fine. But cash only. I can't risk another paper trail. How much?"

Sandra smirked and glanced around conspiratorially. "Let's just say, enough to make it worth my while to forget I ever heard anything."

Chad dug into his pocket, pulling out a wad of cash. "This is all I have on me right now," he said, thrusting the bills into her hand. "But I can get more."

Sandra counted the money, then nodded. "A paltry start, but I'll give you the benefit of the doubt that you can come up with more, a lot more," she replied, slipping the cash into her purse. "And soon. I don't like waiting."

Chad nodded hurriedly, his face slick with sweat. "Yeah, yeah, you'll get it. Just keep your mouth shut."

She hopped off the stool just as Lindsay returned to join Chad. "Oh, what a cute top."

Lindsay beamed. "Thank you. It's Lululemon."

"Well, you wear it well, darlin'. Ciao!"

Sandra gave Chad a final, knowing look before turning and walking away, her heart pounding in her chest. She made her way outside, where Maya was waiting in the car, the recording device still running.

Sandra slid into the passenger seat. "How was I?"

Maya smiled, her eyes gleaming with satisfaction.

"Emma Stone better watch her back." Maya grabbed her phone from the car cupholder and tapped in a number. "Detective Hart, please. It's Maya Kendrick."

At the South Portland Police Precinct, Detective Beth Hart sat behind her desk in her office, listening intently as Maya and Sandra played the recording. The detective's stern expression softened into a smile of triumph. "This is exactly what we needed," she said, quickly adding, "Not that I approve of you two horning your way into my investigations. But that said, well done."

"Thank you, Beth," Maya replied appreciatively.

Hart sat back in her chair. "But there's one more thing. Shrek has an alibi for the night of the murder."

Sandra's brow furrowed. "An alibi? Are you sure?"

Hart nodded. "Positive. Shrek was miles away, at a poker game with half a dozen witnesses. But Chad, we all know he was at the reunion. He had motive, opportunity, and now, thanks to this recording, we have evidence of his desperation to cover it up." She picked up her phone. "We're going to need an arrest warrant so let's get the ball rolling on that."

Within hours, Chad Bryce was in handcuffs, led out of his plush office by a pair of uniformed officers. The press swarmed like vultures, cameras flashing as he was bundled into a police car. Reporters shouted questions, their voices blending into a cacophony of accusations and demands for answers.

Chad, his face flushed with anger and fear, turned to

the crowd. "I didn't kill my wife!" he shouted, his voice cracking with desperation. "This is all a mistake! I didn't do it! I loved Tawny!"

The press surged forward, eager for a soundbite. "Mr. Bryce, what about the evidence? The recording?" one reporter yelled.

Chad shook his head vehemently. "I didn't go through with it! I was desperate, yes, but I didn't kill her! You've got to believe me!"

Sandra watched from a distance. Something in his eyes, in the way he pleaded, gnawed at her. She turned to Maya, who stood beside her, arms crossed. "You know—"

Maya raised a hand. "Stop. I know what you're thinking. There's a part of you that believes him."

"He's admitting to the murder-for-hire plot, but denying he went through with it—why?"

"Because there's a difference between twenty years for conspiracy to commit murder and life without parole for murder in the first degree. He's hedging his bets, trying to get the lesser charge."

Sandra considered this. "Maybe."

"He's lying, Sandra," Maya said flatly. "We have him on tape admitting to trying to hire a hitman. He had motive and opportunity."

"I just don't think Chad would be stupid enough to strangle Tawny at the high school reunion. Why not wait until they were at a more convenient, more private location, just the two of them, where he could control the situation, dispose of the body, make it look like she ran off or something," Sandra mused, her voice thoughtful. "I'm just not one hundred percent sure this is open and shut. There are still missing pieces of the puzzle."

Maya frowned. "Sandra, he tried to hire someone to kill Tawny. He admitted it."

"True," Sandra conceded, "but what if someone else knew about the plan and decided to act on it? Or what if Chad's panic is because he's being set up?"

Maya sighed, rubbing her temples. "Alright, let's say for a moment that he's telling the truth. Who else would have a motive?"

Sandra thought back to their investigation, to the people they had interviewed. "What about Lindsay?" she suggested. "She benefits from Tawny's death too, doesn't she? With Tawny gone, she could have Chad all to herself."

Maya considered this, nodding slowly. "It's possible. But our client is Alyssa. We were hired to clear her name, and as far as I'm concerned, it appears we've done just that. Honestly, you should let this go. We've done our job. If Chad is innocent, then let his lawyers prove it in court."

Sandra shrugged. "You're probably right."

"Of course I'm right, I'm always right," she cracked with a playful wink. "I'm going to call Alyssa and make sure she knows about the arrest."

Maya stepped away, and Sandra watched as the press continued to hound Chad, his protests of innocence ringing out over the din. Sandra could not shake the feeling that the real killer was still out there, and it was up to them to uncover the truth, even though their client would be satisfied that the case involving her was officially closed.

Chapter 29

Alyssa Turner sat at a table in The Blue Spoon, one of the trendiest restaurants in Portland, Maine, nestled in the heart of the Old Port. The atmosphere was a mix of rustic charm and modern elegance, with exposed brick walls and polished wood floors. The noise of the bustling lunch crowd blended with the soft jazz playing overhead, creating a lively yet relaxed ambience. Alyssa's radiant smile and contagious laugh filled the space as she raised her glass of champagne.

"To Maya and Sandra," Alyssa said, her eyes shining with gratitude. "For clearing my name and saving my career."

Maya and Sandra clinked their glasses with Alyssa's, sharing in her relief and joy. The past few weeks had been a whirlwind, but with Chad Bryce's arrest, Alyssa's nightmare seemed to finally be over. The press had shifted its focus, and for the first time in a long while, Alyssa could breathe easily.

Still, Sandra could not shake the nagging feeling

that the case was far from closed. But she also did not want to dissuade a satisfied client who had invited them out to an expensive lunch to celebrate a job well done.

As they chatted and enjoyed their champagne while perusing the menu selections, the restaurant's door swung open, and two familiar faces from their high school days walked in. Kat and Amanda, Tawny Bryce's best friends and former members of her notorious mean girl clique, scanned the room before spotting Alyssa, Maya, and Sandra.

They excitedly whispered to each other, still starstruck by Alyssa, before casually strolling over to the table to say hello.

"My, champagne, la-de-da," Kat said, eyeing the bottle resting in the ice bucket next to the table. "What are we celebrating?"

As if they did not know.

Alyssa took another sip from her glass. "I'm celebrating my friends Maya and Sandra."

Amanda's eyes popped open expectantly. "Why? What did we miss? What did they do?"

Alyssa's smile faltered for a split second before she regained her composure. "Let's just say they're very good at their job."

"Oh, how nice," Amanda cooed.

Kat looked around, her eyes wide with feigned innocence. "We didn't make a reservation, and it's going to be a long wait. Have you ordered yet?"

Maya and Sandra exchanged glances, sensing an opportunity. "No, we just sat down and ordered the champagne. I haven't even looked at the menu," Maya said.

Alyssa hesitated, but knew they would not leave without an invitation. "Why don't you join us?"

Kat and Amanda beamed, pulling up chairs. "Don't mind if we do," Amanda said as she flagged down a passing waiter. "We'll have a bottle of your finest red, and let's start with the lobster bisque and oysters."

The waiter nodded, jotting down their orders before disappearing. Maya and Sandra watched as Kat and Amanda made themselves comfortable. They managed to keep the small talk going until the wine bottle was opened and they were diving into their oysters.

As the wine flowed and the conversation grew more relaxed, Kat and Amanda began to loosen up.

After slurping up an oyster and discarding the shell and washing it down with a big gulp of Pinot Noir, Amanda looked up with a pouty frown that lacked even a modicum of sincerity. "Kat and I were talking on the way over here. This is our first lunch together without Tawny. Can you believe she's gone?"

"No. It's very sad," Alyssa whispered.

"At least the police aren't hounding you anymore, Alyssa. I mean, the idea that you were the one who strangled Tawny, it's just so preposterous."

"Especially when everyone and their mother knew Chad had to be the one who killed her," Kat sniffed, guzzling her own glass of wine and choosing to ignore her own motive with their whole small business going belly-up thanks to Tawny.

Amanda leaned forward, elbows on the table. "He always seemed to be so controlling," she said, her tone conspiratorial.

Kat nodded vigorously in agreement, already pouring herself another generous glass of wine. "Absolutely. And that young slut, Lindsay. You know she had to be a part of it. Chad was her meal ticket. She couldn't risk Tawny ruining her future plans as Mrs. Chad Bryce. Believe me, it's only a matter of time before that one's role in the plot is exposed."

Alyssa forced a polite smile. "It's all such a shock. I never would have guessed."

"I loved Tawny, but she was playing with fire. Humiliating Chad with that video at the reunion? How did she expect him to react? He just lost his senses. It was a crime of passion. Plain and simple," Kat said.

"She told us what she was going to do. We tried to talk her out of it, but she wouldn't listen. She was hell-bent on exacting revenge," Amanda said.

Kat, slightly tipsy, blurted out, "Tawny hadn't been in her right mind for weeks. She never got over her online romance blowing up."

Maya caught the slip immediately. "Wait, what online romance?"

"Kat! Tawny swore us to secrecy!" Amanda scolded.

Kat looked guilty. "I'm sorry. I forgot. It just came out." She swallowed her wine and then topped off her glass from the bottle. After a gulp, Kat wiped her lips with her white linen napkin and looked down at the menu. "I'm thinking of having the halibut with the lemon butter sauce. Has anyone tried it?"

Sandra sat up in her chair. "Kat, you can't just drop a bombshell like that and not provide details."

Kat nervously glanced over at Amanda, who threw her head back in frustration.

"Go ahead. The cat's out of the bag now. And given

the circumstances, it's not like Tawny cares what secrets you spill about her anymore," Amanda sighed.

Kat redirected her attention back to Alyssa, Maya, and Sandra. "Tawny recently met someone online. She was super excited about him. But apparently it ended badly."

"Why?" Maya asked, her curiosity piqued.

Kat shrugged. "She never wanted to talk about it. But he obviously broke her heart. I think she tried to get over him by focusing more on Chad after that."

Sandra, sensing the importance of this lead, pressed gently, "Can you tell us more about this mystery man?"

Amanda sighed, taking a spoonful of lobster bisque. "She didn't tell us a whole lot. She kept the relationship very close to the vest. All we got out of her was that she had met him online and that she called him the 'Anti-Chad'—everything Chad wasn't. She was head over heels."

Kat shook her head, solemnly. "Poor thing. When it blew up in her face, she was devastated, more than we'd ever seen her."

Sandra looked thoughtful, swirling her wine. "I don't know. But if Tawny was so upset, maybe there's more to it. Maybe he knows something."

Kat sighed, dismissing the idea. "It's a waste of time. The killer's already been caught."

Kat and Amanda were eager to change the subject, so they zeroed in on the exciting upcoming film projects and possible co-stars Alyssa was considering for her next movie.

As the conversation wound down, the waiter delivered the check. The total was exorbitant, reflecting the expensive wine and food. Kat and Amanda exchanged awkward glances, making noises about splitting the bill. Kat half-heartedly dropped a hand in her purse in search of a credit card.

Alyssa, sensing their discomfort, reached for her Fendi bag. "I've got it," she said, smiling warmly. "Consider it my treat."

Kat and Amanda looked relieved.

"Thanks, Alyssa," Kat said, trying to sound casual. "That's very generous of you."

As they parted ways, Maya and Sandra exchanged determined looks. They had a new lead: the mystery man who had captured Tawny's heart and then shattered it. Finding him would be their next move. They had to know the truth on the off chance that they, and everybody else looking into this case, had somehow gotten it wrong and arrested an innocent man.

Chapter 30

Maya and Sandra huddled around the small conference table in their office, a map of Tawny Bryce's life spread out before them. The revelations from Kat and Amanda about Tawny's secret lover had set their minds racing. Now they were about to embark on a deeper dive into the tangled web of Tawny's past. With Oscar's help, they were able to obtain her online passwords from hacking into her phone and now had access to her entire life.

Maya leaned forward, her fingers tracing the edge of a printout. "Tawny's financial records show she wired a large sum of money to an unknown recipient about six months ago. It's nearly all she had in the bank."

Sandra, her eyes narrowing, glanced at the printout. "Six months ago . . . That aligns with when her business plans with Kat fell apart. Kat said Tawny was desperate for a new start with a rich guy who could show her the world. What if this mystery lover wasn't just some fling but an online fraudster? Like the Tinder Swindler?"

Maya nodded. "It makes sense. Tawny was so eager for a new life, she might have fallen for one of those romance scams. We need to dig deeper into this angle. Let's see if we can identify this guy."

They spent the next few hours combing through Tawny's online presence. Social media profiles, dating app messages, and email correspondences painted a picture of a woman yearning for escape and reinvention.

Then they struck gold.

Maya scrolled through Tawny's passwords until she found one for the dating app CupidConnect. "Here, this might be it."

She downloaded the app and typed in Tawny's username and password, gaining instant access to her account.

In her profile photo, Tawny stood confidently against a vibrant urban mural. Her shoulder-length hair was freshly styled into loose waves, reflecting a recent makeover. She wore a stylish, fitted blazer over a chic blouse, paired with well-fitted jeans that showcased her modern, sophisticated look. Her makeup was subtle yet elegant, with a hint of bold lipstick that added a pop of color to her ensemble.

She was holding a cup of coffee in one hand, with a slight smile that exuded both warmth and confidence. Her posture was relaxed yet poised, suggesting a newfound self-assurance. The background mural, filled with colorful geometric patterns and inspirational quotes, apparently symbolized her journey of reinvention and her vibrant approach to life.

Her eyes, sparkling with determination, hinted at her readiness to embrace new beginnings. The overall composition of the photo was bright and uplifting, capturing a woman who was ready to take on the world with a fresh perspective and a renewed sense of self.

In other words, they hardly recognized the real Tawny.

She seemed to be attempting to completely reinvent herself.

They scrolled down to read her stats and description of herself.

Username: SecretAdventurer

Age: 35

Maya stopped and glanced at Sandra. "Thirty-five?"

Sandra shrugged. "Lots of women shave off a few years when they sign up for dating apps."

"A few years yes, but *eight*?"

They returned their attention to the profile.

Location: Portland, Maine

About Me: Hello there! I'm a fun-loving, adventurous woman who believes life is too short to spend it all alone. I'm passionate about discovering new places, trying out exotic cuisines, and indulging in good conversation. I value honesty, laughter, and the ability to connect on a deeper level.

Interests: Many!

Traveling to off-the-beaten-path destinations

Cooking gourmet meals and exploring new recipes

Hiking and outdoor adventures

Wine tasting and enjoying cozy nights in

Reading mystery novels and exploring different genres

Looking For: I'm seeking someone who shares my

zest for life and is open to exploring new experiences together. A great sense of humor is a must, and if you love a good adventure, we'll get along just fine. Let's see where this journey takes us!

Fun Fact: I once hiked the entire length of the Appalachian Trail – it was both challenging and incredibly rewarding.

Maya chuckled. "The Appalachian Trail? Tawny? Really?"

"We don't know for sure she made that part up," Sandra offered in Tawny's defense.

"She made it up," Maya concluded confidently.

They went back to reading.

My Ideal Weekend: A perfect weekend would involve a spontaneous road trip to a quaint little town, enjoying a local festival, and ending the day with a candlelit dinner under the stars. If you're up for making memories and having a great time, let's chat!

Disclaimer: I value discretion and believe in living life to the fullest. Let's keep things light and fun!

Maya looked up. "Clearly the disclaimer about discretion was her half-hearted attempt to conceal the fact that she was still a married woman."

Sandra clicked on the message box.

There were about a dozen messages from various suitors who had happened upon her profile within the last month, unaware that she was no longer alive. As they scrolled down the list of correspondence, they reached a string of messages from one man in particular. The suitor, going by the name "Trevor," portrayed himself as a globe-trotting millionaire. The messages started out sweet and flattering, quickly escalating to professions of love and promises of a glamorous future together.

When Maya clicked on the link in the message to bring up the profile, she received a message that the profile no longer existed.

"We need to find out what this guy looked like. He must have sent a private message with his photo," Maya said, continuing to scroll.

They found several messages where Tawny fawned over Trevor and how handsome and sexy she found him, but he apparently had sent all the photos of himself in vanish mode, and they were no longer available to view, having disappeared into the ether.

As they continued pouring over the endless streams of messages, they finally found the piece of the puzzle they had been looking for.

Maya clicked on the message, and their eyes scanned through it quickly. "Here it is. He asked her for a loan to cover a 'trivial' expense. He said his private jet was grounded in Dubai because he needed to pay a sudden customs fee on a valuable piece of art he was transporting. Claimed it was just a technicality, and he'd repay her as soon as it got sorted."

Sandra's eyes widened. "He needed fifty thousand dollars to cover the fee. Tawny wired him the money and . . . of course, that's when he vanished."

"This would explain why Tawny had to unexpectedly pull out of her business venture with Kat," Maya guessed.

They sat in silence for a moment, the weight of their discovery sinking in. This was not just a story of heartbreak; it was one of exploitation and betrayal.

"We need to find out more about this 'Trevor,'" Maya said, determination hardening her voice. "If he's done this before, there will be a trail."

Hours later, their persistence paid off. They found forum posts and blog entries by women describing a man matching Trevor's description using CupidConnect to scam users. He used various pseudonyms, but always the same tactics: portraying himself as a wealthy suitor, gaining trust, and then disappearing after receiving a loan.

"I'm seeing a pattern here," Maya said, scanning through the posts. "These women are describing similar stories. A sudden expense, a grounded jet, an urgent customs fee, and then poof, he's gone."

Sandra clicked on a blog entry from a woman named Rachel who detailed her encounter with a man she called "Ethan." "Look at this," she said, reading aloud. "'Ethan' told me he was stuck in Monaco with a valuable shipment and needed a loan to cover unexpected fees. I wired him ten thousand dollars, and that was the last I heard from him.'"

Maya quickly typed a message to Rachel, explaining who they were and asking for more details about her experience. They repeated the process with several other victims, creating a list of potential leads.

"If they respond, we can start piecing together more information on this guy's real identity," Sandra said.

Maya nodded, a spark of hope in her eyes. "We just need one to get back to us, then she can lead us to more."

As they sent out more emails and messages, a sense of determination filled the office. The answer to Tawny's murder might lie in their stories, and Maya and Sandra were ready to uncover the truth, no matter how elusive it seemed.

As the night stretched on, they were growing more and more frustrated with the lack of response. Perhaps a lot of these women were embarrassed by what had happened to them and did not want to relive the humiliating details with a total stranger.

But then, close to midnight, just as Maya and Sandra were ready to call it a night, there was a ping alerting them to a new message.

It was from a woman named Rachel Calloway.

And she was ready to talk.

Chapter 31

Maya and Sandra arrived at Rachel Calloway's modest townhouse in Bay Village in Boston just as dusk settled over the city. Rachel, a woman in her mid-thirties with kind eyes and an air of quiet strength, greeted them at the door. Her home was warm and inviting, well-kept, obsessively polished and clean.

"Thank you for meeting us, Rachel," Maya said as they settled into the living room.

"Can I offer you a drink, some coffee, tea, maybe something stronger? I could use something stronger. I'm very nervous."

"You have no reason to be," Sandra assured her.

"I'm still processing everything that happened, all the money lost, obviously the emotional toll. I never had trust issues, but lately I barely want to leave my house. I used to love to go out with my friends, on dates, but he did such a number on me, now most days it's just me, my cat. and the *New York Times* crossword puzzle."

As if on cue, Rachel's Maine coon cat sauntered in, tail wagging, demanding attention.

"That's Rufus," Rachel said with a smile.

Sandra patted the top of Rufus's head, and he purred appreciatively. "Rachel, did you ever meet this man?"

"Ethan, at least that's what he called himself in his profile. I'm embarrassed to say I never did. Not in person. We Zoomed a couple of times. And he sent me pictures, and we talked on the phone constantly. He was always jetting off to someplace glamorous. He kept promising to fly into Boston so we could spend the weekend together in his usual suite at the Newbury. At first, I couldn't believe someone like him would be interested in me, but he was so good at making me feel beautiful, special, that I actually began believing fate had played a hand in bringing us together. Can you believe that? God, how could I have been so foolish? I'm so ashamed."

"He's the one who should be ashamed, not you," Maya said forcefully.

"By the time I realized it was a scam, he'd already vanished. I guess I should be grateful he only managed to squeeze ten grand out of me, not fifty like poor Tawny. I felt so sorry for her."

Maya leaned forward. "You mentioned you met Tawny through a support group?"

Rachel nodded, her eyes sad. "Yes, on Zoom. Tawny was so ashamed. She had lost so much money. She was terrified of what her husband, Chad, would do when he found out."

"So she was honest about still being married to Chad?" Maya asked.

Rachel nodded. "Yes. We're a safe space. No judgments. We understood how unhappy she was and that she was desperate to start over with someone new and that she was just testing the waters with CupidConnect, like we all were."

"So Chad never knew about the money?" Sandra asked.

"Not at first. During one of our calls, she admitted she hadn't told anyone the truth about where the money went. She made up excuses, but Chad had found out when he applied for a personal loan from a friend of hers at the bank. He was furious, to put it mildly. I have a recording of that call if you want to see it."

Rachel played the video on her phone. The screen flickered to life, showing a group of women, their faces marked by shared anguish. Tawny, looking more vulnerable than ever, recounted her story. Her voice trembled as she described her fear and humiliation.

"I told no one," Tawny said in the recording. "But Chad found out when he applied for a personal loan at our bank. He was out of his mind with anger. He demanded to know what happened. I couldn't very well tell him I gave it all to a man I thought was in love with me. I just made up some story about making a bad investment, I think I said something about a pasta company that went belly-up, how I didn't do enough due diligence before investing. At any rate, he called me every name in the book. Stupid. An idiot. A gullible fool. Sucker. Easy prey. Imbecile. Brainless. Moronic. And that was just in the first few minutes after I confessed to losing the money. The awful part is, he's right."

Tawny sniffed, fighting back tears, but failing. She reached off camera for a tissue to dab at her eyes.

The recording ended, and the room fell silent.

Rachel offered a tight smile. "Actually, I have something to share right away. I've arranged an online support group meeting with other victims. You can observe and ask questions. We're scheduled for four o'clock this afternoon."

It was already fifteen minutes until four.

Sandra looked at Maya, her eyes widening in surprise. "That's incredible. Thank you, Rachel. This could be exactly what we need."

Rachel nodded, eyes downcast. "I just want to help catch the man who did this to us and maybe get some justice for Tawny, who is no longer with us to fight the good fight."

As the clock struck four, Maya and Sandra joined Rachel at her computer for the Zoom call. One by one, the women appeared on the screen, each with a story similar to Rachel's, but each with a slightly different twist. They shared details of their encounters with the scammer, who used different names but the same tactics.

A woman named Lisa spoke first. "He called himself 'Alex' when he contacted me. He said he was in Morocco and needed money for customs fees on some handwoven Berber rugs he just had to own."

"What was his reason for not being able to pay the fee himself? I mean, he presented himself as such a successful, wealthy man," Maya wondered.

Lisa smiled derisively. "Oh, he had that covered. Apparently, the customs fees had to be paid in cash upon delivery, and unfortunately, his accounts were currently under audit due to a recent business restructuring. As a precautionary measure, he was unable to access his funds directly at that time. However, he assured me that once the audit concluded in a few weeks, he would have full access again and could reimburse me immediately." She shook her head. "I know, I know, as I say it out loud now, it sounds so obvious he was pulling one over on me, but my heart clouded my judgment."

Another woman, Carol, chimed in. "For me, he was 'Daniel' from Paris. Same story about customs fees, but he needed it for a shipment of vintage wine. I lost over five thousand dollars before I figured it out."

"He was 'James' from London for me," added Emily. "He needed money for a charity event. Same excuse about a business audit that had temporarily frozen his assets. I fell for it completely."

Maya and Sandra asked each woman for more details about the scammer's appearance. Most of them had only seen the photos he sent, which vanished from their message chains shortly after he ghosted them.

"Could the photos have been fake?" Sandra asked.

Emily piped in. "No, because we did have a flurry of Zoom calls the first couple of weeks, none of which I recorded, unfortunately, and he was clearly the same man who was in all of the photos."

Maya rubbed her chin. "So what did he look like?"

"He was tall, maybe six feet," Lisa said. "Dark hair, well-built."

Carol nodded in agreement. "He had piercing blue eyes. Looked like he worked out regularly."

Sandra took notes diligently. "Did anyone manage to get a photo that didn't vanish?"

There was a pause, then a woman named Sophie spoke up. "I met him in person while he was in New York."

Some of the women gasped.

"You did?" Rachel whispered.

Sophie nodded. "Yes. He wined and dined me on his dime, told me all these grand stories, how he wanted to whisk me off to his favorite resort in Bali, or his flat in London, or his country house in Tuscany. He had already dangled some story about how he was on the cusp of closing a massive business deal, how it was a once-in-a-lifetime opportunity, but there was a hiccup—a small, temporary liquidity issue. The funds he needed for the final transaction were tied up in an offshore account until the following week. I think he agreed to meet me in person because he felt I was close to agreeing and he really needed to seal the deal with an in-person meeting."

"So when you met, did you offer him money?" Sandra asked with a sense of dread.

"No. Don't get me wrong. I felt a rush of adrenaline at the prospect of being his business partner, the excitement of being the woman by his side as he navigated the high stakes world of international business. I was close, very close, but a little voice inside me miraculously kept urging me to put on the brakes, at least until I had some more time to consider.

"He kept pressing me, explaining how urgent it was, how it was going to change everything for him, for us. I felt so much pressure. The more he saw me hesitate, the more he turned on the charm, flattering me, telling me he had never met a woman like me before, whispering in my ear what he wanted to do with me when we got back to his hotel. The whole thing made me uncomfortable, and so I excused myself, told him I had a headache, and went home. The next day, he had deleted his profile, and all the photos of him were gone. I breathed a huge sigh of relief. I really felt as if I had dodged a bullet."

The other women on the Zoom call had not been so lucky, and you could feel the tension in the air.

"You said you took a photo?" Sandra asked.

Sophie nodded. "By that time, I suspected something was off, so when we walked out of the restaurant and I was waiting for my Uber, I secretly took a photo of him. It's blurry, but you can make him out. I'll email it to you."

Maya told Sophie her number, and moments later, Maya's phone pinged. She opened the email and squinted at the photo. It was blurry, but the man's features were somewhat discernible. Her brow furrowed as she studied the image, the pieces slowly falling into place.

"Maya, what is it?" Sandra asked, sensing the tension.

Maya's hand shook as she held up her phone, showing Sandra the photo. It was hard to identify him, but a creeping realization dawned on her, this man who had ensnared so many in his cruel web of deceit.

"It's definitely him," Maya whispered, her voice filled with disbelief. "But we know him by a different name."

Before Sandra could press further, Maya was texting Alyssa: *Emergency. We're on our way back to Portland from Boston and need to see you right away.*

The revelation hung in the air, heavy and foreboding. As they rushed out of Rachel's home, their minds raced with the implications of what they had just uncovered. The shadows of Tawny's past were darker and more twisted than they had imagined, and the real killer was closer than they had ever thought.

Chapter 32

Maya and Sandra pushed through the revolving doors of the opulent Press Hotel, their faces etched with urgency. The polished marble floor gleamed under the chandelier's light, a stark contrast to the turmoil brewing within their minds. They headed directly for the elevators, dodging a group of businesspeople chatting animatedly in the lobby. The elevator ride felt interminable, the soft classical music doing nothing to soothe their anxiety.

As the doors opened to the twelfth floor, Maya and Sandra hurried to Room 1208 and knocked on the door. Alyssa answered and ushered them inside, her expression full of both relief and apprehension. "Wow, you made it here in record time. You must have broken speed records on ninety-five."

She was in the midst of packing. Her suite was a whirlwind of designer clothes, open suitcases, and various toiletries scattered across the plush carpet. She walked back over to one of her open suitcases and continued folding clothes and placing them inside. "By the way, we have to make this fast. I'm on my way to my parents' house for a farewell dinner before heading to the airport. I'm catching a late flight to New York because I have to be up at five a.m. for a live interview with Gayle King during the first segment of *CBS Mornings* tomorrow."

Sandra raised an eyebrow. "You're doing a TV interview?"

"Actually, it was my publicist's idea. She thought now that Chad's been arrested and my name has been cleared, why not get out there and share my story? How I was targeted by an unscrupulous DA and convicted by an overzealous press. All the morning shows were vying for me to appear. I got personal calls from Savannah Guthrie, Robin Roberts, but Gayle—well, I can picture myself going out for cocktails with Gayle and having a good laugh, so I went with her."

She suddenly noticed Maya and Sandra standing close together in silence, contemplating how best to proceed, and it began making her slightly uncomfortable. "Your text had me worried. You sounded so serious. What's this all about?"

"Alyssa, we need to talk," Maya said, closing the door behind them.

Alyssa paused, a silk blouse hanging limply from her hand. "Okay, now I've gone from worried to scared. What's happening? What did you find?"

Maya and Sandra exchanged a tense glance.

Alyssa's eyes darted from one to the other. "What? Tell me."

Maya pulled out her phone, her fingers trembling

slightly. "We found a blurry photo of a man who has been romancing women on CupidConnect."

"The dating app?"

Sandra nodded. "We think you need to see it."

Alyssa frowned, dropping the blouse into her suitcase. She took the phone from Maya, her eyes scanning the image. Her face paled, and she visibly recoiled, but she quickly composed herself. "I . . . I don't recognize him," she said, though her voice wavered.

"Alyssa, we can see the shock on your face," Maya said gently. "You must see what we see."

"Okay, yes, there is a resemblance to Aaron, but, honestly, it's so blurry, who can really tell?"

"We believe it's him," Sandra said confidently.

Alyssa sat down on the edge of the bed, her hands clasped tightly in her lap. After a moment of tense silence, she sighed deeply. "Are you saying he's cheating on me? How do we know he wasn't on this app before we met? And for the record, I did not hire you to investigate Aaron; I hired you to prove I didn't kill Tawny, so why are you going behind my back like this?"

"This man, if it is Aaron, has been conning women out of money and then vanishing into thin air. We found at least a dozen victims, and we're confident there are a lot more we just need to find," Maya said firmly.

"Aaron doesn't need to con women. He's a film producer. He's got his own money. He treats me all the time," Alyssa blurted out defensively, although they could both almost see her mind reeling. "He's never once asked me for money!"

"Because you're a big catch," Maya explained. "The mother lode. He was playing the long game with you."

Sandra knelt beside her. "How much do you really know about him, Alyssa?"

Alyssa hesitated, then began to recount the story of her first encounter with Aaron. "We, uh, we met at a party at Ashton and Mila's house."

Ashton Kutcher and Mila Kunis, a Hollywood A-list couple.

"I was with some girlfriends, and I spotted him working the room like a pro. It certainly looked like he belonged there. People seemed to know him. I asked who he was, and one of my friends thought he came with Leonardo."

"DiCaprio?" Sandra asked.

Alyssa nodded. "It doesn't get more legit than that. But she could have been wrong. I don't know. It was a crowded party with lots of big industry names."

"So it's possible he crashed," Maya suggested.

Alyssa grimaced. "Yes, I suppose it's possible."

"Who introduced you?" Sandra asked.

"No one. We ran into each other at the bar. We both ordered the same cocktail. The Boulevardier. The bartender had never heard of it, so Aaron had to describe it to him. Bourbon, sweet vermouth, and Campari. I was impressed he knew what it was. I first had one when I was shooting a movie in Paris, where it was invented, but people here in the States are less familiar with it. Aaron told me he had spent a summer in Paris working on a screenplay and had fallen in love with it at his favorite bar, the Little Red Door. From there we just started talking, and I felt so comfortable around him. At the end of the evening, he asked for my number, and I guess I was just tipsy enough to give it to him. He waited a week before he called me, which drove me a little crazy, but when he finally did, I played hard to get, said I was too busy to meet. So we just talked on the phone for days, then weeks, before I finally agreed to have dinner with him, at Church and State, my favorite French restaurant in downtown LA, where he ordered us two Boulevardiers, of course."

"Smooth operator," Maya remarked.

"He paid for everything," Alyssa quickly added.

No doubt with the money he had conned out of his marks on CupidConnect, Sandra thought to herself.

Alyssa snapped out of her reverie and shot to her feet. "Okay, let's assume Aaron is the man in the photo. And let's further assume, although you have not convinced me yet, that he did date various women who might have invested their money in some of his projects. What does any of that have to do with me being accused of Tawny's murder?"

"Because Tawny Bryce was one of the women Aaron targeted on CupidConnect," Maya whispered.

Alyssa's knees buckled.

Sandra leapt to her side, taking hold of her elbow, fearing she might collapse on the spot.

"No . . ." Alyssa moaned.

"She paid him fifty thousand dollars out of her and Chad's savings, and then he ghosted her," Maya quietly explained.

"I-I don't understand," Alyssa stammered. "For a film project?"

Sandra shook her head. "He wasn't a movie producer, and he wasn't going by the name Aaron at the time. He created a whole new identity every time he pursued a different woman online. With Tawny, he was an art collector."

"This—this is madness!" Alyssa cried.

"Like all his other victims, once Tawny wired him the money, he just disappeared, moving onto the next mark. But something went terribly wrong with Tawny. He never expected to ever see her again. But he did. At the reunion."

Alyssa gasped. "No! I can't believe I've been sleeping with a murderer."

"Think about it, Alyssa," Sandra said cautiously. "Aaron was finally on his way to legitimacy, with a famous actress girlfriend and a promising career. But then he made the mistake of accompanying you to your high school reunion, where he came face-to-face with one of his past victims. That's why Tawny was so desperate to talk to you. She was trying to warn you. Aaron couldn't risk being exposed, not at such a critical point, so he lured her behind the bleachers and strangled her. The music was so loud, no one heard a thing."

Alyssa's hand flew to her mouth, her eyes wide with horror. She grabbed her phone and dialed Aaron's number, her fingers moving faster than her thoughts. "I need to talk to him," she said, her voice shaking."

Maya tried to stop her. "Alyssa, wait!"

Alyssa ignored her, dashing across the room away from her.

The call went to voicemail.

"Aaron, it's me. Call me the moment you get this message!" Alyssa said, her voice shaky.

Then, before Maya and Sandra could say a word,

she was making another call to his assistant. "Erica, it's Alyssa. Where's Aaron? Well, when will they be done shooting the scene? Okay, I need to talk to him right away. It's important."

She ended the call, dropping the phone on the bed as she rubbed her temples with both hands.

"Alyssa, please don't tell him anything yet," Maya pleaded. "We need more information and evidence. If he knows we're onto him, he might disappear again, and then we'll never catch him."

Alyssa slumped back onto the bed, her eyes filling with tears. "I'll try," she whispered, "but I don't know how long I can keep this to myself."

Maya and Sandra exchanged worried looks. They knew Alyssa was on the brink of an emotional breakdown, and their entire investigation hung in the balance.

"We'll find more evidence," Sandra assured her. "Just hold on a little longer. We'll get to the bottom of this."

Alyssa nodded, though the doubt in her eyes was unmistakable.

The three women sat in silence, the weight of the situation pressing down on them like an unbearable burden.

Her phone suddenly rang, and she jumped. She scooped it up to look at the screen. "It's Aaron."

"Put it on speaker," Maya commanded.

Taking a deep breath, Alyssa answered and pressed the speaker button. "Hey, where are you?"

"Just finished shooting," Aaron replied smoothly. "Scarlett nailed it. Of course, no disrespect to her, but I couldn't stop thinking about what you would have done with that scene. But I'll just keep holding out hope you'll star in my next film."

"Maybe, we'll see," Alyssa said, trying to act casual.

"Shouldn't you be on a plane back to LA now that all that nasty business in Maine has been resolved?"

"No, I'm still in Portland. I'm flying to New York later tonight to do a TV interview in the morning. I'm staying at the Greenwich."

"De Niro's hotel? Awesome," Aaron said. "Should I meet you there?"

She hesitated. "Um, I need to get a good night's sleep before I face the cameras tomorrow and was planning to fly back to LA directly after the interview."

"Stay an extra day. We can have a date night. Maybe dinner at Joanne Trattoria? The food is supposed to be incredible. You know, the owners are Lady Gaga's parents. I can make a reservation."

He certainly loved dropping names.

"Uh, yes, maybe, um, can I call you later and let you know for sure?"

"Is everything okay?" he asked, a hint of concern in his tone.

"Yeah, just . . . a lot going on," she said, her heart pounding so hard she placed a hand on her chest to calm herself. "I'll call you from the airport."

As she hung up, Sandra could sense the cold knot of fear in Alyssa's stomach.

"He totally suspected I was upset," she said, her voice tinged with panic. "What if I gave it all away?"

Maya stepped forward, placing a reassuring hand on Alyssa's shoulder. "It's going to be okay. Just keep playing it cool until we can gather more evidence. We can't let him know we're onto him."

"I'll try," Alyssa promised, though her voice was unsteady. "I'll do my best."

Sandra nodded, her eyes shining with determination. "We're here with you, Alyssa. We won't let you down."

Alyssa nodded, taking a deep breath to steady herself. The next twenty-four hours would be the most challenging of her life. She had to maintain her composure, to act as if everything was normal, all while the truth threatened to unravel her world.

As the sun set over the city, the three women steeled themselves for the battle ahead, knowing that the stakes had never been higher.

Chapter 33

Maya and Sandra strode into the bustling precinct. Coming here was always fraught for Maya, who had once been a police officer serving under her husband, the now-disgraced captain. She steeled herself for the looks from the other officers who were around at the time of Max's arrest and the intense scrutiny she had faced as suspicion mounted about her possible complicity in his crimes. Living under a microscope at work quickly took its toll, and she felt she had no choice but to resign, leading her to get her private investigator's license. She was raising a daughter alone and needed income now that Max was serving a five- to ten-year sentence. Since she could barely type, she fell back on the one line of work she knew something about.

The desk sergeant gave Maya a curt nod as they passed him, knowing Maya and Detective Hart were friends. The door to Hart's office was open, and they found her sitting behind her desk, buried in paperwork, her expression one of grim concentration.

Maya cleared her throat, capturing Hart's attention. "Lieutenant, we need to talk."

Hart's eyes narrowed. "Make it quick. I'm swamped."

Sandra stepped forward. "We have new information about Tawny Bryce's murder."

Hart leaned back, crossing her arms. "I've already arrested the husband. His arraignment is tomorrow. Case closed."

Sandra placed her hands down on the edge of Hart's desk and said with confidence, "We believe Aaron Hoffman, Alyssa Turner's boyfriend, is the real killer."

"But we questioned him at the scene and cleared him. He had no connection to the murder victim," Hart insisted.

"That we knew of at the time," Maya quickly added. "Now we know there *was* a connection. A big one."

Hart leaned forward, intrigued.

"Aaron is an online hustler. He scams women on dating apps. It turns out Tawny was one of his victims, and we think they ran into each other by coincidence at the reunion, and he killed her to keep her quiet," Maya explained.

Hart's eyes flickered with interest but quickly hardened. "Do you have any solid evidence?"

"Not yet," Sandra admitted. "But we're working on it."

"Come on, Beth, use your resources," Maya urged. "Bring him in for questioning. Confront him with this new information; maybe you'll even get a confession out of him."

"Where is he now?" Hart asked.

"We're not sure. Last we heard, he was on a film set somewhere producing his first major motion picture, but we know he might be meeting Alyssa in New York tomorrow."

Hart cocked an eyebrow. "New York?"

"You need to scoop him up before he starts to suspect we're onto him. Time is of the essence," Maya urged.

"And you should probably also have the DA drop the charges against Chad Bryce," Sandra added.

Hart threw her head back and sighed. "Look, for the record, I don't work for you. I can't just let a murder suspect go based on speculation. Find me more evidence. Concrete evidence."

Maya's frustration bubbled over. "Or is it that you don't want to admit you made a mistake by arresting Chad?"

Hart's eyes flashed with anger. "Watch it, Maya. I don't appreciate being second-guessed."

Maya took a deep breath. "I'm sorry. We just need more time. We will prove Aaron did it. Somehow."

Hart leaned back, her demeanor cooling. "The CSI guys packaged hair and fiber samples that were an exact match to Chad Bryce. It doesn't get any more clear-cut than that," Hart said emphatically.

"Beth, they lived in the same house. Of course she had some of his DNA on her body. How could she not?" Maya sighed.

"What about skin underneath her fingernails? She could've been fighting for her life and managed to scratch him on the neck or face or something," Sandra said.

"None. Also, no one we questioned, including your Aaron guy, had any visible scratches that night."

Maya's mind raced. "He could've attacked her from behind in a chokehold, or maybe pushed her to the floor and straddled her and pinned her arms down with his knees while he strangled her so she couldn't fight back."

The idea of that made Sandra shudder.

"Is it possible he left fingerprints on her neck when he strangled her?" Sandra asked.

"It's possible, but that kind of evidence disappears very quickly. They most likely had already faded by the time the CSI team arrived, if the killer wasn't wearing gloves."

"Was there any DNA evidence on Tawny's body that was not a match to Chad?" Maya pressed.

Hart paused.

"Beth, what is it? Was there other DNA evidence?"

Beth pulled her chair closer to her desk and tapped some keys on her computer keyboard, bringing up the coroner's report. She scrolled down, her eyes darting back and forth as she reviewed the report.

"There were faint traces of saliva on her right ear lobe that did not belong to her husband."

Maya banged her fist down on Hart's desk. "That's it. Maybe some spit from the corner of his mouth dribbled onto Tawny as he was strangling her!"

"Or the saliva was from the dozens of people she kissed and hugged that night at the reunion," Hart said, playing devil's advocate. "We ran the sample through the database and came up empty."

"Because Aaron, or whatever his real name is, doesn't have a criminal record, and I would suspect a con man wouldn't be too anxious to mail in his DNA to 23 and Me," Sandra noted.

"Can't you use his misdeeds on CupidConnect as a pretense to drag him in here for questioning and get a DNA sample while you're at it?"

"The online scam isn't my jurisdiction, especially since the apparent lone local victim, Tawny, is dead. The judge would dismiss the case on that alone. Find me something solid on the murder, and I'll act." Hart stood up and gestured toward the door. "Now, if you'll excuse me, I have other cases that demand my attention."

Maya and Sandra bowed out of the office and hurried back down the hall, both more convinced than ever they had Aaron checkmated if they could somehow get a sample of his DNA.

Maya and Sandra arrived at Alyssa's parents' house, the cozy home filled with the lingering aroma of a recent family dinner. Alyssa greeted them at the door. Her parents, Doug and Edie, stood behind her, their faces etched with worry.

"Come in," Alyssa said, leading them to the living room. "We just finished dinner."

Doug offered them seats, while Edie brought in a tray of tea and cookies. "We're very worried about Alyssa," Edie said, her voice trembling. "This whole situation is just awful."

Maya and Sandra exchanged a glance, then Maya spoke up. "Alyssa, we have some new information."

"What is it?" Alyssa asked, her voice tinged with fear.

"The CSI team found traces of saliva DNA on Tawny's right earlobe," Sandra explained. "It wasn't a match to Chad."

Doug put a comforting arm around his daughter. "But I thought the police had already arrested him for the murder. Isn't that right, Alyssa?"

Maya and Sandra hesitated.

She had not told her parents what they all suspected.

Alyssa, voice quivering, explained, "Yes, Dad, he has. But Maya and Sandra don't believe he was the one who did it."

"If not him, then who?" Doug asked, confused.

Alyssa turned to her father and whispered, "Aaron."

Edie dropped her teacup to the floor. *"What?"*

"Why didn't you tell us?" Doug wanted to know.

"I didn't want to worry you," Alyssa said quietly.

Doug turned to Maya and Sandra. "Are you absolutely certain it was Aaron? Why? What motive would he have to kill Tawny Bryce?"

There was little time to explain, but Alyssa's parents were not going to rest until they knew, so Maya and Sandra quickly brought them up to speed on the whole CupidConnect business.

Edie left the cracked teacup on the floor and joined her husband, her face pale. They sat side by side on the couch, trying to process it all.

"Dear Lord, we invited that man to spend time with us at our summer house in West Bath," Edie whispered.

Finally, Doug spoke. "Honey, I don't want you going anywhere near that man ever again."

Edie grabbed Doug's shirtsleeve. "She said at dinner he was flying into New York tomorrow to meet her." She whipped her head in her daughter's direction. "You need to text him right now and tell him not to come."

Maya, trying to be as gentle as possible, moved closer to Doug and Edie. "The thing is, in order to arrest Aaron and make sure he never hurts anyone ever again, the police need hard evidence. And the only way to get it is to have someone close to him get hold of a soda can or a utensil, something he might have used that would have his DNA on it."

Doug's face darkened. "Absolutely not. Alyssa is not going anywhere near a man who is capable of murder."

"Sandra and I can go with her to New York. We'll be near her, safely out of sight the whole time. We'll make sure nothing goes wrong," Maya promised.

"I'm sorry. It's just too dangerous," Doug bellowed.

"Aaron will never know. He's too swept up in the idea of being Alyssa Turner's boyfriend. He's working very hard to keep her happy. He's too blinded by ambition to suspect anything at this point," Maya said.

Edie glanced at her daughter, trying to guess what she was thinking. "Alyssa?"

Alyssa hugged herself. "It might be the only way, Mom."

Doug shook his head. "Alyssa, don't let them put you in this position. There must be another way to get this guy's DNA. I think you should cancel the Gayle King interview and just stay here with us until they have enough to arrest him."

Maya tried reading the room, afraid she might push too hard and get them kicked out of the house.

Luckily, Alyssa was beginning to understand the stakes.

"If we wait too long, he might get wind that the police are onto him and pull a disappearing act, and then he will be out there free, ready to victimize someone else, or show up wherever I am to stalk me, or worse."

"She's right," Maya said quietly. "If we're going to do it, we need to do it now."

Doug and Edie did not give their blessing to the plan.

But they stopped trying to prevent it from happening.

Sandra was on her phone booking two seats on Alyssa's flight to New York, which was leaving in less than two hours.

"Mom, when Braden shows up tell him I had to go, I'll be fine, and I'll call him tomorrow."

Doug grimaced. "He's not going to be happy you ditched him."

As she hurried for the door ahead of Maya and Sandra, Alyssa turned and said, "He works for me. He'll get over it."

"Please," Edie begged. "Just be careful."

CHAPTER 34

The turbulence hit just as Maya finished reading the text message from Max on her phone. He was surprised to learn she was not coming home tonight and that she was on a flight to New York City, but Max had changed since his time in prison. Once he had been controlling and demanding of her time, but he had been humbled and now was much more supportive and understanding.

She loved him more than ever.

Maya glanced at Sandra, who was flipping through a travel magazine, seemingly unbothered by the plane's sudden shudder.

Alyssa Turner, sitting across the aisle, clutched her armrests, her knuckles white.

"Are you okay?" Maya leaned over, her voice calm and reassuring.

Alyssa nodded, though her eyes betrayed her fear. "Just a bit nervous. About everything."

Sandra looked up and smiled. "We'll get through

this, Alyssa. Just focus on the interview tomorrow. We'll handle the rest."

The flight to LaGuardia seemed longer than it actually was, tension hanging in the air between them. Each was lost in their thoughts, preparing for what lay ahead. Alyssa was shuffling through some interview questions the *CBS Mornings* producers had sent her in preparation for her sit-down live on the air with Gayle King in the morning. There was no doubt in her mind that Gayle would bring up Tawny Bryce's murder and how she had been in the center of the storm until the recent arrest of Tawny's husband. Maya could see Alyssa's mouth moving as she practiced her responses.

When they finally landed, the bustling energy of New York City enveloped them as they were driven across the bridge into Manhattan and then down the FDR Drive by a private limousine service. The driver could not help stealing glances in the rearview mirror, excited to be driving a bona fide Hollywood movie star.

Once they arrived in Tribeca at the Greenwich, a luxury hotel in a kind of rustic, elegant, trendy industrial style, a young bellhop grabbed their luggage, fumbling his greeting because he was so starstruck at the sight of Alyssa.

As they approached the reception desk, Sandra glanced at Maya, who was already sizing up the lobby, mentally noting exits and security cameras.

Once a cop, always a cop.

Alyssa smiled at the receptionist, a petite young woman trying desperately to act casual. After all, a Hollywood legend owned the hotel. De Niro was synonymous with Tribeca. It was her job to play it cool.

"We have two rooms reserved. The name is Priestly," Alyssa said, slapping a platinum credit card down on the desk.

"Of course, Ms. Priestly," the receptionist replied with a practiced smile, tapping on her keyboard.

Maya leaned in whispering in Alyssa's ear. "Priestly?"

Alyssa chuckled. "It's the name I use whenever I travel. Miranda Priestly. My absolute favorite Meryl Streep character."

The Devil Wears Prada.

A classic.

The receptionist handed Alyssa two key cards. "You're in rooms 1502 and 1508. I know you requested adjoining rooms, but unfortunately none were available. We're nearly fully booked. I was lucky to get you two rooms on the same floor."

"It's fine," Alyssa muttered.

But Maya could tell she was not fine.

"Alvin will bring up your bags shortly," the receptionist chirped. "Enjoy your stay."

"Thank you," Alyssa said, taking the cards. She handed one to Maya and kept the other.

On the elevator ride up to their floor, Sandra placed a hand on Alyssa's arm. "We'll be right down the hall if you need *anything*."

"I know. I'll sleep better knowing I'm not here all on my own."

After parting ways, Maya and Sandra went to their shared room a few doors down and waited for their overnight bags to arrive before settling onto their beds.

Maya checked her phone again, noting the time.

"We should get some rest," she said. "Tomorrow's going to be a long day."

Sandra nodded, though she did not seem ready to sleep. Instead, she pulled out her phone and scrolled through her messages.

A text from Lucas popped up.

She grimaced.

Maya noticed her expression. "What is it?"

"Lucas wants to know if I'm free for dinner tomorrow night," Sandra said with a sigh. "I forgot to let him know I left the state."

Maya gave her a knowing look. "Are you still worried about the age difference?"

Sandra shrugged. "I am, but he's persistent. And sweet. It's complicated."

Maya smiled. "He's a good guy, Sandra. If he makes you happy, that's what matters."

"I know . . ." Her voice trailed off, still unconvinced.

Sandra put her phone away and lay back on her pillow. "I just want this case to be over so we can get back to our lives."

"It has been one of the tougher ones," Maya agreed. "But we'll get him. We're so close."

They drifted off to sleep, but it was not long before the shrill ring of the phone jolted them awake. Maya groggily answered, her voice thick with sleep.

"Maya, it's Alyssa. You need to come to my room. Now."

"Why? What happened?"

"Please, just hurry!"

Maya and Sandra exchanged pensive looks, then

quickly threw on their clothes and rushed down the hall to Alyssa's room. They found her pacing, her face pale and eyes wide with panic.

"Alyssa, what is it?" Sandra asked, closing the door behind them.

"Aaron," Alyssa said, her voice trembling. "He was here."

"*Here*? In your room?"

Alyssa nodded, still shaken. "He must have sensed something was wrong when we talked on the phone. He surprised me."

"But how did he get in here?" Maya gasped.

"We've traveled together a number of times. He knows all the security codes and passwords the hotel requires to allow him access. I never thought to change them."

Maya's eyes narrowed. "What did he say?"

"When I walked in, he was sitting on the bed, staring out the window at the skyline, like he was lying in wait for me. When he saw me, he just popped up and started talking about his day like it was the most natural thing in the world for him to be in my hotel room. I was so stunned, I didn't know what to say. He could tell I was upset. He kept asking what was wrong, and I just kept repeating over and over 'nothing,' 'nothing,' but he didn't believe me. He kept pressing, and I was so thrown off, I slipped about his online scam. I could see he was taken aback. He asked me where I was getting this information, and I couldn't stop myself. I just started calling him out on his lies. I'm sorry, I totally blew it. Now he knows we're on to him."

Sandra put a comforting arm around Alyssa's shoulders. "Now come on, he ambushed you. Anyone would have been blindsided by that. It's not your fault."

"I was nominated for an Academy Award, and I couldn't even pull off playing a cool version of myself," she lamented.

Maya took a step toward her. "Once you confronted him, then what?"

Alyssa shrugged. "He just kept denying it. He insisted that whoever was feeding me this fake news was just trying to sabotage our relationship. I shouldn't believe a word of it. It was one vociferous denial after the other, followed by declarations of his love for me and wanting a future together. After a while, he could tell he wasn't making much headway, and so he said we'd talk more later, that he had to get back to the set, and he left my room. I called you immediately."

"We need to know where he's going. Alyssa, do you have the number for Aaron's assistant? Can you call her?"

"Yes," Alyssa said, picking up her phone from the nightstand and speed dialing. "Hi, Erica, it's Alyssa." She put the call on speaker so Maya and Sandra could listen in. "Have you heard from Aaron? I'm trying to locate him."

Erica sounded frazzled. "I was about to call you. He's not shown up at the film set all day," she said. "We have major problems with the production. An unhappy star threatening to walk off, inclement weather screwing with the schedule, and a stunt performer sidelined by an accident. Aaron's not answering his phone, and we need him here."

"Okay, I'll keep looking and will call you the moment I hear anything," Alyssa said.

"Thanks, Alyssa, I would appreciate it," Erica replied, her voice full of desperation.

Alyssa ended the call.

Maya and Sandra exchanged concerned looks.

"He's no doubt already gone into hiding," Sandra said. "We'll probably never get a sample of his DNA now."

Maya stared at Alyssa intently. "Think carefully. Did he touch anything, eat or drink something from the minibar, use the bathroom? Anything we might possibly use?"

Alyssa shook her head. "No, nothing. All I could think about was getting rid of him. I was so disgusted by him, I could barely hide it. When he kissed me, it made my skin crawl."

Maya's eyes widened. "He kissed you?"

Alyssa nodded, confused. "Why? What's important about that?"

Maya's face lit up with realization. "DNA. When you kiss someone, you exchange DNA. We can use that."

Sandra's eyes danced as she caught on. "You're right. I've read about studies that show DNA can be detected in saliva for at least an hour after a kiss. We could get a sample."

Alyssa looked between them, hope dawning on her face. "What do we need to do?"

Maya quickly explained, then handed Alyssa a glass. "Spit into this. We'll call Oscar, our friend at the Portland Police Department. Maybe he can connect us with a lab tech here in New York who can fast-track the sample."

Alyssa did as instructed, and Maya called Oscar. After a brief conversation, she hung up and turned to the others. "Apparently Oscar has a buddy who lives downtown in the East Village who is a real night owl and works for a lab. They play Dungeons and Dragons together over Zoom three times a week. Yes, it's as nerdy as it sounds. He's going to text me the lab's address so I can go meet him there with the sample."

"What about me?" Sandra asked.

"You stay here with Alyssa in case Aaron decides to come back. I'll go meet Morthos."

"Morthos?" Sandra asked, confused. "That's his name?"

"I'm sure that's the name he uses when he plays Dungeons and Dragons. He's Morthos the Human Warlock," Alyssa said. "Remember, I'm a big nerd at heart too."

Maya shook her head. "You can't make this stuff up."

Maya's phone pinged, and she glanced at the screen. "Got it. I'm out. I'll call you in the morning when I have the results."

Maya bolted out the door and, with Alvin the bellhop's help, caught a taxi downtown, where she met Oscar's buddy outside a nondescript brick building in the village near NYU.

Morthos, whose real name was Mike, was not what Maya had expected. He was disheveled, with a five o'clock shadow and wrinkled shirt, but he was also undeniably attractive in that dorky cute kind of way.

She noticed a Dungeons & Dragons book peeking out from his backpack.

"Oscar told me you'd be hot," Mike said, shaking her hand. "He wasn't kidding."

Maya gave him a half smile, but did not respond.

Mike got the feeling he had crossed a line and got down to business. "Let's get that sample processed. We don't have much time."

As they entered the lab's reception area and Mike turned on all the lights, Maya handed over the sample from a laundry bag she had taken from the hotel. He explained the process, detailing how he would isolate the DNA and compare it to the sample found on Tawny's ear lobe, using the genetic code of the sample Oscar had forwarded from Portland.

He accessed the lab with his security card, and Maya tried following him, but he stopped her. "Sorry, you're going to have to wait out here. They've got security cameras everywhere. No guests allowed. They're very serious about contamination."

"Understood," Maya said, taking a seat in reception.

Mike disappeared, and as Maya waited, the tension she felt was palpable. What if there was not enough DNA to be conclusive? What if it had somehow been contaminated en route from the hotel to the lab?

But hours later, just as Alyssa was sitting down at CBS Studios to start her interview with Gayle King, Mike emerged from the lab with a happy smile on his face.

The DNA matched.

Aaron was the killer.

Chapter 35

When Maya returned to the Greenwich Hotel, she made a beeline for Alyssa's room and knocked on the door.

After a moment, she heard Alyssa's strained voice. "Who is it?"

"It's Maya," Maya assured her.

The door opened, and Alyssa, a bundle of nerves, peered out, her face relaxing at the sight of Maya. She swung the door open and quickly ushered her inside, where Sandra was sitting on the bed, closing the door behind her and sliding the security chain in place.

"Have you heard from Aaron?" Maya asked.

"No, not a word. Why? What's happening?"

Maya took a deep breath. "It was a match. Aaron did it. He killed Tawny Bryce."

Alyssa's knees wobbled, and she had to sit down on the edge of the bed next to Sandra. "Oh my God . . ."

Maya glanced at the clock on the nightstand, each

tick amplifying their urgency. She turned to Sandra. "We need to call Detective Hart," she said, reaching for her phone.

Sandra patted Alyssa's knee reassuringly. "We'll find him. Don't you worry."

Alyssa gave her a skeptical smile. "I hope so."

Maya tapped the number for the Portland Police Department, her fingers trembling slightly. "Detective Hart, please. Maya Kendrick." She waited. After a few rings, Detective Hart's gruff voice answered. "Hart here."

Maya put the call on speaker.

"Beth, it's Maya and Sandra. We're here with Alyssa. We have new information on Aaron. We need your help, and fast."

Hart sighed on the other end. "I know. Oscar already brought me up to speed. He told me his friend in New York tested Aaron's DNA on Alyssa against the DNA on the victim. I chewed him out for overstepping bounds, but I felt confident issuing the warrant. Aaron's dangerous, and we need to move quickly."

"Thank you, Detective," Maya said, relief washing over her. They finally had Hart taking them seriously. "What's our next move?"

"I'm hooking you up with two FBI agents who want to meet with you at their New York office. They've got a lot of questions. I'll text you the address. Get there as soon as you can. They're waiting for you."

Maya's eyes widened. "The FBI? But this is a state murder investigation."

"They'll explain everything when you get there. Now

get a move on. The clock is ticking. This guy could be trying to flee the country as we speak and may have resources under multiple identities."

"Understood. We're on our way," Maya replied.

Alyssa's mouth dropped open. "The FBI is involved?"

"Appears so," Maya said. "We'd better get going. But first we need to move you to another hotel. Maybe something a little less flashy, more discreet, where there is very little chance he could find you."

"The Frederick is nearby. Stephen and I stayed there when we brought the boys to town to see *The Lion King* when they were in eighth grade."

"Great, see if you can get a reservation, and use a different name, not Miranda Priestly," Maya urged.

"Okay, what name should I use?"

"Julia Child," Alyssa said. "My second favorite Meryl Streep character."

Sandra was on her phone opening the Expedia app. Within minutes, she had secured a room.

They stood and hustled for the door.

"We can drop you off on the way," Maya said.

After Maya and Sandra checked Alyssa into the Frederick, updating her security clearances with new passwords and measures, hopefully making it impossible for Aaron to find her, they grabbed a taxi to the FBI office located in the Jacob K. Javits Federal Building on Foley Square in the Civic Center neighborhood in Lower Manhattan.

An hour later, Maya and Sandra were ushered into a conference room, where two familiar faces awaited them, Agents Tabitha Markey and Jane Rhodes.

Maya and Sandra both stopped short.

"Hello, Maya, Sandra," Markey said with a sly smile.

"Well, I didn't expect to see you two here," Maya marveled. "I thought you were both based in DC."

"We are, but FBI Chief Katz sent us up here because we're very aware of the activities of Aaron Hoffman, aka Donnelly Smith, aka Sam Weaver, aka the list goes on and on."

Maya and Sandra had met Agents Markey and Rhodes down in Washington DC several years ago when they were chaperoning their kids' high school class trip to the nation's capital and got involved in a murder case. Sandra's now ex-husband, Stephen, had been falsely accused of murdering a pretty young intern who had been working in his office. They had clashed fiercely with the two agents, but the four ultimately learned it behooved them all to work together in order to bring the rightful killer to justice. That was the last time Maya and Sandra had had any contact with Markey and Rhodes.

Until now.

Sandra glanced at Maya. "Why do I get the feeling there's a lot more about Aaron we still don't know?"

"There certainly is," Markey replied, her dark eyes sharp and focused. "We were briefed by Detective Hart. The Tawny Bryce case is not the first murder case in which he's been a suspect."

Rhodes nodded, her red hair gleaming under the fluorescent lights. "We've been building a case against Aaron for some time. He was a suspect in the murder of a wealthy widow, Ann Betancourt, in Baltimore. He romanced her, cleaned out her accounts, and then vanished. We've been tracking him ever since."

Maya and Sandra exchanged shocked glances.

Maya took a deep breath. "This changes everything. He's even more dangerous than we thought."

"There was no physical evidence tying him to the Ann Betancourt case, but now, thanks to you, we have enough to arrest him for the Tawny Bryce murder," Markey said. "We've frozen all of Aaron's assets, so he can't access his money."

"But what if he has other resources available to him under multiple identities that he can use to escape?" Sandra asked.

"We highly doubt it," Rhodes assured her. "He's been wining and dining a Hollywood star; he needs as much cash as he can possibly gather in order to impress her. We believe he's consolidated all his money into the Aaron Hoffman accounts in order to give the impression he's a successful movie producer. And now we've locked him out of that. He's going to get desperate."

Markey nodded in agreement. "He knows there's a warrant out for his arrest, and he'll likely try to secure funds quickly from another victim."

"We suspect he'll go back to his old ways," Rhodes added. "Creating a new identity and using CupidConnect to find another target."

Sandra's mind raced. "We need to smoke him out online before he finds his next victim."

"We'll have to find another female agent to create a profile that will attract him. He likes to video chat to make sure his mark isn't lying about her own profile, and he already knows me and Tabitha from when we questioned him in the Ann Betancourt investigation."

"There's no time to look for someone else," Sandra

insisted. "We need to move now. I'll do it. I'll create a profile on CupidConnect."

Maya frowned. "Sandra, that won't work. He already met both of us at the reunion. Plus, you're a public figure. You used to be married to a United States senator."

Sandra shook her head. "We only met briefly. I'll disguise myself enough in the profile photos. He won't recognize me, and I don't plan on ever meeting him in person. We just need to draw him out, right?"

Markey looked at Rhodes, then back at Sandra. "It's risky, but it might work. We'll monitor everything closely. You won't be in any real danger."

Sandra nodded, her resolve firm. "Let's do it. We can't let Aaron escape."

Maya marveled at Sandra's pure joy at taking on undercover assignments. She must have watched a lot of *Charlie's Angels* reruns when she was a kid.

Under the supervision of Markey and Rhodes, Sandra and Maya spent the next few hours crafting the perfect profile. They used buzzwords and phrases that had attracted Aaron to his previous victims—lonely, wealthy, looking for companionship. Sandra's photos were carefully chosen and edited to ensure she looked different enough from her real self but still pretty enough to attract him.

Finally, they were satisfied they had come up with an enticing profile to dangle in front of him.

Username: CoastalDreamer

Location: Ogunquit, Maine

Just enough outside of Portland so as not to arouse his suspicions.

Bio: Recently single and looking to connect with

someone special. I enjoy quiet evenings with a good book, exploring the city's hidden gems, and meaningful conversations. Financially secure and seeking a genuine connection with someone who appreciates the finer things in life. Let's see where this journey takes us.

They then uploaded tastefully edited images showcasing a sophisticated yet approachable woman with a warm smile and an air of mystery.

As a new profile, it was sure to be sent to Aaron's mailbox as a suggestion for a possible connection.

As they hit "publish" on the profile, a sense of anticipation filled the room. They knew it was a gamble, but it was their best shot at catching Aaron before he vanished for good.

"We'll monitor his activity," Markey assured them. "The moment he takes the bait, we'll be ready."

Just after midnight, a notification pinged on Sandra's phone. Aaron, clearly recognizable from the photos, but using a new alias, Kevin McAllister, had taken the bait. His profile name was EliteVoyager, and his message was charming and carefully worded:

Hello there, CoastalDreamer. Your profile caught my eye, and I must say, you seem like an intriguing and wonderful person. I'd love to hear more about you and see if we share common interests. Hope to chat with you soon!

"He's hooked," Sandra whispered, her heart pounding. "Now we reel him in."

The next phase of their plan began. They had to keep Aaron engaged, drawing him in while keeping the net tight. With Markey and Rhodes monitoring every move, they were ready to strike the moment Aaron made a mistake.

As the night stretched on, the tension in the room was palpable. The game of cat and mouse had begun, and there was no turning back. Now they just had to wait.

Chapter 36

Sandra sat at the computer in Detective Hart's office, her fingers hovering over the keyboard, her heart pounding. Maya stood behind her, hands on her shoulders, giving her a reassuring squeeze.

"You've got this, Sandra," Maya said, her voice calm and steady. "Remember, he's already taken the bait. Just stay cool and follow the script. We're right here with you."

Sandra touched the silver locket around her neck nervously. Maya could tell she was worried. The locket, which had a photo of her two sons inside, was her touchstone. She rarely did not have it around her neck; she wore it always to remind her of what was most important in her life, to calm herself whenever she felt stressed.

Detective Hart and Agents Markey and Rhodes stood off to the side, far enough away from Sandra not to crowd her or distract her. She needed to be singularly focused on the task at hand.

Reeling in Aaron Hoffman.

Sandra took a deep breath. She clicked on the message from Kevin McAlister—Hoffman's alias—and began to read a second message he had just sent. Patience was not a luxury he could afford.

Hi CoastalDreamer, I'm Kevin. Your profile really stood out to me. I'd love to get to know you better. What do you say?

Sandra glanced at Maya, who nodded encouragingly. She began to type her response.

Hi Kevin! Thanks for reaching out. I'm Sabrina. Your profile is impressive. I'd love to get to know you too. Judging from your profile name, EliteVoyager, I'm guessing you love to travel. What's the most exciting place you've been to?

To her surprise, he responded almost immediately.

Hey Sabrina! Thanks for the compliment. The most exciting place? That's a tough one. Probably the Maldives. Crystal clear waters, private bungalows . . . paradise. What about you?

Sandra felt a rush of adrenaline. This was happening. She had to stay focused.

The Maldives sound incredible! I've always wanted to go there. It's definitely on my list. I think my favorite place so far is Santorini. The sunsets are magical.

Within seconds, he responded again. Sandra could tell he was going all in to charm her.

Santorini is beautiful. You have great taste, Sabrina. What do you do for a living, if you don't mind me asking?

Sandra typed furiously.

I don't mind at all. I manage a bed-and-breakfast on the ocean in Kennebunkport and a seafood restaurant that's been in my family for generations. It keeps me busy, but I enjoy it. What about you?

She could see he was typing.

Then up came another response.

I run a few tech startups. It keeps me on my toes, always flying from one meeting to the next. But it's rewarding. I travel so much for work I'm a million miler on American. That's me humble bragging.

Self-effacing.

He was pulling out all the stops.

Sandra could feel the tension in the room. Maya, Hart, Markey, and Rhodes were all focused on her screen, watching the conversation unfold.

Sandra kept typing.

Do you ever get tired of all the travel?

Brief pause.

More typing on his end.

Sometimes, but it's worth it. Meeting new people, experiencing new cultures . . . it's invigorating. But I do miss having someone to share it with.

Maya shook her head in disbelief. "This guy is good."

Sandra quickly responded.

I know what you mean. It's nice to have someone to come home to, someone to share those experiences with.

Maya leaned down, squeezing Sandra's shoulder and whispering in her ear. "Nice."

Almost two minutes passed without a reply.

Sandra glanced up at Maya, worried. "Do you think he got cold feet? Did I say something wrong?"

"You're doing great," Hart piped in. "Give him a little time."

Finally, a message popped up.

Exactly. So, Sabrina, tell me more about you. What do you do for fun?

Sandra did not want to answer him too fast after the lag time on his end, so she waited almost a minute before typing back.

I love sailing. There's something so freeing about being out on the open water. I also enjoy cooking, trying out new recipes. What about you?

His next response came much quicker.

Sailing sounds amazing. I've been on a few yachts, but never really sailed. And cooking . . . I must admit, I'm more of a takeout kind of guy. Maybe you could cook for me sometime?

Sandra's fingers flew across the keyboard.

I'd love that. My family's sailboat growing up wasn't exactly what you'd call a yacht, no kitchen to speak of, just a picnic basket with lobster rolls and a cooler with wine and beer. But I do have a cousin who works for Morris Yachts up in Bar Harbor who helps custom build the boats for all the millionaires and billionaires, but I can't honestly say I've ever gone yachting myself.

All of that was true.

Sandra knew if she stuck as close to the truth as possible, there was less of a chance she would screw up. Her heart pounded as she typed each response, aware that any misstep could tip Aaron off. She had to keep him engaged, keep him believing she was real.

Sabrina, I've really enjoyed talking to you. I feel like we have a connection.

Sandra smiled.

She had him.

I feel the same way, Kevin. It's been wonderful getting to know you.

Another agonizing pause.

Had he suddenly signed off?

But then they could see him typing again.

How about we take this to the next level? How about a video chat right now?

Sandra's heart skipped a beat. This was the moment they had been preparing for. She had to play it cool, not let him see her nerves.

She quickly typed her response.

I'd love that. Give me an hour to freshen up and make myself presentable.

He sent a smiling emoji.

Then typed some more.

I'm sure you're as beautiful without makeup as you are all made up, but take your time. I'll be here waiting.

Sandra turned to the others, her face pale. "He wants to video chat. I need an hour to get ready."

"Go," Maya urged. "We'll set up a secure connection while you prepare."

An hour later, Sandra sat in front of her laptop, her hair styled and makeup carefully applied to match her profile photos. Under the watchful eyes of Hart, Markey, and Rhodes, all carefully out of the view of the camera, she clicked on the video-call link.

The screen flickered to life, and there he was. Aaron, or Kevin, appeared charming and confident, just as she had expected.

"Hi, Sabrina," he said with a warm smile.

"Hi, Kevin. It's nice to finally see you," she replied, matching his smile.

They chatted casually for a while, discussing their supposed travels and interests. Sandra could see he was testing her, looking for any signs of deception. She maintained her composure, answering each question with practiced ease.

"So, Sabrina, you said you manage a couple of family businesses. What kind of businesses are they?" he asked, his eyes narrowing slightly.

Sandra felt a moment of panic.

She thought she had told him during their previous chat.

But her mind was blank.

She had to recall precisely what she had told him.

If she took too long, she was dead in the water.

"We own a bed-and-breakfast on the ocean and a seafood restaurant," she said, forcing a smile.

"In Ogunquit?"

She was about to say yes, but thankfully remembered at the last second what she had told him before. "No, Kennebunkport."

He leaned closer to the camera, his gaze intense. "Interesting. What's the name of the bed-and-breakfast?"

Sandra hesitated for a split second, her mind racing. "It's . . . the Coastal Comfort Inn. That's how I came up with my profile name CoastalDreamer. It's a very relaxing atmosphere, plenty of time to daydream."

Aaron's eyes flickered with suspicion, but he smiled. "I'd love to visit sometime."

"I'd love to show you around," Sandra replied, trying to keep her voice steady.

After the call ended, Sandra let out a shaky breath. "I think I blew it," she said, turning to the others.

But then, a notification popped up on CupidConnect.

I really enjoyed our chat. How about we meet in person? Ogunquit, tomorrow at noon. There's a beautiful walking path overlooking the ocean. We can meet there and take a nice stroll together.

Sandra's heart raced as she showed the message to Maya, Hart, Markey, and Rhodes.

"We have to do it. It may be our only chance," Rhodes said firmly. "We'll be there, but out of sight."

Sandra quickly wrote back. **Marginal Way. I walk that path all the time. We can meet in front of the Sparhawk Resort and make our way down to Perkins Cove and perhaps grab some lunch.**

Moments later Aaron wrote, **Perfect. See you then.**

The next day, Sandra arrived at the Ogunquit walking path and sat down on a bench overlooking the ocean at the Sparhawk Resort. She was wired for surveillance, able to talk to Maya, Hart, Markey, and Rhodes, who were hidden nearby, ready to pounce at the first sign of Aaron.

"I'm here," Sandra whispered into the hidden mic. "Do you see anything?"

"Not yet," Hart replied. "Stay alert."

Minutes passed, then an hour.

Sandra's anxiety grew with each passing moment.

"I think someone's approaching," Maya's voice crackled in her ear. Sandra's heart leapt as she looked around, but it was just a jogger, oblivious to her presence.

He passed her by.

"False alarm," Markey said. "Keep your eyes open."

As the minutes ticked by, Sandra felt a creeping sense of dread. What if he had figured it out?

"I don't see him," Sandra whispered, her voice trembling. "He may not be coming."

"Stay calm," Rhodes replied. "We're watching."

Suddenly, Sandra felt a prickling sensation on the back of her neck, as if she were being watched. She turned slowly, scanning the area. In the distance, she spotted a man standing near a tree, partially obscured by shadows.

"I see someone," she whispered. "He's by the tree, about fifty yards away."

The man noticed her looking and took off, disappearing into the crowd of tourists ambling along Shore Road.

"He's running!" Sandra exclaimed, jumping to her feet.

"Stay put," Hart ordered. "We're on it."

But by the time they reached the spot, the man was gone, and there was no sign of him.

Sandra sat back down onto the bench, her heart sinking. "He's gone, isn't he?"

Maya, Hart, Markey, and Rhodes gathered around her, all of them frustrated.

"He might be," Markey admitted. "But we'll keep looking. We won't let him disappear into the ether."

Sandra looked out over the ocean, a sense of determination settling in. They might have missed him this time, but they would not give up.

Not until Aaron Hoffman was brought to justice.

Chapter 37

As Maya drove Sandra back home from Ogunquit to Portland, they sat in silence, contemplating the stakes of this case, the danger Aaron posed the longer he was on the loose. He had killed twice already, so there was no guarantee he would hesitate to do it again if he was backed into a corner.

Sandra's phone rang.

She glanced at the screen and saw it was her friend Molly, who ran the real Coastal Comfort Inn. Molly had been a key player in Sandra's ex-husband's political campaign, helping him win his Senate seat. Over the years, Molly and her parents and siblings had become more like family to Sandra, and Sandra often felt a protective bond with Molly's children. When Aaron, aka Kevin, put her on the spot about the bed-and-breakfast she owned, Sandra had quickly come up with the Coastal Comfort Inn because she knew the owners and felt confident she could convince them to play a role in confirming to Aaron that she was telling him the truth.

"Hello?" Sandra said, trying to keep her voice steady.

"Sandra, it's Molly. I got a call from a man inquiring about the family that owns the inn. I answered just as you instructed me, but I was nervous. I may have stumbled a few times. I really didn't want to screw up. But I think he was satisfied with what I told him about you owning the inn."

Sandra breathed a sigh of relief. "Thank you, Molly. That helps a lot. I'm sure you did just fine."

"No problem. Just be careful, okay? This sounds serious."

"Always. How are Mike and the kids?"

"We're all doing fine, happy the season's starting to wind down, ready for a break."

"Well, we should all get together soon when Jack and Ryan are both home for a weekend."

"Sounds fun. Take care."

"Will do," Sandra replied, hanging up. She turned to Maya, who was focused on the road. "Molly got a call from Aaron, or Kevin, or whatever his real name is. He appeared to buy the story."

"Good. At least that's one thing going our way," Maya responded.

They pulled up to Sandra's house, a sprawling, two-story New England colonial home with a welcoming front porch. Sandra felt a fleeting sense of safety as they parked in the driveway.

"Let's call Alyssa," Sandra suggested as they headed inside.

Maya dialed Alyssa's number and put her on speaker.

It rang a few times before she answered.

"Hello?" Alyssa's voice was tense.

"It's us," Maya said. "Sandra's safe, but we've got news. Aaron called the Coastal Comfort Inn. Molly handled it, but he was a no-show at the meeting spot, so we need to stay on high alert."

There was a long pause.

Then Alyssa sighed, the fear palpable in her voice. "I came back to my parents' place from New York. I don't dare go back to my house in Pacific Palisades. I don't feel safe there. I'm even thinking about pulling out of my next movie. What if Aaron shows up again?"

"Don't worry, Alyssa," Sandra said firmly. "We won't let that happen. We're going to catch him."

"Exactly," Maya added. "You focus on your safety, and we'll take care of finding Aaron."

Alyssa hesitated before replying, "Okay. Thank you both."

They ended the call, and Maya got ready to leave. "Call me if anything happens. I'll be on standby."

"Thanks, Maya," Sandra said, walking her to the door.

As Maya drove away, Sandra received a call from Lucas. She answered, her voice weary. "Hey, Lucas."

"Hey, beautiful, I've been trying to call you."

She checked her phone.

She had one voicemail and two texts from him.

"Sorry, I've been busy working. What's up?"

I was thinking maybe we could get together tonight. I could come over. How about it?"

"It sounds nice, but I'm exhausted, Lucas."

"I could cook. I can make my world-famous chicken Parmesan casserole, maybe toss a salad, heat up some garlic bread in the oven, oh, and pop open a bottle of wine . . . or two. You can just put your feet up and let me serve you."

It was an enticing offer.

But after the intense pressure she had been under all day, Sandra just wanted to go to bed early. However, she knew she had been distant with Lucas lately, and the last thing she wanted to do was give him the impression she was pushing him away.

"Can we meet for breakfast instead?"

Lucas paused, then asked, "How's the case going?"

Sandra hesitated, then said, "We had a close call with Aaron. Almost had him, but then he disappeared, and now we're trying to find him again. It's been intense."

"Aaron? You mean the guy Alyssa Turner's dating?"

Sandra suddenly realized she had not discussed much of the case with Lucas, so she brought him up to speed.

When she finished, there was dead silence on the line.

"Lucas? Are you still there?"

Lucas's voice tightened with concern. "Sandra, this sounds dangerous. What if something happens to you? Is this job really worth it?"

Sandra gripped the phone, suddenly tense. "Lucas, I didn't expect this from you. I thought when it came to my job, you were eyes wide open."

"No, no, I am, I am. It's just that this sounds so, so next level. I mean, I guess I never really pictured you going undercover to lure in a killer and the ramifications of that. It's a lot to take in."

Sandra felt a surge of frustration. There was a long silence before she spoke again. "Lucas, this is my passion. This is what I do. If you can't accept that, then there's no way for us to move forward."

She did not mean to sound as harsh and cold as she did.

Lucas definitely felt the chill and quickly backtracked. "You're right. I get it. I'm sorry. I won't bring it up again. But I want to see you. Can I come over to personally apologize?"

She paused.

"Let me tuck you in. I won't bother you, I'll let you sleep, but I'll be there in case you need anything."

She had to admit, his presence did sound nice.

But she knew if he did come over, she would not sleep. They would have a glass of wine, talk, and then one thing would lead to another, and her bones were just so achingly tired.

"Let's stick to breakfast," Sandra replied, softening. "I'll see you at eight a.m."

"Okay. Goodnight, Sandra. I love you."

This was not the first time he had said those three words.

And it was unfair of her not to respond in kind.

Because she did love him.

She just was not certain they should be together.

But he needed to know where she stood.

"Love you too," she blurted out. "Good night."

Before he could make a big deal about it—he had been waiting months for her to say it—Sandra hung up.

As she ascended the stairs to her bedroom, she felt a pang of loneliness and instantly regretted telling Lucas to stay home. She thought about calling him back to tell him she'd changed her mind and he should jump in his car and come right over, but it was already going on ten o'clock. She thought of her sons, Ryan and Jack, both away at college. She longed to hear their voices but did not want to bother them too much. She thought perhaps she had been calling them too much lately and was coming across as an overbearing mother. Instead, she headed to bed, hoping for a few hours of rest.

After removing the heavy makeup she had applied as part of her CupidConnect disguise, she shimmied out of her clothes and threw on some sweats and a T-shirt and hit the bed, snuggling under the covers.

Just as she was about to drift off, she heard a noise outside. Her eyes snapped open, heart racing. She got up and peeked out the window and saw some kids running down the street, but then she noticed a man standing under a streetlight in the shadows, seemingly watching her house.

Sandra's heart pounded as she watched the man. He did not move. He just stood there, staring. She tried to make out his features, but the light cast eerie shadows across his face. For what felt like an eternity, they were locked in a silent standoff. Finally, she mustered the courage to hurry down the stairs and walk outside, but as soon as she stepped onto the porch, the man disappeared into the night.

Was it the same man she had spotted on Marginal Way?

Was it Aaron?

Or someone else?

Unease settled in her gut as she went back inside, locked the door, and headed to bed.

The next morning, Sandra woke up early and prepared to meet Lucas at their favorite diner, which served up greasy comfort food. She texted him that she would be there at eight. As she got dressed, a message notification from CupidConnect made her stomach churn. She opened it, and her blood ran cold.

The message read: **I know who you are.**

It was not from Kevin McAllister, Aaron's latest false identity.

It had been sent from a new account.

The profile name was just a number and there was no photo.

Her hands trembled as she grabbed her keys and headed out the door. She needed to meet Maya right away, texting her that she was on her way to the office. Then she stopped at the driver's side door of her sleek black Mercedes to text Lucas to cancel, when she suddenly felt a presence behind her. Spinning around, she was face-to-face with Aaron, his face twisted with anger.

"Get in the car," he ordered, shoving a gun in her side.

She glanced around the neighborhood, but it was still early and no one was outside, not even anyone walking their dog.

Sandra's heart pounded as she obeyed, sliding into the driver's seat.

Aaron climbed in beside her, his grip tight on the weapon.

"Drive," he commanded, and she started the engine with shaking hands.

As they pulled away from the curb, Aaron's eyes bored into her. "I know you were married to a powerful US senator. So since you and the cops have cut me off, you're going to get me the money I need to get out of the country."

Sandra swallowed hard, trying to keep her voice steady. "I can't do that."

Aaron's face contorted with rage. "Don't lie to me! Your friend Molly, who quote unquote works for you at the Coastal Comfort Inn, slipped and called you Sandra instead of your fake name Sabrina. I only know one Sandra, the woman I met at Alyssa's reunion, the private detective. I know you've been setting me up."

"I won't help you," Sandra said, her voice firmer now. "You can't force me."

Aaron's grip tightened on the gun, his eyes wild with desperation. "The thing is, Sandra, I know all about you. You're a public figure. Your famous husband. Your two sons. It was stupid of you to think you were going to fool me."

Sandra's mind raced, searching for a way out. She needed to stay calm, think strategically. She took a deep breath, focusing on the road ahead, hoping for an opportunity to escape before it was too late.

Chapter 38

Lucas banged on the glass door of Maya and Sandra's private investigations office, his eyes wild with panic. Maya, who had been reviewing some notes at her desk, looked up and immediately sensed something was wrong.

Lucas was never this frazzled.

She quickly got up and unlocked the door, ushering him inside.

"Maya, she's gone," Lucas blurted out as soon as he was inside. His voice was strained, almost breaking. "Sandra didn't show up for our breakfast date this morning. I've been calling her nonstop, but she's not answering."

Maya felt a chill run down her spine. Sandra was always punctual, especially when it came to Lucas. "Calm down, Lucas. Let's think this through. Did she mention anything unusual last night?"

Lucas shook his head frantically. "No, nothing. I

wanted to come over, but she said she was too tired. We talked about meeting up this morning, and she seemed fine. I don't know what's happened."

Maya grabbed her keys. "I'm going over to her house and check things out."

Lucas tried following her, but she spun around and stopped him with a hand placed on his chest. "No, Lucas. You need to stay put and calm down. I will call the minute I have any more information. I promise."

He was reluctant to sit idly by and do nothing, but he could tell from Maya's stern, determined expression that she was not about to tolerate any argument from him.

He took a small step back and nodded solemnly.

Maya then raced down the hall toward the elevator.

As she drove to Sandra's house, Maya's mind raced. They had been so close to snaring Aaron yesterday.

But what had gone wrong?

Had he somehow figured out their plan and taken Sandra as leverage?

The thought made her grip the steering wheel tighter.

Upon arriving at Sandra's house, Maya noticed the front door was locked, and Sandra's black Mercedes was nowhere to be seen. She walked around the property, looking for any signs of disturbance. Then she saw it: a small, inconspicuous object lying near the edge of the driveway. She bent down to pick it up and recognized it immediately.

It was Sandra's silver locket, something she never left home without. It had popped open, revealing two pictures of her sons, Jack and Ryan, when they were little boys.

Maya's heart pounded. This was Sandra's signal. She was in trouble. Maya quickly snapped a picture of the locket with her phone and sent it to Detective Hart with a message: **Sandra's been taken. Meet me at her house ASAP.**

Detective Hart, along with a couple of officers, arrived within minutes, her face grim. "We need to move fast," she said. "Let's search the house for any more clues."

"It's locked," Maya informed her.

"We can't just bust in. The police are not authorized for any breaking and entering," Hart reminded her. "Unless we have a warrant or permission."

Maya was already rifling through her bag. "Sandra once gave me a key to her house in case of an emergency. This is an emergency, so technically we have her permission." Maya finally found the key and hurried up the porch steps to open the door, with Hart and her officers on her heels.

They methodically went through each room, looking for anything out of the ordinary. Drawers were untouched, rooms looked undisturbed, and there were no signs of a struggle. It was now clear Sandra had been taken outside, likely in the driveway.

"We need to canvas the neighborhood," Hart said. "Someone must have seen something."

They split up and, along with the two officers, began knocking on doors, asking neighbors if they had noticed anything unusual that morning. Most were still waking up and had not seen anything.

A man walking his dog nearby was their last hope.

"Excuse me, sir," Maya called out, approaching him. "Did you happen to see anything suspicious this morning? A woman being forced into a car, perhaps?"

The man shook his head, looking concerned. "Sorry, I didn't see anything. I wish I could help."

Hart sighed in frustration and called Agents Markey and Rhodes. "Get in touch with Senator Stephen Wallage in Washington and bring him up to speed. We need all hands on deck."

Maya and Detective Hart rushed to the police station. They entered an office where Agents Markey and Rhodes were in the middle of a heated video conference call with Senator Wallage, Sandra's ex-husband.

"Senator, we need you to stay calm and avoid any public statements," Agent Markey was saying. "If the press gets wind of this, it could push Aaron to do something drastic. We need to keep this under wraps to protect Sandra."

Senator Wallage's voice was tight with barely controlled panic. "You find her, you hear me? Do whatever it takes."

Maya could see the desperation in the senator's eyes, even through the video call. As soon as the call ended, she spoke up. "Sandra left a clue. Her silver locket. Aaron's got her. We need to act fast."

Agent Rhodes nodded. "We'll get IT on tracking her phone immediately. Does she have location sharing enabled with anyone?"

Maya nodded. "Yes, Sandra and I typically share our locations on our phones so we can constantly keep in touch, but I've never used it to locate her. Maybe Oscar can help us."

Minutes later, they were joined by Oscar in Hart's office. Oscar, looking as if he had just climbed out of bed, with wild hair and mismatched clothes, was hunched over a laptop in the corner of the room, a steaming cup of coffee next to him, Maya's phone next to him.

He muttered to himself as he tapped away at the keys. "Come on, come on . . . got it! Sandra's phone is active. She's on the move."

The room buzzed with activity. Detective Hart, Agents Markey and Rhodes, and Maya all gathered around Oscar. "Where is she?" Hart demanded.

"She's heading north, just outside the city limits," Oscar replied, pointing to a map on his screen. "They're moving fast. Could be on the highway. Most likely on 295."

Lucas burst into the room, his face pale and drawn. "Did you find her? What's happening?"

"I thought I told you to stay at the office," Maya scolded.

"I want to help find her."

She understood where he was coming from.

Sitting alone was probably driving him crazy.

He had to feel like he was doing something.

Anything so he would not feel so helpless.

But she could not have him hovering over her shoulder, second-guessing her every move when time was of the essence.

Maya placed a hand on his shoulder. "Lucas, we're doing everything we can. Right now, I need you to go home and wait. We'll keep you updated. We have a line on her whereabouts. We're going to find her and bring her home. But we can't have you involved in the search. You're too emotional right now. It's dangerous. For you and, more importantly, for Sandra."

Lucas opened his mouth to argue, but Maya's steely gaze stopped him. He nodded reluctantly and left the room.

Hart turned to the agents. "We need to move. Now. Markey, Rhodes, you coordinate with local law enforcement along the route. Maya, you're with me."

The team moved with precision, each second feeling like an hour. As they sped down Franklin Street toward I-295 North, the tension in the car was thick. Hart kept glancing at her phone, waiting for updates from Oscar.

Suddenly, Oscar's voice crackled over the speaker. "She's stopped. Looks like a residential home on Quaker Point Road in West Bath, Maine, along the New Meadows River."

Maya's eyes widened. "Alyssa's parents mentioned having a summer home in West Bath. Aaron must have known about it. It's been sitting empty."

Hart pressed the accelerator harder, her face set in determination.

Maya whispered to no one in particular, "Hang on, Sandra. We're coming."

They were racing against time, the car cutting through the early-morning light as they sped north on 295 toward West Bath. Each passing mile felt like an eternity. Maya's thoughts were consumed with Sandra, her friend, her partner, hoping they would reach her before it was too late.

The road signs blurred past. Hart's hands gripped the wheel tightly, her knuckles white. The team was silent, focused, every second bringing them closer to their destination.

As they neared the address, the sun was casting a warm glow over the landscape. Maya looked at Hart, her face set in grim determination.

"We're almost there," Hart said, her voice steady. "Just a little farther."

Maya nodded, her heart racing. They had to find Sandra. They could not afford to be too late.

Chapter 39

The tranquility of the late morning belied the tension inside Alyssa's family lake house. Aaron's breaths came in short, rapid gasps as he pushed Sandra into a chair, tying her wrists to the arms with a length of rope he had found in the garage. Her eyes bore into him, defiant and unyielding despite the fear she tried to mask.

"You don't have to do this, Aaron," Sandra said, her voice steady. "The police know everything. They're going to find you. It will only get worse for you if you try to run. Don't make things harder on yourself. It's over. Just let me go."

"Shut up!" Aaron snapped, running a hand through his disheveled hair. "Just shut up. I need time to think."

"Alyssa also knows you're a fraud, so you can forget about that revenue stream. It's only a matter of time before all this ends. So why not let me go? We can figure something out."

Aaron laughed bitterly. "Figure something out? You

really think there's a way out of this for me that doesn't involve me going to prison? No, Sandra, I can't go to prison. That is definitely off the table. So I need another plan."

"There is no other plan. The FBI has frozen your assets. They've got you in a corner."

Aaron waved his gun menacingly. "I still got this. I can still shoot my way out like Butch and Sundance."

"They both died at the end of that movie," Sandra reminded him.

He scowled. "What about you?"

"What about me?"

"You're loaded. You're married to a fancy United States senator," Aaron spit out.

"*Was* married. We're divorced."

"And I can just imagine what kind of rich settlement you got," Aaron guessed. "I'm thinking maybe fifty grand might be enough get me out of the country with a fake passport."

"Sorry to remind you, but there's something like a three-hundred-dollar limit on an ATM withdrawal."

"You must have mobile banking. We can do a transfer."

"No way."

"Make the transfer, and I'll let you live."

Sandra met his gaze. "You'll kill me as soon as you get what you want. I won't help you, Aaron."

Aaron's eyes darkened, and he clenched his fists. "You're smart, Sandra, but not smart enough. You're going to transfer the money, or I swear, I'll—"

"You'll what? Kill me? Drown me in the lake?" Sandra spat out. "You think that will help you escape?

Then you'll have nothing. They're going to catch you. There's nowhere to hide."

Aaron's face twisted with rage and desperation. He leaned in close, his voice a harsh whisper. "Stop saying that. You're going to make me angry, and you wouldn't like me when I'm angry."

"Are you quoting *The Incredible Hulk* now? Are you going to turn into a giant green monster and burst out of your clothes?"

"I'm warning you . . ."

Sandra took a deep breath, trying to stay calm. "Look, even if I wanted to help, your accounts are frozen. Even if I could transfer the money, you won't be able to access the account."

Aaron's eyes flickered mischievously as he broke out into a wide smile. "Yes. All the Aaron Hoffman accounts. But I did keep one account open under a previous identity that the cops probably missed. We can use that one."

Sandra's heart sank.

Then she glared at him defiantly and growled, "No, I won't do it."

Aaron slammed his fist on the table, making Sandra flinch. "Then maybe I'll go to someone else in the esteemed Wallage family to help me. One of your sons, perhaps? What are their names? Jack and Ryan? Was your husband a Tom Clancy fan? Say, isn't one attending Boston College? That's only about a two-hour drive from here."

Sandra looked into his eyes, seeing the madness growing there. She knew that reasoning with him was useless. And there was no way she was going to risk her sons' safety. She had to bide her time, look for an opportunity. "Fine," she said finally. "But I need my laptop. It's in my bag."

Aaron eyed her suspiciously but nodded. "Where's your bag?"

"In the car. You need to go get it."

Aaron considered this, then nodded again. "Don't try anything funny, Sandra."

He turned and headed toward the car, leaving Sandra momentarily alone. She tested the ropes, finding them too tight to slip free.

She needed to think of another plan.

Aaron returned moments later with her laptop. He placed it on the table in front of her, keeping a wary eye on her every move. "Get to work."

"You're going to have to untie me. I can't type like this."

Aaron sighed, annoyed. He loosened the rope enough that she was able to free her hands.

Sandra powered on the laptop, her mind racing. She needed to stall, to find a way to alert Maya and the police without Aaron noticing.

She typed in her bank's web address, typing slowly.

"What's the account number for the transfer?" Sandra asked quietly.

"First, get into your account and set up the transfer, then I'll give you the number. Hurry up."

Sandra was not connecting to the website.

She kept hitting the refresh button.

"I need to connect to the internet. There's no signal out here."

"What are you talking about? I know they have internet here. I saw a router in the kitchen."

"Well, it's not working."

"It has to be working!"

She hit the "refresh" button again.

Still nothing.

"Maybe you should try rebooting it!"

His face contorting in frustration, Aaron stomped off to the kitchen.

With her hands free, Sandra quickly reached into her back pocket for her phone. She needed to text Maya, let her know where they were. Her fingers trembling, she managed to type out **Alyssa's summer house. West Bath. Old Quaker**

But then she heard Aaron coming back and had no choice but to shove her phone back in her pocket before she was able to finish the text and hit "send."

She would have to look for another opportunity.

Aaron hovered behind her, reaching down and impatiently pounding the key with his finger to connect the computer with the Turner family's Wi-Fi network.

"There! Now get to it!"

Sandra nodded, her fingers still trembling as she finally managed to connect to the Wi-Fi. She opened the bank's website and pretended to type in her password.

It was incorrect.

"What's wrong? Why didn't it work?" Aaron demanded to know.

"Ever since my husband and I divorced and separated our financial accounts, I can never remember my new password. It's really long and complicated for security reasons."

She was stalling.

"You must have it stored somewhere on your laptop!"

"Of course not! What if some hacker took over my computer? They could clean me out. I must have it written down somewhere, maybe in my bag," Sandra said, acting innocent.

She glanced at Aaron, who was now pacing the room, muttering to himself.

Sandra pretended to rifle through her bag looking for a scrap of paper, buying more time.

"Hurry," Aaron barked, his eyes darting to the window.

Sandra stared into the contents of her bag. "I can't seem to find it. It's probably in my office somewhere or at home."

Aaron marched over, pushed her aside, and went into her system settings, where he saw that she had stored passwords and only needed a four-digit passcode to access them. He raised the gun close to her face, fingering the trigger. "Don't tell me you can't remember a simple four-digit passcode."

She wanted to stall some more.

But she thought of Jack and Ryan.

And the last thing she wanted was to antagonize this guy even more to the point where he would carry through on his threat to show up on Jack's campus.

She typed in the passcode.

Within seconds, they were in her account.

Aaron leaned in, his breath hot on her neck. "No more games, Sandra. Just get it done."

Suddenly, Sandra's phone buzzed in her pocket. She glanced at Aaron, who heard it.

"You still have your phone on you? You said you left it in the kitchen when we were driving here!"

Sandra kept mum.

He put his hand out. "Give it to me."

Left with no choice, Sandra pulled out the phone and dropped it in his palm.

He glanced at the screen. "Your ex-husband's calling you. What does he want?"

"How should I know?" Sandra asked, trying to keep her voice calm.

The call finally went to voicemail.

That's when Aaron saw the incomplete text to Maya.

His eyes widened in fury. "When did you write this? When I was in the kitchen?"

Sandra stayed silent, her mind racing.

Then he was hit with a sudden realization. "They're probably tracking this phone, aren't they? They're probably on their way here right now."

Aaron's panic was palpable, his movements becoming more erratic. He glared at the phone, and just as he did, the ringtone went off again.

Stephen's name appeared on the screen.

He was calling again.

Aaron stared at the phone, momentarily distracted. Sandra saw her chance. She lunged forward, shoving Aaron with all her strength. He stumbled back, and she bolted for the door.

"Get back here!" Aaron shouted, regaining his balance and sprinting after her.

Sandra ran through the trees, her heart pounding. She could hear Aaron's footsteps behind her, growing louder. She pushed herself harder, dodging branches and leaping over rocks. The sun flickered through the leaves, casting confusing shadows on the ground.

Just when she thought she had lost him, Aaron burst through the underbrush, tackling her to the ground. She screamed, struggling to free herself, but his grip was too strong.

"Stop fighting!" Aaron hissed, dragging her back toward the summer house. "You're only making this worse on yourself."

Sandra kicked and screamed, trying to get away, but Aaron's grip was unrelenting. He pulled her back into the house, slamming the door behind them.

"We can't stay here," Aaron muttered, pacing the room. "We need to move. Now."

Sandra's eyes fell upon her phone, smashed to pieces on the floor. Aaron must have destroyed it with the heel of his shoe as she tried to escape. It was a gut punch, her hopes of a rescue now fading.

Aaron yanked Sandra to her feet, his eyes wild with desperation. "You're coming with me."

Sandra's heart sank. She knew Aaron was serious. And she knew her only hope was to continue to try and stall for more time, to give Maya and the police a chance to find them. As Aaron dragged her toward the car, she prayed they would arrive soon.

Chapter 40

The gravel crunched beneath their boots as they advanced in silence. Maya's heart raced in sync with every step, anxiety gnawing at her resolve. The Turner family summer house loomed ahead. She glanced at Detective Hart, who signaled for the team to halt. FBI agents Markey and Rhodes positioned themselves strategically. The officers spread out, forming a perimeter around the house.

Maya's phone buzzed, breaking the tense silence. She glanced at the screen.

It was Lucas.

She stepped back, trying to keep her voice low. "Lucas, this isn't a good time—"

"Maya, where are you? I overheard at the station that you're going to Alyssa's family's summer house."

"What? How? Were you eavesdropping outside Oscar's office?"

"It doesn't matter. I need to know where it is. I want to come out there."

Maya took a deep breath, trying to keep her voice calm. "Lucas, you need to stand down. If you show up, you'll just make things worse."

"But I feel so helpless. I can't just sit here and do nothing. Sandra needs me."

"I understand, but you have to trust us. We're doing everything we can to find her. If you come, you'll only get in the way, and I won't risk Sandra's safety."

There was a brief silence.

He knew she was right.

Lucas's voice cracked with desperation. "I'm scared, Maya. What if something happens to her?"

"I know, Lucas. I'm scared too. But you need to stay put. Let us handle this. We have a plan."

There was another pause on the line, then Lucas sighed heavily. "Alright, I'll stay. Just, please, find her and bring her home."

"We will. I promise." She hung up, shoving her phone back into her pocket. Every second counted, and she could not afford any more distractions.

Immediately, she dialed Max. "Max, I need you to do something for me."

"Maya, Lucas has been calling. He says he knows where Aaron might have taken Sandra. Where are you? I can't just sit here."

Maya sighed.

Men.

Always wanting to play the hero.

"I know, but I need you to do something for me. Keep an eye on Lucas. He's frantic and might do something stupid. He was at the station and overheard our location. Please, I need you to go over to his place and babysit him so he doesn't get in the way."

Max's voice was tight with frustration. "I swear, if Aaron hurts her, I'll kill him myself. My parole be damned."

"Max, you can't. You already have one foot back in prison thanks to your temper. I need you to stay far away from this. Please, just go look after Lucas. Make sure he doesn't do anything reckless."

Max sighed, the tension clear in his voice. "Alright, I'll go over there. But be careful, Maya. And call me the minute you have news."

"I will. Thank you."

"I love you."

"Love you, too."

She hung up, shoving her phone back into her pocket. Maya moved back into formation, nodding to Detective Hart.

She returned the nod and motioned for the team to proceed.

They approached the house cautiously, staying in the shadows.. The wooden porch creaked under their weight as they ascended the steps. Maya's eyes darted to the windows, looking for any signs of movement inside. She held up a hand, signaling the team to stop.

"We go in quietly," she whispered. "No guns blazing. We can't risk Sandra getting hurt."

The team nodded, understanding the gravity of the situation. Maya took a deep breath and reached for the doorknob. To her surprise, it turned easily in her hand. She exchanged a puzzled glance with Detective Hart before pushing the door open slowly.

The house was eerily silent. They moved through the dimly lit hallway, their footsteps muffled by the thick carpet in the foyer. Maya's heart pounded in her chest as they approached the living room. She held her breath, praying they were not too late.

As they rounded the corner, the scene before them made Maya's blood run cold. The room was empty, save for a few overturned chairs and a smashed phone lying on the floor.

Sandra's phone.

"Damn it," Hart muttered under her breath. "We missed them."

Maya felt a wave of despair wash over her. She knelt down, picking up the broken phone pieces. "He's getting desperate," she said softly.

Agents Markey and Rhodes began searching the room for any clues, while the officers spread out to check the rest of the house.

Maya stood, clutching the shattered remains of Sandra's phone.

Her mind raced with possibilities.

Somehow tipped off, they had already fled the location.

Where could Aaron have taken her?

Hart placed a reassuring hand on Maya's shoulder. "We'll find her. We won't give up."

They finished searching the house, but came up empty. No clues, no sign of where Aaron might have taken Sandra.

Maya's heart sank.

As the team regrouped outside, the sense of dread deepened.

Maya exchanged a grim look with Beth. "We're back to square one. We have no clue where they are."

Hart nodded, her face set in determination. "We'll find them, Maya. Trust me."

Maya desperately wanted to trust Hart.

She knew she was a good detective.

But as the day wore on, while the officers turned the house upside down in search of something, anything that might indicate their whereabouts, Maya could not shake the feeling of helplessness.

Time was running out, and with each passing minute, the danger to Sandra increased exponentially.

But Maya refused to lose hope.

Not yet.

Chapter 41

Maya stood in the center of the Turner family's summer house. The weight of the situation pressed down on her, making it difficult to breathe.

Think, Maya thought to herself.

Think.

Sandra was out there somewhere, held captive by Aaron, and their best lead had just disintegrated into a million tiny pieces.

There must be something she had not thought of, something they could use to smoke him out.

The echoing silence of the house was suffocating, amplifying the frantic pace of her thoughts.

Detective Hart, standing by the window, spoke up, breaking the oppressive silence. "We need a new plan, and fast. Every minute we waste is a minute Sandra doesn't have."

Maya nodded, trying to suppress the rising panic. "The trail's gone cold. How are we supposed to find her now?"

Her phone buzzed in her pocket, a text from Max: **Went over to Lucas's place to keep him out of your way. He's not there. Lucas is out there and a loose cannon. Sorry. I know this is not news you want to hear. I'm here if you need me.**

Maya's heart sank further.

One more wild card in an already chaotic situation.

Alyssa.

Alyssa had to be the key.

Aaron was obsessed with her.

He had come so close to the life of his dreams, with her by his side, before it all went to hell.

If anyone could cause him to trip up, it was her.

Maya knew she had to get to Alyssa, to see if they could come up with something, anything that might give them a new lead.

She knew Alyssa was at her parents' house, huddled with Edie and Doug Turner.

She turned to Detective Hart. "Beth, I need to try something. Maybe it'll help, maybe it won't, but I'm going to head back to Portland."

"Go, whatever it takes. But keep me in the loop."

Maya nodded and bolted out the door.

The air was thick with tension when Maya arrived at the Turner house, the gravity of the situation clearly weighing on everyone. She quickly updated the family.

Upon hearing the news that Aaron had Sandra as his captive, the blood drained from Alyssa's face, and her eyes welled up with tears. Her father, Doug, put a comforting arm around her shoulders.

"I can't believe he went to the summer house," Alyssa

said, her voice trembling. "He only visited once, months ago. Why would he go there?"

"He's desperate and unpredictable," Maya replied. "We need to find a way to draw him out, Alyssa. We need something that will make him show himself."

Alyssa buried her face in her hands. "This is all my fault. If I hadn't panicked and confronted him at the hotel that night . . ."

"No," Maya interrupted, her tone firm. "This is not your fault. Aaron is unhinged. But we need to use that to our advantage."

Doug Turner, his face pale and drawn, spoke up. "What are you thinking, Maya?"

"We need to make Aaron believe he's still got a chance with Alyssa. He sees her as the ultimate prize. If we can give him some hope, make him think she's still interested, we might be able to lure him out."

Alyssa looked up, her eyes wide with fear. "You want me to pretend to . . . to want him back? He'll never buy it."

Maya's gaze was steady. "Aaron's a narcissist. He believes he can charm anyone, win anyone over. If you play to that, we might just have a shot."

Edie clutched Alyssa's hand. "Are you sure about this? It sounds dangerous."

"It's a risk," Maya admitted. "But we don't have any other options. Alyssa, you're our best weapon."

Alyssa took a deep breath, her resolve hardening. "What do you need me to do?"

Maya outlined the plan. Alyssa would post on Instagram, a carefully crafted message that hinted at regret and confusion about her feelings toward Aaron, pretending to be clueless regarding Sandra's kidnapping.

It was a dangerous game, but it was their only shot.

As Alyssa typed out the post on her laptop, Maya hovered over her shoulder, offering guidance.

@AlyssaTurnerOfficial: I've been doing a lot of thinking lately. I lashed out at Aaron, but maybe I was too harsh. Maybe I was wrong. I don't know. I just want to talk, to understand where we went wrong. I feel so lost right now . . .

She attached a photo of the two of them in happier times, smiling, a beautiful, famous power couple.

Catnip to Aaron.

Alyssa hit "post," and the waiting began. The seconds ticked by like hours, the tension in the room palpable.

Maya paced the room, consumed with worry.

Aaron had to take the bait.

He had to.

Sandra's life depended on it.

Alyssa's phone buzzed with notifications as fans and followers reacted to the post, but there was nothing from Aaron. The clock was ticking.

Maya glanced at Alyssa, seeing the fear and determination in her eyes. But despite the danger, despite the uncertainty, there was a sliver of hope.

For the first time in hours, Maya felt a glimmer of optimism.

This just might work.

They still might be able to save Sandra and finally bring Aaron to justice.

Now they could only wait and see if their desperate gamble would pay off.

But an hour passed.

Then two.

And still nothing.

Chapter 42

Sandra's heart pounded as Aaron's grip on her arm tightened. They had arrived back at her house, pulling her car into the garage and quickly closing the door so as not to arouse any suspicion from the neighbors.

Inside, Sandra felt a gnawing sense of dread. She had always thought of her home as her sanctuary.

Now, eerily quiet, it felt more like a prison.

Aaron believed this was the last place the police would look for them.

But Sandra knew better.

Maya was out there, trying to track him down.

Sandra's thoughts raced as Aaron led her into the living room, his fingers digging into her flesh. She needed to stay calm, to think clearly, to survive this. She cast a quick glance around, hoping against hope that there might be something—anything—that could help her.

"Sit down," Aaron growled, pushing her toward the

living room sofa. Sandra complied, her mind working overtime to find a way out of this nightmare.

That's when they heard a sound.

Like someone coughing.

Aaron raised his gun in the air, alert. "What was that?"

Sandra shrugged.

"Did you hear that?"

She shook her head, defiant.

"Is someone here?"

"I don't know!"

Just then, the door to the home office creaked open. Sandra's heart skipped a beat as she saw her ex-husband, Stephen, step into the room.

His eyes widened in shock as he took in the scene. "Sandra?" he called out, his voice full with concern. "I thought I heard voices. What's going on? Are you alright?"

Her voice was a whisper. "Stephen, what are you doing here?"

"I heard you were in some kind of trouble." He glanced nervously at Aaron, who now held the gun by his side. "I flew up from DC as soon as I could."

"Are you the husband?" Aaron spat out, slowly raising the gun.

"I am," Stephen barked. "Who the hell are you? What the hell do you think you're doing? Do you seriously believe kidnapping my wife is going to somehow help you escape from the authorities? Be smart. And let her go. Now."

Sandra felt a sudden wave of fear for his safety.

"Stephen, you need to leave," she urged, trying to keep her voice steady.

"No one's going anywhere," Aaron spat, his eyes narrowing as he glared at Stephen. "I've seen you on C-Span in your fancy suits and expensive haircut and wearing a Rolex. And wouldn't you know, I could use my own Daddy Warbucks right about now."

Stephen stood his ground, his gaze shifting between Sandra and Aaron, trying to assess how he might take control of the situation. "If you think I'm going to give you money—"

Sandra tried to silently warn him not to play hero.

It was too dangerous.

And it could get them both killed.

Aaron's grip on the gun tightened. "Cash, credit cards, whatever you got, I'll take."

Stephen's eyes hardened. "I'm not giving you a damn thing."

Aaron's face twisted in rage. "Give me the money, or I swear I'll . . ." He swung the gun toward Sandra, who recoiled on the couch.

With Aaron's eyes off him for a split second, Stephen lunged at Aaron, trying to wrest the gun from his hand. The two men grappled violently, crashing into furniture as they fought. Sandra watched in horror, her mind racing for a way to help. Stephen managed to land a punch, but Aaron retaliated with a brutal strike to Stephen's head with a heavy bookend from the mantle.

Stephen crumpled to the floor, unconscious.

"No!" Sandra screamed, rushing to her ex-husband's side. She pressed her fingers to his neck, relieved to feel a pulse.

She lowered her right ear to his lips and could hear his breathing, labored but steady.

Relief washed over her, but it was short-lived as Aaron's wild eyes bore into her.

She feared for a moment he might shoot her on the spot.

Then Aaron's phone buzzed, drawing his attention.

A smile crept across his lips as he read the message.

Sandra noticed the change in his demeanor.

"What is it?" Sandra asked, trying to sound casual.

Aaron glanced at her but said nothing, his smile lingering.

"What's so funny?" Sandra pressed, her curiosity piqued. "You're smiling."

Aaron hesitated, then shrugged. "It's nothing."

Sandra leaned forward, her eyes wide with interest. "Come on, Aaron. It's just the two of us here. You can tell me. What's so important?"

"It's just an Instagram post," Aaron snapped.

"From who?"

"It's none of your business!"

She suspected it might be Alyssa.

He had been checking social media the entire time he had been holding her captive, as if he was hoping she might reach out to him.

"Is it her? Is it Alyssa? What did she say?"

He silently read the post again, trying to make sense of it, to tell if it was real or not.

Aaron's grip on his phone tightened, and he finally relented. "Alyssa posted on Instagram that she's conflicted, that she might still have feelings for me."

Sandra's heart skipped a beat. She knew this had to be a ploy, Maya's way of tracking Aaron.

But she needed to keep him engaged.

"It's true, Aaron," she said softly.

His eyes narrowed. "What are you talking about?"

"When Alyssa hired us, she couldn't stop raving about you, how she had never met a man like you, how you had turned her whole world upside down in the most wonderful way."

Aaron scoffed and threw his phone down on the coffee table. "Stop trying to con a con man."

"I'm not. Look, you can believe me or not. I have no reason to lie. I just want to get out of this alive." She hesitated. "But it doesn't surprise me, even after all this, that she never stopped loving you."

"She seemed pretty much over me that night in the hotel room when she found out what I had done . . ."

"There's only one way to find out for sure. Text her."

Aaron's gaze flickered with doubt, but the allure of Alyssa's supposed affection was too strong. "You think so?" he muttered.

Sandra nodded, her voice gentle. "Just reach out. See what she says. Maybe your ending hasn't been written yet."

"No! Stop it! I don't need to be listening to you. Just stay out of it," Aaron snapped.

Had she gonc too far?

Sandra waited a few moments, giving him some space to contemplate, but then persisted.

"Aaron, you have nothing to lose. Maybe she can help us," she said soothingly.

Sandra could almost see his mind at work. Alyssa's

resources and support could be the escape hatch he needed from all the trouble he was in. She said nothing, letting that thought sink in.

After a moment of hesitation, Aaron sighed and grabbed his phone, his fingers flying over the screen as he composed a text message to Alyssa.

At Doug and Edie Turner's house, Maya stood with the police and FBI, who had all gathered there, her nerves on edge. Detective Hart and FBI Agents Markey and Rhodes coordinated their teams. Cyber genius Oscar was setting up his equipment, ready to trace the exact location of Aaron's texts by coordinating with the cell phone company providing Aaron's service.

"We need to keep him texting," Maya urged Alyssa, who was visibly nervous. "Every second counts."

Alyssa took a deep breath and began typing, responding to Aaron's message.

Aaron: Alyssa, I've missed you. I know I messed up big-time, but maybe we can work things out if you give me another chance. Maybe we can meet somewhere, out of the country, away from all the chaos.

A place with no extradition agreement with the US, Maya thought to herself.

Alyssa: Aaron, I'm so confused. Who is the real you? Is it the person who loves me or the person who has done all these terrible things?

It went back and forth like this for twenty minutes. There were long spells between texts as they each worked on crafting the perfect response.

Oscar's eyes lit up as the signal began to triangulate. "We're getting closer. Keep him engaged."

Aaron: The real me loves you. I don't want to lose you. You mean everything to me, Alyssa.

Alyssa's hands shook, but she continued the conversation, keeping Aaron hooked with promises and nostalgia.

Finally, Oscar pinpointed the location.

"It's Sandra's house," Oscar announced. "We've got him."

Maya's mouth dropped open in shock.

But in some strange way, it made sense.

The last place they would expect to find them.

The police and FBI raced to the Wallage home, Maya and Alyssa in tow. Maya kept a close eye on Alyssa, making sure she stayed focused on keeping Aaron busy until they arrived.

As they pulled up, a car screeched to a halt nearby.

Maya's heart sank as she recognized Lucas, jumping out of his Prius, his face pale with fear and determination.

"That's Lucas," Maya explained to the agents. "Sandra's boyfriend. He's here to help, but he doesn't know what he's walking into."

Markey and Rhodes exchanged a glance, their concern evident. "We can't let him ruin the element of surprise," Markey said.

She signaled to two male agents in flak jackets, who darted across the street toward the house, quietly approaching Lucas from behind. Maya watched, her stomach in knots. She knew Lucas was only trying to help, but his unexpected arrival could jeopardize everything.

Just as Lucas reached the front door, his hand inches from the knob, the two agents pounced, grabbing him from behind, one clapping a hand over his mouth, pulling him away from the scene before he could make a sound.

Inside the house, Sandra saw Aaron engrossed in his phone. Stephen was still crumpled on the floor, unconscious, and Sandra knew she had to buy more time. She kept talking, feeding Aaron's ego, his biggest liability.

"I can tell Alyssa really loves you," Sandra said softly. "She's been waiting her whole life for someone like you."

He glanced up at her.

Sandra grimaced, fearing she had gone overboard, laying it on too thick.

But then she could see Aaron's eyes gleaming with a twisted hope. He continued texting Alyssa, his attention fully absorbed.

As Aaron typed another message, Stephen groaned, slowly regaining consciousness. Aaron spun around, dropping his phone and grabbing for his gun.

Sandra could see he was distracted and knew she had to seize the moment. She grabbed a fire poker from the fireplace and, with all her strength, swung it at the back of Aaron's head. Aaron howled in pain, but the whack did not knock him out; it just infuriated him even more as he grabbed the back of his head and glowered at Sandra, full of rage.

Aaron retaliated, grabbing at the fire poker, trying to wrest it from her grip. They struggled fiercely, and Sandra felt herself losing control. But Stephen, now more alert, crawled to his knees and lunged for Aaron's gun, which had fallen to the floor during the scuffle.

He grabbed it and pointed it at Aaron.

"Enough!" Stephen shouted, his voice commanding.

Aaron froze, his eyes wide with fear.

He let go of the fire poker, releasing it to Sandra.

She tossed it aside and rushed to Stephen's side, grabbing him by his arm, helping to lift him up so he was standing on his feet. He steadied the gun, keeping it trained on Aaron. "We need to tie him up."

"I think we have some rope in the pantry," Sandra said, scooting into the kitchen and returning moments later with enough to tie Aaron's hands and feet, securing him.

As Sandra went to phone for help, she could see out the large bay window the police and FBI surging toward the house.

She hurried to greet them at the door, calling out, "He's down! He's down!"

She did not want them storming into her home, guns blazing unnecessarily. Markey and Rhodes and several agents fanned out, ensuring the scene was safe.

Sandra leaned against the doorway, exhaustion washing over her. She smiled wearily at the officers.

"Welcome to my home," she said. "I can offer you coffee, and my homemade apple cider donuts are in the kitchen if anyone's hungry."

Always the consummate hostess.

Detective Hart approached her, a look of admiration on her face as her eyes fell upon Aaron trussed up in the living room. "You did great, Sandra."

Sandra nodded, her eyes filling with tears. "Thank you."

As Detective Hart talked to Stephen to make sure his injuries were not serious, Sandra watched as the FBI agents led a cuffed Aaron out of the house as Maya and Alyssa were running up the driveway.

Aaron's eyes locked onto Alyssa's, realization dawning on him. "You were lying," he snarled, his face contorted with rage. "You *never* loved me."

Alyssa stood firm, her voice cold. "It was all a trap, Aaron. You're sick, and you're going to pay for what you did."

Aaron's face fell as the reality of his situation sank in. The FBI agents led him away, and Sandra finally felt a tsunami of relief wash over her.

The nightmare was finally over.

Chapter 43

Maya and Sandra parked their car outside the elegant colonial house. They took a moment to gather their thoughts before making their way to the front door.

Before they could ring the bell, the door swung open, revealing Edie Turner with her welcoming smile. Her eyes sparkled with the same charm and warmth as her daughter's. "Maya, Sandra, come in, come in! Alyssa is just finishing up packing," she said, ushering them into the living room.

"Thank you, Mrs. Turner," Maya said, returning the smile. She and Sandra followed Edie, taking in the comfortable, cozy surroundings that felt like a haven of normalcy after the whirlwind of the past few weeks.

Doug Turner appeared from the kitchen, carrying a tray laden with lobster rolls and iced tea. "It's great to see you both. Thank you for everything you've done for Alyssa."

No one wanted to say his name.

They were all trying to forget the havoc he had caused, the irreparable damage done.

"We're glad it all worked out," Sandra replied, though her tone was softened by genuine gratitude that the whole ordeal was behind them, all of them.

As they settled into the plush couches, Alyssa descended the staircase, looking more relaxed than Maya and Sandra had seen her in a while. Her relief was evident, her eyes brighter, her posture more relaxed. "Hey, you two! Just in time for lunch," she greeted them with a hug.

"Ready for France?" Sandra asked, taking a lobster roll from Doug.

"More than ready," Alyssa said, her smile widening. "It's a romantic comedy, so it should be a nice change of pace. I think I need it. I jumped on the project when Emma Stone dropped out at the last minute. Honestly, I welcome the distraction of working on something lighthearted and being out of the country."

Edie exchanged a knowing glance with Doug. "And I hear you might have some company over there?" she teased.

Alyssa blushed, a rare sight for the seasoned actress. "Mom, please . . ."

Maya and Sandra perked up.

"Oh?" Sandra asked with a raised eyebrow.

"I've been exchanging texts after we reconnected at the reunion. I didn't say anything before, not with all the drama with Aaron going on, but he's been so sweet, always checking in on me, and we just clicked . . ."

Maya leaned forward, curious. "Don't keep us in suspense."

Sandra gasped. "Noah!"

Alyssa's radiant smile confirmed that Sandra had guessed correctly.

"Who knew I'd wind up dating a guy I met in Chess Club," Alyssa laughed.

"Of course, the former nerd turned tech mogul," Maya said, recalling the bespectacled boy from high school, always in the library or the computer lab, who had completely transformed into a brainy hunk when they saw him at the reunion.

"He's joining me in a few weeks," Alyssa continued, a dreamy look crossing her face. "It's been nice, you know, talking to someone who knew me before all the Hollywood craziness. He's . . . different now, but in a good way."

Doug chuckled. "Well, I'm happy if you're happy. And I have to say, I'm thrilled my daughter is interested in the one man who makes more money than her!"

They all laughed as Alyssa rolled her eyes, and Sandra added, "It's amazing how much he's changed. So confident and self-assured. And, let's be honest, he's such a hottie now. Who would have thought?"

"Definitely a glow-up," Alyssa agreed, her eyes twinkling.

As they dove into their lobster rolls, there was a quick knock at the door, and the door swung open. Alyssa's brooding security guard, Braden, stepped in, his dark eyes locking onto Maya.

"Lobster roll, Braden?" Doug offered.

"No, thank you, sir, I'm just going to load Alyssa's

luggage in the car. We need to leave for the airport soon."

Edie jumped to her feet. "Well, you need to eat at some point. I'll wrap a couple up and get a doggie bag ready."

She dashed off into the kitchen.

Maya shifted uncomfortably as he stared at her for a second too long. She braced herself as he approached.

"Maya, can we talk?" Braden asked, his tone serious.

Maya gave Sandra a quick glance before setting her plate down and joining Braden in the foyer out of earshot of Doug and Sandra and Alyssa, who continued chatting.

Maya took a deep breath.

"Listen, I know I was out of line with you. I normally don't act like that. I typically keep my feelings pretty close to the vest, but when I first laid eyes on you, I was smitten, and I should've managed my feelings better. I regret not acting more professionally."

"I'm flattered, Braden, really I am," Maya said softly.

He smiled at her warmly.

A complete one eighty from his usual dour demeanor.

She could see a faint look of hope on his face.

That he might still have a chance.

"Braden, I appreciate everything you've done for Alyssa, and for us," Maya began, her voice firm. "But I need to be clear—I'm deeply in love with my husband, Max. There's no room for anyone else."

A flicker of disappointment crossed Braden's face

as she shut him down once again, but he nodded. "I understand. I just had to try."

With a brief, respectful nod, he turned and left the room, leaving behind an awkward silence that Doug quickly dispelled with one of his corny dad jokes. They spent the next twenty minutes chatting and reminiscing, the heavy weight of recent events lifting, replaced by a lightness that felt long overdue.

As they prepared to leave, Maya's phone buzzed with a message from Max.

Meeting in 30 minutes with Dee Kaplan. Meet you there?

She looked at Sandra, her earlier lightheartedness replaced by intense worry. "I've got to go. Max and I have an appointment with his parole officer. They're deciding whether or not to revoke his parole."

Sandra's eyes widened with concern. "Because of the fight with Shrek?"

Maya nodded, her heart heavy. "I can't bear the thought of him going back to prison, Sandra."

Sandra squeezed her hand. "I know, but Max has a good case. Shrek has a lengthy police record. The parole officer has to take that into account."

"I hope you're right," Maya said, her voice tinged with anxiety. "But I'm not so sure. We've faced worse, but this feels different."

As they said their goodbyes to Alyssa and her parents, Maya could not shake the anxiety gnawing at her. The drive to the parole office in Sandra's Mercedes was filled with tense silence, and when they arrived, Sandra hugged her tightly.

"Good luck. Call me as soon as you know something," Sandra said.

Maya nodded, taking a deep breath before walking inside. She could only hope that their love and determination would be enough to keep Max free. As she entered the building, her heart pounded in her chest, each step echoing her fears. This was not just about Max—it was about their future, and she could not imagine facing it alone.

Chapter 44

Maya sat next to Max in the cramped, fluorescent-lit office of his parole officer, Dee Kaplan. The room felt oppressive. Maya clasped Max's hand tightly, both of them nervously waiting for Kaplan to arrive. Max's jaw was set, and Maya could feel the anxiety radiating off him.

"Max," she began, her voice barely a whisper, "we're going to get through this."

He looked at her, his eyes dark with worry. "Maya, you have to prepare yourself. I might be going back to prison. We need to talk about what happens if—"

"No," she interrupted, her grip tightening. "Not yet. Let's just wait to hear what Kaplan has to say."

Max sighed, nodding. The silence between them stretched out until the door finally opened, and Dee Kaplan walked in. Kaplan, with a no-nonsense demeanor and a hardened edge from years of dealing with parolees, took her seat behind the desk. She glanced at them over her reading glasses, her expression unreadable.

"Max, Maya," Kaplan began, her tone even. "Let's get right to it. Max, you never should have been at that bar that night. You know the conditions of your parole. You never should have engaged with Shrek, who is a known felon."

Maya's heart pounded as Kaplan continued. "Although Detective Ramos, who was at the scene in plainclothes, did not see you strike Shrek first, the bartender did. He confirmed that you punched Shrek first, which set off the physical fight."

Maya opened her mouth to protest. "Shrek grabbed me, he was about to assault me. Max was just defending me—"

Max placed a hand on her knee, a silent plea to let Kaplan finish.

Kaplan's eyes softened for a moment before she continued. "Unfortunately, Detective Ramos was preoccupied at the time, on his phone, and did not see the situation unfold, only the resulting physical altercation."

Maya whispered under her breath, "But I did. I was there."

Kaplan nodded, acknowledging her, but with a hint of skepticism. "But you're his loyal wife, who doesn't want to see her husband go back behind bars. So your version of events may be questioned. That's the reality."

Max took a deep breath, preparing for the worst.

"And as far as the parole board is concerned . . ." Kaplan paused, her expression shifting. "However, the bartender had gone back to the storeroom to get a case of beer and returned just in time to witness the altercation. He was able to corroborate your story as you explained it. Shrek threatening you, physically grabbing you, and Max stepping in, demanding Shrek let you go. Shrek's refusal led to the fight."

Maya and Max exchanged hopeful looks, a flicker of relief starting to break through the tension.

"Additionally," Kaplan continued, "Shrek is desperate to make a deal on some other pending charges. He has offered to drop the assault charge against Max, which I will include in my report to the parole board and the DA's office. Bottom line, Max is probably not going back to prison."

Max released a huge sigh of relief, his shoulders sagging as the weight lifted off him. "Thank you, Ms. Kaplan."

Kaplan offered a rare smile. "Don't thank me yet. You need to stay out of trouble, Max. It might be a very good idea not to insert yourself in your wife's private investigations. They are a minefield of potential parole violations."

Max nodded earnestly. "I promise. I'll help out in the office, not in the field."

Kaplan extended her hand, and Max shook it. "Good. I'll see you at your next appointment in a month. Until then, stay out of trouble."

They left the office, the tension still clinging to Maya's shoulders. As soon as they were outside, she could not hold it in any longer. She broke down, sobbing, the relief washing over her like a tidal wave. The case was finally solved, and now the only goal was to keep Max out of prison. The stress of the past few weeks, the fear of losing Max again, all came crashing down.

Max pulled her into his arms, holding her tightly. "It's okay, Maya," he murmured into her hair. "We're going to be okay." Maya clung to him, her tears soaking his shirt. For the first time in years, she felt true peace. They had faced so many trials, and now, finally, they would not be split apart again like they were all those years when Max had languished in prison for his police corruption conviction. She took a deep breath, pulling herself together, feeling the weight lift from her shoulders.

"I'm not going anywhere," Max whispered. "I promise."

Maya nodded, her heart full. Their family would stay together, and they could finally start to rebuild their lives. The road ahead was still long, but for the first time, it felt like they were on the right path.

Chapter 45

Settled in a cozy corner of Fore Street, a beloved restaurant in the Old Port of Portland, Sandra and Lucas had just sat down. The dim lighting and soft hum of conversation created an intimate atmosphere.

As the waiter, an older man with kind eyes, approached, Sandra stiffened slightly. She knew him personally. He had served her many times before, back when she used to come here with Stephen.

"Good evening, folks. Can I start you off with something to drink?"

"We'll have a bottle of the 2014 Domaine Leflaive Puligny-Montrachet," Lucas replied, selecting an expensive white wine, before adding, "And we'll also take an order of the Wood Oven Roasted Maine Rope-Cultured Mussels to start, please. They're my favorite."

The waiter nodded. "Excellent choice. I think we may have just one order left. They've been very popular tonight." Then he did a double take. "Mrs. Wallage! It's been a while."

"Hello, Hank," Sandra said with a tight smile.

"So good to see you again. And with . . . someone new."

Lucas looked a little intimidated, but Sandra quickly explained, "Lucas, I used to come here all the time with Stephen when we were married."

The waiter chimed in, "In fact, I believe they had their first date here." Realizing his faux pas, he backtracked, "Oh, I mean, I had just started working here, and they were one of the first tables I waited on. It's been over twenty years now."

The waiter gave a slight nod, then left to get their wine.

Lucas took it in stride, smiling. "At least I didn't choose the restaurant where he proposed."

There was a long silence.

"Please tell me this is not the place where he proposed," Lucas moaned.

"No, that happened on a cruise to the Caribbean, and I was terribly seasick and just didn't have the energy to say no," Sandra joked.

Lucas fidgeted with his napkin, his usual calm demeanor replaced by an anxious energy. "Sandra," he started, his voice breaking slightly, "I can't tell you how worried I was. When I heard you were taken hostage, my mind went to the darkest places."

"Lucas," Sandra interjected, trying to calm him.

At that moment, the waiter returned with the wine, interrupting Lucas's emotional confession. He expertly popped open the bottle and poured two glasses.

"Be right back with your mussels," the waiter promised.

"A toast?" Lucas suggested once the waiter was gone, raising his glass with a knowing smile. "To you, Sandra, and your bravery during what must have been a terrifying ordeal—"

Sandra raised a hand to stop him from talking and then lifted her own glass. "How about we just toast to us?"

"That totally works for me. To us," Lucas echoed, and they clinked glasses. The brief interruption allowed Lucas to collect himself, and then he continued.

"You mean everything to me, Sandra. I know there's this age difference that bothers you, but I don't care. I love you. I love you more than I've ever loved anyone."

"Lucas, please," Sandra said, her voice firmer this time. But he was on a roll, the words pouring out of him like a flood he could not hold back.

"No, I just need to get this out." He took a breath and exhaled, gathering the courage. "I've never felt this way before. When I thought I might lose you, I realized just how much you mean to me."

"Lucas!" she said more loudly, trying to get his attention. But he was lost in his emotions, oblivious to her attempts to speak.

"You're my world, Sandra. I don't care about anything else. Just you."

"Lucas!" she finally shouted, startling him into silence. "Would you please just shut up and kiss me?"

He stared at her, stunned, for a heartbeat. Then he moved, standing up so quickly his chair nearly toppled over. He rounded the table, pulled her up from her seat, and planted his lips on hers.

It was not a gentle kiss. It was fierce and passionate, a culmination of all the fear and love and relief that had been building up inside him. Sandra responded in kind, her reservations melting away in the heat of the moment.

Fireworks exploded behind her closed eyelids, and she clung to him, feeling his arms wrap around her, holding her tight as if he never wanted to let go. When they finally pulled apart, they realized the entire restaurant was watching them. Blushing, they sat down quickly, embarrassed but smiling.

Sandra hesitated, her mind racing. She could feel Lucas's eyes on her, waiting.

He leaned forward, whispering, "Come on, I know you can say it."

She laughed nervously, looking down at her hands. "I . . . I . . ."

"Just three little words. I know you can do it. But slower. Not so fast like the last time. Like you were dreading having to say it," he said, smiling.

She opened her mouth to speak.

At that precise moment, the waiter arrived with the mussels, setting the platter down on the table between them along with two bowls for the empty shells.

Lucas shook his head and cracked, "Super awesome timing, man."

The sarcasm was apparently lost on the waiter. "Yes, it turns out this was our last batch of mussels. Five minutes later, and you would have been fresh out of luck. I'll be right back to get your entrée order."

As he left, Lucas called after him, "Take your time." Then he returned his gaze to Sandra.

"I love you, Lucas," she finally managed, the words coming out in a rush.

His face lit up with a brilliant smile. "What a coincidence, because I love you too, Sandra," he said without hesitation.

They both turned to the mussels, laughing a little at the awkwardness of the moment. Lucas took a bite, savoring the flavor, then looked at Sandra with newfound boldness. "Now that we've finally gotten that out of the way, what are we waiting for?"

Sandra picked up her fork and began tearing the mussel out of its shell. "What are you talking about?"

"Why not just go ahead and make it official?" he said, setting down his fork. "We could just—"

"Stop!" she interrupted, holding up her hand. "Let's not push it, okay?"

Lucas winked at her. "Too soon?"

"Yes!" Sandra declared. "Way, way, way too soon!"

"Okay. I'm sure glad I didn't try to hide an engagement ring in one of these mussels for you to find," he said softly. He knew when to stand down, and for now, that was enough. But then he could not resist adding, "But it wasn't a hard pass, so at least I have a little hope to hang on to, right?"

They shared a laugh, leaving the door open to whatever the future might hold.